AF555931

Shree Durga Saptashati

श्री दुर्गा सप्तशती

Shree Durga Saptashati

श्री दुर्गा सप्तशती

Published in Sanskriti Press
by Rupa Publications India Pvt. Ltd 2025
161-B/4, Gulmohar House,
Yusuf Sarai Community Centre,
New Delhi 110049

Sales centres:
Bengaluru Chennai
Hyderabad Kolkata Mumbai

P-ISBN: 978-93-7003-229-3
E-ISBN: 978-93-7003-387-0

First impression 2025

10 9 8 7 6 5 4 3 2 1

Printed in India

Contents

दुर्गा सूक्तम

Durga Suktam

जातवेदसे सुनवाम सोममरातीयतो निदहाति वेदः ।।
स नः पर्षदति दुर्गाणि विश्वा नावेव सिन्धुं दुरितात्यग्निः ।।१।।

Jātavedase Sunavāma Somam-ārātīyato ṇidahāti Vedah ।।
Sa ṇah Parssad-āti ḍurgānni Viśvā ṇāve[a-ī]va
Sindhum ḍurita-āty[i]-āgnih ।।1।।

We offer oblations of Soma unto Agni. May he burn those who are against us. May that Agni lead us beyond all difficulties, like a boatman takes his boat across a river.

तामग्निवर्णां तपसा ज्वलन्तीं वैरोचनीं कर्मफलेषु जुष्टाम् ।।
दुर्गां देवीँशरणमहं प्रपद्ये सुतरसि तरसे नमः ।।२।।

ṭām-āgni-Varnnām ṭapasā Jvalantīm Vairocanīm
kharma-Phalessu Jussttām ।।
ḍurgām ḍevī[ngu]m-ṣarannam-āham
Prapadye Su-ṭarasi ṭarase ṇamah ।।2।।

I take refuge in that Goddess, who has the lusture of fire, who is radiant due to her penance, who gives the fruits of all actions, and who is difficult to obtain. O Durga, we bow to you who are skilled in making us cross all difficulties.

अग्ने त्वं पारया नव्यो अस्मान् स्वस्तिभिरति दुर्गाणि विश्वा ।।
पूश्च पृथ्वी बहुला न उर्वी भवा तोकाय तनयाय शंयोः ।।३।।

āgne ṭvam Pārayā ṇavyo āsmān
Svastibhir-āti ḍurgānni Viśvā ।।
Pūś-Ca Prthvī Bahulā ṇa ūrvī
Bhavā ṭokāya ṭanayāya ṣamyoh ।।3।।

Oh Agni! You are worthy of all praise. Lead us safely beyond all difficulties. May our land and our earth be abundant. Bless our children and their children with happiness.

विश्वानि नो दुर्गहा जातवेदः सिन्धुं न नावा दुरितातिपर्षि ।।
अग्ने अत्रिवन्मनसा गृणानोऽस्माकं बोध्यविता तनूनाम् ।।४।।

Viśvāni ṇo ḍurga-ḥā Jātavedah
Sindhum ṇa ṇāvā ḍurita-āti-Parssi ।।
āgne ātrivan-ṃanasā ġrnnāno-[ā]smākam
Bodhy[i]-āvitā ṭanūnām ।।4।।

O destroyer of all difficulties! Rescue us from difficulties, just as one crosses a river by means of a boat. O Agni! Protect our bodies vigilantly like Atri (who is concerned with the welfare of all beings).

पृतनाजितँसहमानमुग्रमग्निँ हुवेम परमात्सधस्थात् ।।
स नः पर्षदति दुर्गाणि विश्वा क्षामद्देवो अति दुरितात्यग्निः ।।५।।

Pṛtanā-[ā]jita[ngu]m-Sahamānam-
ūgram-āgni ḥuvema Paramāt-Sadhasthāt ॥
Sa ṇah Parssad-āti ḍurgānni Viśvā
<u>kh</u>ssāmad-ḍevo āti ḍurita-āty[i]-āgnih ॥5॥

We invoke Agni from the highest assembly, who charges and vanquishes his enemies and is fearsome. May that Agni protect us and lead us beyond all that is transient, all difficulties, and all sins.

प्रत्नोषि कमीड्यो अध्वरेषु सनाच्च होता नव्यश्च सत्सि ॥
स्वां चाग्ने तनुवं पिप्रयस्वास्मभ्यं च सौभगमायजस्व ॥६॥

Pratnossi <u>kh</u>am-īiddyo ādhvaressu
Sanāc-Ca ḥotā ṇavyaś-Ca Satsi ॥
Svām Ca-āgne ṭanuvam Piprayasva-āsmabhyam
Ca Saubhagam-āayajasva ॥6॥

O Agni! You who are adored in sacrifices multiply our joy. You are present in the sacrifices and are always laudable. Grant us happiness thinking of us as your own body. Bring us good fortune from all corners.

गोभिर्जुष्टमयुजो निषिक्तं तवेन्द्र विष्णोरनुसंचरेम ॥
नाकस्य पृष्ठमभि संवसानो वैष्णवीं लोक इह मादयन्ताम् ॥७॥

ġobhir-Jussttam-āyujo ṇissiktam
ṭave[a-ī]ndra Vissnnor-ānusamcarema ॥
ṇākasya Prssttham-ābhi Samvasāno
Vaissnnavīm ḻoka īha ṃādayantām ॥7॥

O all-pervading Indra who is unattached ! We shall follow you blessed with cattle and happiness. May those who live in the upper reach of the heavens bless me with the world of Vishnu in this life.

ॐ कात्यायनाय विद्महे कन्याकुमारि धीमहि
तन्नो दुर्गिः प्रचोदयात् ॥

khātyāyanāya Vidmahe khanyākumāri ḍhīmahi
ṭan-ṇo ḍurgih Pracodayāt ॥

We perceive the daughter of Katyayana; we meditate on that young virgin. May that Durga inspire us (to reach that goal).

ॐ शान्तिः शान्तिः शान्तिः ॥

Oṃ śāntiḥ śāntiḥ śāntiḥ ..

Om peace peace peace.

अथ देव्याः कवचम्

Durga Kavach

अथ श्रीदुर्गाः कवचम्

Atha śrīdurgāḥ kavacam

ॐ अस्य श्रीचण्डीकवचस्य ब्रह्मा ऋषिः, अनुष्टुप् छन्दः,
चामुण्डा देवता, अङ्गन्यासोक्तमातरः बीजम्, दिग्बन्धदेवताः तत्त्वम्,
श्रीजगदम्बाप्रीत्यर्थे सप्तशतीपाठाङ्गत्वेन जपे विनियोगः।

oṁ asya śrī-caṇḍī-kavacasya brahmā ṛṣiḥ, anuṣṭup chandaḥ,
cāmuṇḍā devatā, aṅganyāsokta-mātaro bījam,
digbandha-devatās tattvam,
śrī-jagadambā-prītyarthe saptashatī-pāṭhāṅgatvena
jape viniyogaḥ.

This verse is a viniyoga or statement of intent for reciting the Śrī Caṇḍī Kavacha, a protective hymn from the Devī Mahātmyam (Durga Saptashatī). It declares that the sage (ṛṣi) of the hymn is Brahmā, the meter (chandaḥ) is Anuṣṭup, and the presiding deity is Caṇḍī (Cāmuṇḍā). The seed (bīja) of the hymn consists of the divine Mothers invoked during the body-touching ritual (aṅganyāsa), and the essential principle (tattva) relates to the guardian deities

of the directions (digbandha-devatās). This recitation is to be performed as part of the Durga Saptashatī, with the goal of pleasing Śrī Jagadambā, the Divine Mother.

ॐ नमश्चण्डिकायै ॥

॥ namaścaṇḍikāyai ॥

॥ मार्कण्डेय उवाच ॥

ॐ यद्गुह्यं परमं लोके सर्वरक्षाकरं नृणाम् ॥
यन्न कस्य चिदाख्यातं तन्मे ब्रूहि पितामह ॥१॥

॥ mārkaṇḍeya uvāca ॥

Om yadguhyam paramam loke sarva rakṣākaram nṛṇām ॥
yanna kasya cidākhyātam tanme brūhi pitāmaha ॥1॥

Thus spoke Markandeya:

1) O Brahmadeva, please tell me that what is so very secret and has not been told by anyone to anybody else and which Protects all human beings in this world.

॥ ब्रह्मोवाच ॥

अस्ति गुह्यतमं विप्रा सर्वभूतोपकारकम् ॥
दिव्यास्तु कवचं पुण्यं तच्छृणुष्वा महामुने ॥२॥

॥ brahmovāca ॥

asti guhyatamam viprā sarva bhūtopakārakam ॥
divyāstu kavacam puṇyam tacchṛṇuṣvā mahāmune ॥2॥

Thus spoke Bramha:

O Brahmin, there is Devi Kavach which is the most secret and useful to all beings. Please listen to that, O Great Sage. Durga is known by these Names:

प्रथमं शैलपुत्री च द्वितीयं ब्रह्मचारिणी ।।
तृतीयं चन्द्रघण्टेति कूष्माण्डेति चतुर्थकम् ।।३।।

prathamam śailaputrī ca dvitīyam brahmacāriṇī ।।
tṛtīyam candraghaṇṭeti kūṣmāṇḍeti caturthakam ।।3।।

The first form is SHAILAPUTRI- Daughter of the King of Himalayas; second is BRAHMACHARINI One Who observes the state of celibacy; third is CHANDRAGANTA- One Who bears the moon around Her neck fourth is KOOSHMANDA- Whose Void contains the Universe

पञ्चमं स्कन्दमातेति षष्ठं कात्यायनीति च ।।
सप्तमं कालरात्रीति महागौरीति चाष्टमम् ।।४।।

pañcamam skandamāteti ṣaṣṭham kātyāyanīti ca ।
saptamam kālarātrīti mahāgaurīti cāṣṭamam ।।4।।

Fifth is SKANDAMATA- Who gave birth to Karttikeya; Sixth is KATYAYANI Who incarnated to help the Devas; Seventh is KALARATRI- the fiercest form of Durga; Eight is MAHAGAURI- One Who made great penance

नवमं सिद्धिदात्री च नव दुर्गाः प्रकीर्तिताः ।।
उक्तान्येतानि नामानि ब्रह्मणैव महात्मना ।।५।।

navamam siddhidātrī ca nava durgāḥ prakīrtitāḥ ।।
uktānyetāni nāmāni brahmaṇaiva mahātmanā ।।5।।

Ninth is SIDDHIDATRI- One Who grants Moksha. Those who remember You with great devotion indeed have prosperity. Undoubtedly, O Goddess of the Gods, You Protect those who remember You.

अग्निना दह्यमानस्तु शत्रुमध्ये गतो रणे ।।
विषमे दुर्गमे चौव भयार्ताः शरणं गताः ।।६।।

agninā dahyamānastu śatrumadhye gato raṇe ।।
viṣame durgame caiva bhayārtāḥ śaraṇam gatāḥ ।।6।।

न तेषां जायते किञ्चिदशुभं रणसङ्कटे ।।
नापदं तस्य पश्यामि शोकदुःखभयं न ही ।।७।।

na teṣām jāyate kiñcidaśubham raṇasaṅkaṭe ।।
nāpadam tasya paśyāmi śokaduḥkhabhayam na hī ।।7।।

यैस्तु भक्त्या स्मृता नूनं तेषां वृद्धिः प्रजायते ।।
ये त्वां स्मरन्ति देवेशि रक्षसे तान्न संशयः ।।८।।

yaistu bhaktyā smṛtā nūnam teṣām vṛddhiḥ prajāyate ।।
ye tvām smaranti deveśi rakṣase tānna samśayaḥ ।।8।।

Those who are frightened, having been surrounded by the enemies on the battlefield, or are burning in fire, or being at an impassable place, would face no calamity, and would never have grief, sorrow, fear, or evil if they surrender to Durga.

प्रेतसंस्था तु चामुण्डा वाराही महिषासना ॥
ऐन्द्री गजसमारूढा वैष्णवी गरुडासना ॥९॥

pretasamsthā tu cāmuṇḍā vārāhī mahiṣāsanā ॥
aindrī gajasamārūḍhā vaiṣṇavī garuḍāsanā ॥9॥

The Goddess Chamunda sits on a corpse, Varahi rides on a buffalo, Aindri is mounted on an elephant and Vaishnavi on a condor.

माहेश्वरी वृषारूढा कौमारी शिखिवाहना ॥
लक्ष्मीः पद्मासना देवी पद्महस्ता हरिप्रिया ॥१०॥

māheśvarī vṛṣārūḍhā kaumārī śikhivāhanā ॥
lakṣmīḥ padmāsanā devī padmahastā haripriyā ॥10॥

Maheswari is riding on a bull, the vehicle of Kaumari is the peacock, Lakshmi, the Beloved of Shri Vishnu, is seated in a lotus and is also holding a lotus in Her Hand.

श्वेतरूपधारा देवी ईश्वरी वृषवाहना ॥
ब्राह्मी हंससमारूढा सर्वाभरणभूषिता ॥११॥

इत्येता मातरः सर्वाः सर्वयोगसमन्विताः ॥
नानाभरणशोभाढया नानारत्नोपशोभिताः ॥१२॥

śvetarūpadhārā devī īśvarī vṛṣavāhanā ॥
brāhmī hamsasamārūḍhā sarvābharaṇabhūṣitā ॥11॥

ityetā mātaraḥ sarvāḥ sarvayogasamanvitāḥ ॥
nānābharaṇaśobhāḍhayā nānāratnopaśobhitāḥ ॥12॥

(11-12) The Goddess Ishwari, of white complexion, is riding on a bull and Brahmi, Who is bedecked with all ornaments is seated on a swan. All the mothers are endowed with Yoga and are adorned with different ornaments and jewels.

दृश्यन्ते रथमारूढा देव्याः क्रोधसमाकुलाः ।।
शङ्खं चक्रं गदां शक्तिं हलं च मुसलायुधम् ।।१३।।

dṛśyante rathamārūḍhā
devyāḥ krodhasamākulāḥ ।।
śaṅkham cakram gadām śaktim
halam ca musalāyudham ।।13।।

खेटकं तोमरं चैव परशुं पाशमेव च ।।
कुन्तायुधं त्रिशूलं च शाङ्र्गमायुधमुत्तमम् ।।१४।।

kheṭakam tomaram caiva paraśum pāśameva ca ।।
kuntāyudham triśūlam ca śārṅgamāyudhamuttamam ।।14।।

दैत्यानां देहनाशाय भक्तानामभयाय च ।।
धारयन्त्यायुद्धानीथं देवानां च हिताय वै ।।१५।।

daityānām dehanāśāya bhaktānāmabhayāya ca ।।
dhārayantyāyuddhānītham devānām ca hitāya vai ।।15।।

(13-15) All the Goddesses are seen mounted in chariots and very Angry. They are wielding conch, discus, mace, plough, club, javelin, axe, noose, barbed dart, trident, bow and arrows. These Goddesses are wielding Their weapons for Destroying the bodies of demons, for the Protection of Their devotees and for the benefit of the Gods.

नमस्तेऽस्तु महारौद्रे महाघोरपराक्रमे ।।
महाबले महोत्साहे महाभयविनाशिनि ।।१६।।

namaste'stu mahāraudre mahāghoraparākrame ।।
mahābale mahotsāhe mahābhayavināśini ।।16।।

Salutations to You, O Goddess, of very dreadful appearance, of frightening valour, of tremendous strength and energy, the Destroyer of the worst fears.

त्राहि मां देवि दुष्प्रेक्ष्ये शत्रूणां भयवर्धिनि ।।
प्राच्यां रक्षतु मामैन्द्रि आग्नेय्यामग्निदेवता ।।१७।।

trāhi mām devi duṣprekṣye śatrūṇām bhayavardhini ।।
prācyām rakṣatu māmaindri āgneyyāmagnidevatā ।।17।।

दक्षिणेऽवतु वाराही नैर्ऋत्यां खड्गधारिणी ।।
प्रतीच्यां वारुणी रक्षेद् वायव्यां मृगवाहिनी ।।१८।।

dakṣiṇe'vatu vārāhī nairṛtyām khaṅgadhāriṇī ।।
pratīcyām vāruṇī rakṣed vāyavyām mṛgavāhinī ।।18।।

(17-18) O Devi, it is difficult to have even a glance at You. You increase the fears of Your enemies, please come to my rescue. May Goddess Aindri Protect me from the east. Agni Devata (Goddess of Fire) from the south-east, Varahi

(Shakti of Vishnu in the form of the boar) from the south, Khadgadharini (Wielder of the sword) from the south-west, Varuni (The Shakti of Varuna, the rain God) from the west and Mrgavahini, (Whose vehicle is the deer) may Protect me from the north-west.

उदीच्यां पातु कौमारी ऐशान्यां शूलधारिणी ॥
ऊर्ध्वं ब्रह्माणी में रक्षेदधस्ताद् वैष्णवी तथा ॥१९॥

udīcyām pātu kaumārī aiśānyām śūḷadhāriṇī ॥
ūrdhvam brahmāṇī mem rakṣedadhastād vaiṣṇavī tathā ॥19॥

The Goddess Kaumari (The Shakti of Kumar, that is Karttikeya) Protect me from the north and Goddess Shooladharini from the north-east, Brahmani, (The Shakti of Brahma) from above and Vaishnavi (Shakti of Vishnu) from below, Protect me.

एवं दश दिशो रक्षेच्चामुण्डा शववाहाना ॥
जाया मे चाग्रतः पातुः विजया पातु पृष्ठतः ॥२०॥

evam daśa diśo rakṣeccāmuṇḍā śavavāhānā ।
jāyā me cāgrataḥ pātuḥ vijayā pātu pṛṣṭhataḥ ॥20॥

अजिता वामपार्श्वे तु दक्षिणे चापराजिता ॥
शिखामुद्योतिनि रक्षेदुमा मूर्ध्नि व्यवस्थिता ॥२१॥

ajitā vāmapārśve tu dakṣiṇe cāparājitā ॥
śikhāmudyotini rakṣedumā mūrdhni vyavasthitā ॥21॥

(20-21) Thus Goddess Chamunda, Who sits on a corps, Protects me from all the ten directions. May Goddess Jaya Protect me from the front and Vijaya from the rear; Ajita from the left and Aparajita from the right. Goddess Dyotini may Protect the topknot and Uma may sit on my head and Protect it.

मालाधारी ललाटे च भ्रवो रक्षेद् यशस्विनी ॥
त्रिनेत्रा च भ्रुवोर्मध्ये यमघण्टा च नासिके ॥२२॥

mālādhārī lalāṭe ca bhruvo rakṣed yaśasvinī ॥
trinetrā ca bhruvormadhye yamaghaṇṭā ca nāsike ॥22॥

शङ्खिनी चक्षुषोर्मध्ये श्रोत्रयोर्द्वारवासिनी ॥
कपोलौ कालिका रक्षेत्कर्णमूले तु शङ्करी ॥२३॥

śaṅkhinī cakṣuṣormadhye śrotrayordvāravāsinī ॥
kapolau kālikā rakṣetkarṇamūle tu śaṅkarī ॥23॥

(22-23) May I be Protected by Maladhari on the forehead, Yashswini on the eye-brows, Trinetra between the eye-brows, Yamaghanta on the nose, Shankini on both the eyes, Dwaravasini on the ears, may Kalika Protect my cheeks and Shankari the roots of the ears.

नासिकायां सुगन्धा च उत्तरोष्ठे च चर्चिका ॥
अधरे चामृतकला जिह्वायां च सरस्वती ॥२४॥

nāsikāyām sugandhā ca uttaroṣṭhe ca carcikā ॥
adhare cāmṛtakalā jihvāyām ca sarasvatī ॥24॥

दन्तान् रक्षतु कौमारी कण्ठदेशे तु चण्डिका ।।
घण्टिकां चित्रघण्टा च महामाया च तालुके ।।२५।।

dantān rakṣatu kaumārī kaṇṭhadeśe tu caṇḍikā ।।
ghaṇṭikām citraghaṇṭā ca mahāmāyā ca tāluke ।।25।।

कामाक्षी चिबुकं रक्षेद् वाचं मे सर्वमङ्गला ।।
ग्रीवायां भद्रकाली च पृष्ठवंशे धनुर्धारी ।।२६।।

kāmākṣī cibukam rakṣed vācam me sarvamaṅgalā ।।
grīvāyām bhadrakālī ca pṛṣṭhavamśe dhanurdhārī ।।26।।

नीलग्रीवा बहि:कण्ठे नलिकां नलकूबरी ।।
स्कन्धयो: खड्ग्नी रक्षेद् बाहू मे वज्रधारिणी ।।२७।।

nīlagrīvā bahiḥkaṇṭhe nalikām nalakūbarī ।।
skandhayoḥ khaṅginī rakṣed bāhū me vajradhāriṇī ।।27।।

(24-27) May I be Protected by Sugandha-nose, Charchika-lip, Amrtakala-lower lip, Saraswati-tongue, Kaumari-teeth, Chandika-throat, Chitra-ghanta-soundbox, Mahamaya-crown of the head, Kamakshi-chin, Sarvamangala-speech, Bhadrakali-neck, Dhanurdhari-back. May Neelagreeva Protect the outer part of my throat and Nalakoobari-windpipe, may Khadgini Protect my shoulders and Vajra-dharini Protect my arms.

हस्तयोर्दण्डिनी रक्षेदम्बिका चान्गुलीषु च ।।
नखाञ्छूलेश्वरी रक्षेत्कुक्षौ रक्षेत्कुलेश्वरी ।।२८।।

hastayordaṇḍinī rakṣedambikā cāngulīṣu ca ॥
nakhāñchūleśvarī rakṣetkukṣau rakṣetkuleśvarī ॥28॥

स्तनौ रक्षेन्महादेवी मनः शोकविनाशिनी ॥
हृदये ललिता देवी उदरे शूलधारिणी ॥२९॥

stanau rakṣenmahādevī manaḥ śokavināśinī ॥
hṛdaye lalitā devī udare śūladhāriṇī ॥29॥

नाभौ च कामिनी रक्षेद् गुह्यं गुह्येश्वरी तथा ॥
पूतना कामिका मेढ्रं गुडे महिषवाहिनी ॥३०॥

nābhau ca kāminī rakṣed guhyam guhyeśvarī tathā ॥
pūtanā kāmikā meḍhram guḍe mahiṣavāhinī ॥30॥

(28-30) May Devi Dandini Protect both my hands, Ambika-fingers, Shooleshwari my nails and may Kuleshwari Protect my belly. May I be Protected, by Mahadevi-breast, Shuladharini-abdomen, Lalita Devi-heart, Kamini-navel, Guhyeshwari-hidden parts, Pootana Kamika-reproductive organs, Mahishavasini-excretory organ.

कट्यां भगवतीं रक्षेज्जानूनी विन्ध्यवासिनी ॥
जङ्घे महाबला रक्षेत्सर्वकामप्रदायिनी ॥३१॥

kaṭyām bhagavatīm rakṣejjānūnī vindhyavāsinī ॥
jaṅghe mahābalā rakṣetsarvakāmapradāyinī ॥31॥

(31) May Goddess Bhagavati Protect my waist, Vindhyavasini-knees and the wish-fulfilling Mahabala may Protect my hips.

गुल्फयोर्नारसिंही च पादपृष्ठे तु तैजसी ॥
पादाङ्गुलीषु श्रीरक्षेत्पादाधःस्तलवासिनी ॥३२॥

gulphayornārasimhī ca pādapṛṣṭhe tu taijasī ॥
pādāṅgulīṣu śrī rakṣetpādādhaḥstalavāsinī ॥32॥

(32) May Narashini Protect my ankles. May Taijasi Protect my feet, may Shri Protect my toes. May Talavasini Protect the soles of my feet.

नखान् दंष्ट्रा कराली च केशांशचौवोर्ध्वकेशिनी ॥
रोमकूपेषु कौबेरी त्वचं वागीश्वरी तथा ॥३३॥

nakhān damṣṭrā karālī ca keśāmśacaivordhvakeśinī ॥
romakūpeṣu kauberī tvacam vāgīśvarī tathā ॥33॥

(33) May Danshtrakarali Protect my nails, Urdhvakeshini-hair, Kauberi-pores, Vagishwari-skin.

रक्तमज्जावसामांसान्यस्थिमेदांसि पार्वती ॥
अन्त्राणि कालरात्रिश्च पित्तं च मुकुटेश्वरी ॥३४॥

raktamajjāvasāmāmsānyasthimedāmsi pārvatī ॥
antrāṇi kālarātriśca pittam ca mukuṭeśvarī ॥34॥

(34) May Goddess Parvati Protect blood, marrow of the bones, fat and bone; Goddess Kalaratri-intestines. Mukuteshwari-bile and liver.

पद्मावती पद्मकोशे कफे चूडामणिस्तथा ॥
ज्वालामुखी नखज्वालामभेद्या सर्वसन्धिषु ॥३५॥

padmāvatī padmakośe kaphe cūḍāmaṇistathā ॥
jvālāmukhī nakhajvālāmabhedyā sarvasandhiṣu ॥35॥

(35) May Padmavati Protect the Chakras, Choodamani-phlegm (or lungs), Jwalamukhi lustre of the nails and Abhedya-all the joints.

शुक्रं ब्रह्माणी मे रक्षेच्छायां छत्रेश्वरी तथा ॥
अहङ्कारं मनो बुद्धिं रक्षेन्मे धर्मधारिणी ॥३६॥

śukram brahmāṇī me rakṣecchāyām chatreśvarī tathā ॥
ahaṅkāram mano buddhim rakṣenme dharmadhāriṇī ॥36॥

(36) Brahmani-semen, Chhatreshwari the shadow of my body, Dharmadharini-ego, superego and intellect (buddhi).

प्राणापानौ तथा व्यानमुदानं च समानकम् ॥
वज्रहस्ता च मे रक्षेत्प्राणं कल्याणशोभना ॥३७॥

prāṇāpānau tathā vyānamudānam ca samānakam ॥
vajrahastā ca me rakṣetprāṇam kalyāṇaśobhanā ॥37॥

(37) Vajrahasta-pran, apan, vyan, udan, saman (five vital breaths), Kalyanashobhana-pranas (life force).

रसे रूपे च गन्धे च शब्दे स्पर्शे च योगिनी ॥
सत्वं रजस्तमश्चैव रक्षेन्नारायणी सदा ॥३८॥

rase rūpe ca gandhe ca śabde sparśe ca yoginī ॥
satvam rajastamaścaiva rakṣennārāyaṇī sadā ॥38॥

(38) May Yogini Protect the sense organs, that is, the faculties of tasting, seeing, smelling, hearing and touching. May Narayni always protect satva, rajas and tamas guna.

आयू रक्षतु वाराही धर्मं रक्षतु वैष्णवी ॥
यशः कीर्तिं च लक्ष्मीं च धनं विद्यां च चक्रिणी ॥३९॥

āyū rakṣatu vārāhī dharmam rakṣatu vaiṣṇavī ।
yaśaḥ kīrtim ca lakṣmīm ca dhanam vidyām ca cakriṇī ॥39॥

(39) Varahi-the life, Vaishnavi-dharma, Lakshmi-success and fame, Chakrini-wealth and knowledge.

गोत्रामिन्द्राणि मे रक्षेत्पशून्मे रक्षा चण्डिके ॥
पुत्रान् रक्षेन्महालक्ष्मी भार्यां रक्षतु भैरवी ॥४०॥

gotrāmindrāṇi me rakṣetpaśūnme rakṣā caṇḍike ॥
putrān rakṣenmahālakṣmībhāryām rakṣatu bhairavī ॥40॥

(40) Indrani-relatives, Chandika-cattle, Mahalakshmi-children and Bhairavi-spouse.

पन्थानं सुपथा रक्षेन्मार्गं क्षेमकरी तथा ॥
राजद्वारे महालक्ष्मीर्विजया सर्वतः स्थिता ॥४१॥

panthānam supathā rakṣenmārgam kṣemakarī tathā ॥
rājadvāre mahālakṣmīrvijayā sarvataḥ sthitā ॥41॥

(41) Supatha may Protect my journey and Kshemakari my way. Mahalakshmi may Protect me in the king's court and Vijaya everywhere.

रक्षाहीनं तु यत्स्थानं वर्जितं कवचेन तु ॥
तत्सर्वं रक्ष मे देवी जयन्ती पापनाशिनी ॥४२॥

rakṣāhīnam tu yatsthānam varjitam kavacena tu ॥
tatsarvam rakṣa me devī jayantī pāpanāśinī ॥42॥

(42) O Goddess Jayanti, any place that has not been mentioned in the Kavach and has thus remained unprotected, may be Protected by You.

पदमेकं न गच्छेतु यदिच्छेच्छुभमात्मनः ॥
कवचेनावृतो नित्यं यात्र यत्रैव गच्छति ॥४३॥

padamekam na gacchetu yadicchecchubhamātmanaḥ ।
kavacenāvṛto nityam yātra yatraiva gacchati ॥43॥

तत्र तत्रार्थलाभश्च विजयः सर्वकामिकः ॥
यं यं चिन्तयते कामं तं तं प्राप्नोति निश्चितम् ॥
परमैश्वर्यमतुलं प्राप्स्यते भूतले पुमान् ॥४४॥

tatra tatrārthalābhaśca vijayaḥ sarvakāmikaḥ ।
yam yam cintayate kāmam tam tam prāpnoti niścitam ।
paramaiśvaryamatulam prāpsyate bhūtale pumān ॥44॥

(43-44) One should invariably cover oneself with this Kavacha (by reading) wherever one goes and should not walk even a step without it if one desire auspiciousness. Then one is successful everywhere and all one's desires are fulfilled and that person enjoys great prosperity on the earth.

निर्भयो जायते मर्त्यः सङ्ग्रमेष्वपराजितः ॥
त्रैलोक्ये तु भवेत्पूज्यः कवचेनावृतः पुमान् ॥४५॥

nirbhayo jāyate martyaḥ saṅgrameṣvaparājitaḥ ॥
trailokye tu bhavetpūjyaḥ kavacenāvṛtaḥ pumān ॥45॥

(45) The person who covers himself with Kavacha becomes fearless, is never defeated in the battle and becomes worthy of being worshipped in the three worlds.

इदं तु देव्याः कवचं देवानामपि दुर्लभम् ॥
यः पठेत्प्रयतो नित्यं त्रिसन्ध्यं श्रद्धयान्वितः ॥४६॥

idam tu devyāḥ kavacam devānāmapi durlabham ॥
yaḥ paṭhetprayato nityam trisandhyam śraddhayānvitaḥ ॥46॥

दैवी कला भवेत्तस्य त्रैलोक्येष्वपराजितः ॥
जीवेद् वर्षशतं साग्रामपमृत्युविवर्जितः ॥४७॥

daivī kalā bhavettasya trailokyeṣvaparājitaḥ ॥
jīved varṣaśatam sāgrāmapamṛtyuvivarjitaḥ ॥47॥

(46-47) One who reads with faith every day thrice (morning, afternoon and evening), the 'Kavacha' of the Devi, which is inaccessible even to the Gods, receives the

Divine arts, is undefeated in the three worlds, lives for a hundred years and is free from accidental death.

नश्यन्ति टयाधयः सर्वे लूताविस्फोटकादयः ।।
स्थावरं जङ्गमं चौव कृत्रिमं चापि यद्विषम् ।।४८।।

naśyanti ṭayādhayaḥ sarve lūtāvisphoṭakādayaḥ ।।
sthāvaram jaṅgamam caiva kṛtrimam cāpi yadviṣam ।।48।।

(48) All disease, like boils, scars, etc. are finished. Moveable (scorpions and snakes) and immoveable (other) poisons cannot affect him.

अभिचाराणि सर्वाणि मन्त्रयन्त्राणि भूतले ।।
भूचराः खेचराशचौव जलजाश्चोपदेशिकाः ।।४९।।

abhicārāṇi sarvāṇi mantrayantrāṇi bhūtale ।।
bhūcarāḥ khecarāśacaiva jalajāścopadeśikāḥ ।।49।।

सहजा कुलजा माला डाकिनी शाकिनी तथा ।।
अन्तरिक्षचरा घोरा डाकिन्यश्च महाबला ।।५०।।

sahajā kulajā mālā ḍākinī śākinī tathā ।
antarikṣacarā ghorā ḍākinyaśca mahābal ।।50।।

ग्रहभूतपिशाचाश्च यक्षगन्धर्वराक्षसाः ।।
ब्रह्मराक्षसवेतालाः कूष्माण्डा भैरवादयः ।।५१।।

grahabhūtapiśācāśca yakṣagandharvarākṣasāḥ ।।
brahmarākṣasavetālāḥ kūṣmāṇḍā bhairavādayaḥ ।।51।।

नश्यन्ति दर्शनात्तस्य कवचे हृदि संस्थिते ।।
मानोन्नतिर्भावेद्राज्यं तेजोवृद्धिकरं परम् ।।५२।।

naśyanti darśanāttasya kavace hṛdi samsthite ।।
mānonnatirbhāvedrājyam tejovṛddhikaram param ।।52।।

(49-52) All those, who cast magical spells by mantras or yantras, on others for evil purposes, all bhoots, goblins, malevolent beings moving on the earth and in the sky, all those who mesmerise others, all female goblins, all yakshas and gandharvas are destroyed just by the sight of the person having Kavach in his heart.

यशसा वद्धते सोऽपी कीर्तिमण्डितभूतले ।।
जपेत्सप्तशतीं चणण्डीं कृत्वा तु कवचं पूरा ।।५३।।

yaśasā vaddhate so'pī kīrtimaṇḍitabhūtale ।।
japetsaptaśatīm caṇaṇḍīm kṛtvā tu kavacam pūrā ।।53।।

(53) That person receives more and more respect and prowess. On the earth he rises in prosperity and fame by reading the Kavacha and Saptashati.

यावद्भूमण्डलं धत्ते सशैलवनकाननम् ।।
तावत्तिष्ठति मेदिनयां सन्ततिः पुत्रपौत्रिकी ।।५४।।

yāvadbhūmaṇḍalam dhatte saśailavanakānanam ।।
tāvattiṣṭhati medinayām santatiḥ putrapautrikī ।।54।।

देहान्ते परमं स्थानं यात्सुरैरपि दुर्लभम् ।।
प्राप्नोति पुरुषो नित्यं महामायाप्रसादतः ।।५५।।

dehānte paramam sthānam yātsurairapi durlabham ।।
prāpnoti puruṣo nityam mahāmāyāprasādataḥ ।।55।।

लभते परमं रूपं शिवेन सह मोदते ।।ॐ।। ।।५६।।

labhate paramam rūpam śivena saha modate ।।56।।

(54-56) His progeny would live as long as the earth is rich with mountains and forests. By the Grace of Mahamaya, he would attain the highest place that is inaccessible even to the Gods and is eternally blissful in the company of Lord Shiva.

इति श्री देव्याः कवचं सम्पूर्णम्

iti śrī devyāḥ kavacam sampūrṇam

Thus, the armor (kavaca) of the
Holy Goddess is concluded.

अर्गलास्तोत्रम्

Argala Stotram

Introduction

The Argala Stotram is a powerful hymn dedicated to Goddess Durga, often recited during the Chandi Path or Durga Saptashati. The stotram is composed of verses that invoke the blessings of the Goddess in her various forms, asking for protection, prosperity, victory, and the removal of obstacles. The word "Argala" refers to a "bolt" or "lock," and just as a lock needs to be opened to gain access to something valuable, the recitation of the Argala Stotram is believed to unlock the blessings and grace of the Divine Mother.

ॐ अस्य श्रीअर्गलास्तोत्रमन्त्रस्य विष्णुर्ऋषिः, अनुष्टुप् छन्दः, श्रीमहालक्ष्मीर्देवता, श्रीजगदम्बाप्रीतये सप्तशतीपाठाङ्गत्वेन जपे विनियोगः ॥

ॐ नमश्चण्डिकायै ॥

मार्कण्डेय उवाच

oṃ asya śrīargalāstotramantrasya
viṣṇurṛṣiḥ,anuṣṭup chandaḥ,
śrīmahālakṣmīrdevatā, śrījagadambāprītaye
saptaśatīpāṭhāṅgatvena jape viniyogaḥ..
oṃ namaścaṇḍikāyai..

mārkaṇḍeya uvāca

Oṃ, for the recitation of this Argala Stotram mantra, the seer (Rishi) is Viṣṇu, the meter (Chandaḥ) is Anuṣṭup, the deity (Devata) is Śrī Mahālakṣmī, and it is used in the ritual recitation of the Saptaśatī for pleasing Śrī Jagadambā.

ॐ जयन्ती मङ्गला काली भद्रकाली कपालिनी ।।
दुर्गा क्षमा शिवा धात्री स्वाहा स्वधा नमोऽस्तु ते ।।१।।

oṃ jayantī maṅgalā kālī bhadrakālī kapālinī ।।
durgā kṣamā śivā dhātrī svāhā svadhā namo'stu te ।।1।।

Salutations to you, O Goddess! You are Jayantī (the victorious), Maṅgalā (the auspicious), Kālī (the black-hued one), Bhadrakālī (the benevolent and fierce form of Kālī), and Kapālinī (the one who holds a skull). You are Durgā (the invincible), Kṣamā (the embodiment of forgiveness), Śivā (the auspicious one), Dhātrī (the support of all beings), Svāhā (the invocation for offerings to the gods), and Svadhā (the invocation for offerings to the ancestors). Salutations to you!

जय त्वं देवि चामुण्डे जय भूतार्तिहारिणि ।।
जय सर्वगते देवि कालरात्रि नमोऽस्तु ते ।।२।।

jaya tvaṃ devi cāmuṇḍe jaya bhūtārtihāriṇi ।।
jaya sarvagate devi kālarātri namo'stu te ।।2।।

Victory to you, O Goddess Cāmuṇḍā! Victory to you, the remover of the distress of beings! Victory to you, O all-pervading Goddess, O Kālarātri (night of destruction), salutations to you!

मधुकैटभविद्राविविधातृवरदे नमः ॥
रुपं देहि जयं देहि यशो देहि द्विषो जहि ॥३॥

madhukaiṭabhavidrāvividhātṛvarade namaḥ ॥
rupaṃ dehi jayaṃ dehi yaśo dehi dviṣo jahi ॥3॥

Salutations to the one who bestowed boons after destroying the demons Madhuka and Kaiṭabha. Grant me beauty, grant me victory, grant me fame, and destroy my enemies.

महिषासुरनिर्णाशि भक्तानां सुखदे नमः ॥
रुपं देहि जयं देहि यशो देहि द्विषो जहि ॥४॥

mahiṣāsuranirṇāśi bhaktānāṃ sukhade namaḥ ॥
rupaṃ dehi jayaṃ dehi yaśo dehi dviṣo jahi ॥4॥

Salutations to the one who annihilated Mahishasura and who grants happiness to her devotees. Grant me beauty, grant me victory, grant me fame, and destroy my enemies.

रक्तबीजवधे देवि चण्डमुण्डविनाशिनि ।।
रुपं देहि जयं देहि यशो देहि द्विषो जहि ।।५।।

raktabījavadhe devi caṇḍamuṇḍavināśini ।।
rupaṃ dehi jayaṃ dehi yaśo dehi dviṣo jahi ।।5।।

O Goddess, the slayer of Raktabīja and the destroyer of Caṇḍa and Muṇḍa, grant me beauty, grant me victory, grant me fame, and destroy my enemies.

शुम्भस्यैव निशुम्भस्य धूम्राक्षस्य च मर्दिनि ।।
रुपं देहि जयं देहि यशो देहि द्विषो जहि ।।६।।

śumbhasyaiva niśumbhasya dhūmrākṣasya ca mardini ।।
rupaṃ dehi jayaṃ dehi yaśo dehi dviṣo jahi ।।6।।

O destroyer of Śumbha, Niśumbha, and Dhūmrākṣa, grant me beauty, grant me victory, grant me fame, and destroy my enemies.

वन्दिताङ्घ्रियुगे देवि सर्वसौभाग्यदायिनि ।।
रुपं देहि जयं देहि यशो देहि द्विषो जहि ।।७।।

vanditāṅghriyuge devi sarvasaubhāgyadāyini ।।
rupaṃ dehi jayaṃ dehi yaśo dehi dviṣo jahi ।।7।।

O Goddess, whose feet are worshipped and who bestows all auspiciousness, grant me beauty, grant me victory, grant me fame, and destroy my enemies.

अचिन्त्यरुपचरिते सर्वशत्रुविनाशिनि ।।
रुपं देहि जयं देहि यशो देहि द्विषो जहि ।।८।।

acintyarupacarite sarvaśatruvināśini ।।
rupaṃ dehi jayaṃ dehi yaśo dehi dviṣo jahi ।।8।।

O Goddess of incomprehensible form and deeds, destroyer of all enemies, grant me beauty, grant me victory, grant me fame, and destroy my enemies.

नतेभ्य: सर्वदा भक्त्या चण्डिके दुरितापहे ।।
रुपं देहि जयं देहि यशो देहि द्विषो जहि ।।९।।

natebhyaḥ sarvadā bhaktyā caṇḍike duritāpahe ।।
rupaṃ dehi jayaṃ dehi yaśo dehi dviṣo jahi ।।9।।

O Caṇḍikā, who is always worshipped with devotion and who removes suffering, grant me beauty, grant me victory, grant me fame, and destroy my enemies.

स्तुवद्भ्यो भक्तिपूर्वं त्वां चण्डिके व्याधिनाशिनि ।।
रुपं देहि जयं देहि यशो देहि द्विषो जहि ।।१०।।

stuvadbhyo bhaktipūrvaṃ tvāṃ caṇḍike vyādhināśini ।।
rupaṃ dehi jayaṃ dehi yaśo dehi dviṣo jahi ।।10।।

O Caṇḍikā, destroyer of diseases, you are praised with full devotion. Grant me beauty, grant me victory, grant me fame, and destroy my enemies.

चण्डिके सततं ये त्वामर्चयन्तीह भक्तित: ।।
रुपं देहि जयं देहि यशो देहि द्विषो जहि ।।११।।

caṇḍike satataṃ ye tvāmarcayantīha bhaktitaḥ ।।
rupaṃ dehi jayaṃ dehi yaśo dehi dviṣo jahi ।।11।।

O Caṇḍikā, to those who constantly worship you with devotion, grant me beauty, grant me victory, grant me fame, and destroy my enemies.

देहि सौभाग्यमारोग्यं देहि मे परमं सुखम् ।।
रुपं देहि जयं देहि यशो देहि द्विषो जहि ।।१२।।

dehi saubhāgyamārogyaṃ dehi me paramaṃ sukham ।।
rupaṃ dehi jayaṃ dehi yaśo dehi dviṣo jahi ।।12।।

Grant me good fortune and health, and bestow upon me supreme happiness. Grant me beauty, grant me victory, grant me fame, and destroy my enemies.

विधेहि द्विषतां नाशं विधेहि बलमुच्चकैः ॥
रुपं देहि जयं देहि यशो देहि द्विषो जहि ॥१३॥

vidhehi dviṣatāṃ nāśaṃ vidhehi balamuccakaiḥ ॥
rupaṃ dehi jayaṃ dehi yaśo dehi dviṣo jahi ॥13॥

Bring about the destruction of my enemies and grant me great strength. Grant me beauty, grant me victory, grant me fame, and destroy my enemies.

विधेहि देवि कल्याणं विधेहि परमां श्रियम् ॥
रुपं देहि जयं देहि यशो देहि द्विषो जहि ॥१४॥

vidhehi devi kalyāṇaṃ vidhehi paramāṃ śriyam ॥
rupaṃ dehi jayaṃ dehi yaśo dehi dviṣo jahi ॥14॥

O Goddess, grant me auspiciousness and bestow supreme prosperity. Grant me beauty, grant me victory, grant me fame, and destroy my enemies.

सुरासुरशिरोरत्ननिघृष्टचरणेऽम्बिके ।।
रुपं देहि जयं देहि यशो देहि द्विषो जहि ।।१५।।

surāsuraśiroratnanighṛṣṭacaraṇe’mbike ।।
rupaṃ dehi jayaṃ dehi yaśo dehi dviṣo jahi ।।15।।

O Mother, whose feet are adorned with the crowns of both gods and demons, grant me beauty, grant me victory, grant me fame, and destroy my enemies.

❧

विद्यावन्तं यशस्वन्तं लक्ष्मीवन्तं जनं कुरु ।।
रुपं देहि जयं देहि यशो देहि द्विषो जहि ।।१६।।

vidyāvantaṃ yaśasvantaṃ lakṣmīvantaṃ janaṃ kuru ।।
rupaṃ dehi jayaṃ dehi yaśo dehi dviṣo jahi ।।16।।

Make me learned, famous, and prosperous.
Grant me beauty, grant me victory, grant me fame, and destroy my enemies.

❧

प्रचण्डदैत्यदर्पघ्ने चण्डिके प्रणताय मे ।।
रुपं देहि जयं देहि यशो देहि द्विषो जहि ।।१७।।

pracaṇḍadaityadarpaghne caṇḍike praṇatāya me ।।
rupaṃ dehi jayaṃ dehi yaśo dehi dviṣo jahi ।।17।।

O Caṇḍikā, destroyer of the arrogance of fierce demons, I bow to you. Grant me beauty, grant me victory, grant me fame, and destroy my enemies.

चतुर्भुजे चतुर्वक्त्रसंस्तुते परमेश्वरि ।।
रुपं देहि जयं देहि यशो देहि द्विषो जहि ।।१८।।

caturbhuje caturvaktrasaṃstute parameśvari ।।
rupaṃ dehi jayaṃ dehi yaśo dehi dviṣo jahi ।।18।।

O supreme Goddess, praised in your form with four arms and four faces, grant me beauty, grant me victory, grant me fame, and destroy my enemies.

कृष्णेन संस्तुते देवि शश्वद्भक्त्या सदाम्बिके ।।
रुपं देहि जयं देहि यशो देहि द्विषो जहि ।।१९।।

kṛṣṇena saṃstute devi śaśvadbhaktyā sadāmbike ।।
rupaṃ dehi jayaṃ dehi yaśo dehi dviṣo jahi ।।19।।

O Goddess, constantly praised by Kṛṣṇa with devotion, O Mother, grant me beauty, grant me victory, grant me fame, and destroy my enemies.

हिमाचलसुतानाथसंस्तुते परमेश्वरि ॥
रुपं देहि जयं देहि यशो देहि द्विषो जहि ॥२०॥

himācalasutānāthasaṃstute parameśvari ॥
rupaṃ dehi jayaṃ dehi yaśo dehi dviṣo jahi ॥20॥

O supreme Goddess, praised by the Lord of the daughter of Himācala (Śiva), grant me beauty, grant me victory, grant me fame, and destroy my enemies.

इन्द्राणीपतिसद्भावपूजिते परमेश्वरि ॥
रुपं देहि जयं देहि यशो देहि द्विषो जहि ॥२१॥

indrāṇīpatisadbhāvapūjite parameśvari ॥
rupaṃ dehi jayaṃ dehi yaśo dehi dviṣo jahi ॥21॥

O supreme Goddess, worshipped by Indrāṇī's consort (Indra), grant me beauty, grant me victory, grant me fame, and destroy my enemies.

देवि प्रचण्डदोर्दण्डदैत्यदर्पविनाशिनि ॥
रुपं देहि जयं देहि यशो देहि द्विषो जहि ॥२२॥

devi pracaṇḍadordaṇḍadaityadarpavināśini ॥
rupaṃ dehi jayaṃ dehi yaśo dehi dviṣo jahi ॥22॥

O Goddess, destroyer of the pride of demons with your powerful arms, grant me beauty, grant me victory, grant me fame, and destroy my enemies.

देवि भक्तजनोद्दामदत्तानन्दोदयेऽम्बिके ॥
रुपं देहि जयं देहि यशो देहि द्विषो जहि ॥२३॥

devi bhaktajanoddāmadattānandodaye'mbike ॥
rupaṃ dehi jayaṃ dehi yaśo dehi dviṣo jahi ॥23॥

O Mother Goddess, giver of great joy to your devotees, grant me beauty, grant me victory, grant me fame, and destroy my enemies.

पत्नीं मनोरमां देहि मनोवृत्तानुसारिणीम् ॥
तारिणीं दुर्गसंसारसागरस्य कुलोद्भवाम् ॥२४॥

patnīṃ manoramāṃ dehi manovṛttānusāriṇīm ॥
tāriṇīṃ durgasaṃsārasāgarasya kulodbhavām ॥24॥

Grant me a delightful wife who follows my heart's desires, who helps me cross the difficult ocean of worldly existence, and who comes from a noble family.

इदं स्तोत्रं पठित्वा तु महास्तोत्रं पठेन्नरः ॥
स तु सप्तशतीसंख्यावरमाप्नोति सम्पदाम् ॥२५॥

idaṃ stotraṃ paṭhitvā tu mahāstotraṃ paṭhennaraḥ ॥
sa tu saptaśatīsaṃkhyāvaramāpnoti sampadām ॥25॥

iti devyā argalāstotraṃ sampūrṇam

After reciting this stotra, one should also recite the great stotra. He shall obtain the merit of reciting the entire Saptaśatī and attain great prosperity.

कीलकम्

Sri Kilaka Mantra

ॐ अस्य श्रीकीलकमन्त्रस्य शिवऋषिः, अनुष्टुप् छन्दः,
श्रीमहासरस्वती देवता, श्रीजगदम्बाप्रीत्यर्थं
सप्तशतीपाठाङ्गत्वेन जपे विनियोगः ॥

oṁ asya śrī-kīlaka-mantrasya śiva ṛṣiḥ, anuṣṭup chandaḥ,
śrī-mahāsarasvatī devatā, śrī-jagadambā-prītyarthaṁ
saptashatī-pāṭhāṅgatvena jape viniyogaḥ.

This verse is the *viniyoga* (statement of purpose) for reciting the Sri Kilaka Mantra, which is part of the Durga Saptashati (also known as the Devi Mahatmyam). It states that Shiva is the sage (rishi), Anushtup is the meter (chhanda), and the presiding deity is Sri Mahasaraswati. The mantra is to be recited as an integral part of the Saptashati recitation, with the aim of pleasing Sri Jagadamba, the Divine Mother.

मार्कण्डेय उवाच

विशुद्धज्ञानदेहाय त्रिवेदीदिव्यचक्षुषे ॥
श्रेयः प्राप्तिनिमित्ताय नमः सोमार्धधारिणे ॥१॥

ṃārkannddeya ūvāca

Viśuddha-Jnyāna-ḍehāya ṭri-Vedī-ḍivya-Cakssusse ॥
ṣreyah Prāpti-ṇimittāya ṇamah Soma-ārdha-ḍhārinne ॥1॥

Sage Markandeya said: (I offer my salutations to the one) the essence of whose form is that of pure knowledge (of absolute consciousness) [vishuddha-jnana-dehaya] and whose three divine eyes form the three vedas [tri-vedi-divya-cakssusse], to imbibe that auspiciousness (of pure knowledge). I meditate on Shiva and Shakti in their conscious blissful form. I offer my salutations to Shiva who bears the half-of-soma (soma means moon) and also to Shakti who bears half-of-soma (in her body as ardhanareeswara. Soma here is Shiva). Therefore, she has the same qualities of Shiva, of vishuddha jnana deha and trivedi divya cakssu. Keelaka is pin or nail. The conscious form of Shakti is pinned to all the mantras of devi mahatmyam as the underlying principle through the keelaka stotram.

सर्वमेतद् विजानीयान्मन्त्राणामपि कीलकम् ॥
सोऽपि क्षेममवाप्नोति सततं जाप्यतत्परः ॥२॥

Sarvam-ĕtad Vijānīyān-ṃantrānnām-āpi khīlakam ॥
So-[ā]pi khssemam-āvāpnoti Satatam Jāpya-ṭatparah ॥2॥

All these hymns of Keelaka stotram, one should know, are indeed the keelaka (pin or nail) by which the mantras (of devi mahatmyan are pinned) (i.e. by which the underlying principle of the conscious form of devi are pinned), he who devotes himself to continuously chant these hymns, indeed attains tranquility of mind (i.e. he who continuously meditates on the conscious form of devi in the heart indeed attains tranquility of mind).

सिद्ध्यन्त्युच्चाटनादीनि कर्माणि सकलान्यपि ।।
एतेन स्तुवतां देविं स्तोत्रवृन्देन भक्तितः ।।३।।

Siddhyanty[i]-ūccāttana-[ā]adīni
kharmānni Sakalāny[i]-āpi ।।
ĕtena Stuvatām ḍevim
Stotra-Vrndena Bhaktitah ।।3।।

He accomplishes uccatana (eradication of inner enemies) to the very root, and all related (spiritual) accomplishments, by extolling the devi with devotional fervour with this collection of hymns.

न मन्त्रो नौषधं तत्र न किञ्चिदपि विद्यते ।।
विना जप्येन सिद्ध्येत्तु सर्वमुच्चाटनादिकम् ।।४।।

ṇa ṃantro ṇa-[ā]ussadham ṭatra ṇa <u>kh</u>in.cid-āpi Vidyate ।।
Vinā Japyena Siddhayet-ṭu Sarvam-ūccāttana-[ā]adikam ।।4।।

There are no mantras (hymns) or ousadha (medicine) available, even a trace (which can accomplish uccatana), without chanting (any mantras) one accomplishes uccatana (eradication of inner enemies), all to its very root (by meditating on the conscious form of devi in the heart while reciting the devi mahatmyam).(here reciting devi mahatmyam is not like chanting any mantra to obtain the fruit of uccatana, but for meditation on the conscious form of devi and merging our ego in her.)

समग्राण्यपि सेत्स्यन्ति लोकशङ्कामिमां हरः ।।
कृत्वा निमन्त्रयामास सर्वमेवमिदं शुभम् ।।५।।

Samagrānny[i]-āpi Setsyanti ḻoka-ṣangkām-īmām ḥarah ।।
<u>kh</u>rtvā ṇimantrayāmāsa Sarvam-ĕvam-īdam ṣubham ।।5।।

People had this doubt, how can it be that everything is indeed accomplished (uccatana and other fruits) by reciting the devi mahatmyam which appears to be full of violence; Lord Shiva summoned and pinned the underlying principle of the conscious form of devi to all the mantras of devi mahatmyam; and having done that all this indeed became auspicious (i.e. now the violence in the battlefield became the auspicious force purging us from within).

स्तोत्रं वै चण्डिकायास्तु तच्च गुह्यं चकार सः ।।
समाप्नोति स पुण्येन तां यथावन्निमन्त्रणाम् ।।६।।

Stotram Vai Cannddikāyās-ṭu ṭac-Ca ġuhyam Cakāra Sah ।।
Samāpnoti Sa Punnyena ṭām ẏathāvan-ṇimantrannām ।।6।।

That stotra of devi Chandika (i.e. Keelaka stotra), lord Shiva indeed made it hidden (behind every mantra of devi mahatmyam) thus making the conscious form of devi as the object of meditation, he achieves everything by her auspiciousness, when she is invoked in the right manner by meditating on her eternal conscious form.

सोऽपि क्षेममवाप्नोति सर्वमेव न संशयः ।।
कृष्णायां वा चतुर्दश्यामष्टम्यां वा समाहितः ।।७।।

So-[ā]pi khssemam-āvāpnoti Sarvam-ĕva ṇa Samśayah ।।
khrssnnāyām Vā Caturdaśyām-āssttamyām Vā Samāhitah ।।7।।

He indeed attains tranquility of mind and all other fruits, there is no doubt about it, he who meditates (on the devi) on Krishna paksha chaturdashi or ashtami of a month.

ददाति प्रतिगृह्णाति नान्यथैषा प्रसीदति ।।
इत्थंरूपेण कीलेन महादेवेन कीलितम् ।।८।।

ḍadāti Pratigrhnnāti ṇa-ānyathai[ā-ĕ]ssā Prasīdati ||
īttham-ṟūpenna khīlena ṃahādevena khīlitam ||8||

While meditating on the conscious form of devi during recitation of devi mahatmyam, he should give himself, in surrender to her lotus feet, and receive in return her grace; Otherwise she is not pleased (by mechanical recitation of devi mahatmyam bereft of devotion), in this manner, by the keela (pin of keelaka stotram) Mahadeva pinned the mantras of devi mahatmyam (making the meditation on the conscious form of devi the central theme).

यो निष्कीलां विधायैनां चण्डीं जपति नित्यशः ॥
स सिद्धः स गणः सोऽथ गन्धर्वो जायते ध्रुवम् ॥९॥

ẏo ṇisskīlām Vidhāyai[a-ĕ]nām Cannddīm Japati ṇityaśah ||
Sa Siddhah Sa ġannah Sotha ġandharvo Jāyate ḍhruvam ||9||

He who after unpinning the keelaka makes her manifest (i.e. invokes her conscious form in the heart), and then recites the chandi, by constantly dwelling (on her conscious form), he becomes a siddha (spiritually accomplished), he becomes a gana (an attendent of the devi), he becomes a gandharva (celestial singer who glorifies the devi), truly.

न चौवापाटवं तस्य भयं क्वापि न जायते ॥
नापमृत्युवशं याति मृते च मोक्षमाप्नुयात् ॥१०॥

ṇa Cai[a-ĕ]va-āpāttavam ṭasya Bhayam <u>kh</u>vāpi ṇa Jāyate ॥
ṇa-āpamrtyu-Vaśam ẏāti ṃrte Ca ṃokssam-āapnuyāt ॥10॥

He indeed does not become handicapped (prematurely) with major diseases; fear does not rise in him anywhere (which leads to unnecessary anxiety), he does not become victim of premature death; and after death attains moksha (liberation).

ज्ञात्वा प्रारभ्य कुर्वीत ह्यकुर्वाणो विनश्यति ॥
ततो ज्ञात्वैव सम्पूर्णमिदं प्रारभ्यते बुधैः ॥११॥

Jnyātvā Prārabhya <u>kh</u>urvīta
ḥy[i]-ākurvānno Vinaśyati ॥
ṭato Jnyātvai[ā-ĕ]va Sampūrnnam-
īdam Prārabhyate Budhaih ॥11॥

Only after knowing (the keelakam), he should begin (reciting the devi mahatmyam); if not done in this manner, he is deprived (of the fruits of recitation), therefore only after knowing this fully (i.e. understanding the keelaka fully), the wise men begin reciting the devi mahatmyam.

सौभाग्यादि च यत्किञ्चिद् दृश्यते ललनाजने ॥
तत्सर्वं तत्प्रसादेन तेन जप्यमिदं शुभम् ॥१२॥

Saubhāgya-[ā]adi Ca ẏatkin.cid ḍrśyate ḻalanā-Jane ॥
ṭat-Sarvam ṭat-Prasādena ṭena Japyam-īdam ṣubham ॥12॥

Whatever good fortune, beauty, charm and the like are seen in women, all that is the result of your grace; Therefore women should chant this auspicious stotra and meditate on the auspicious form of the devi.

शनैस्तु जप्यमानेऽस्मिन् स्तोत्रे सम्पत्तिरुच्चकैः ॥
भवत्येव समग्रापि ततः प्रारभ्यमेव तत् ॥१३॥

ṣanaistu Japyamāne-[ā]smin Stotre Sampattir-ūccakaih ॥
Bhavaty[i]-ĕva Samagra-āpi ṭatah Prārabhyam-ĕva ṭat ॥13॥

If this stotra is chanted gently (without haste) (meditating on its true import), one attains (spiritual) wealth of the highest kind, one indeed becomes the whole (i.e. fragmentation of the ego gradually melts and one feels the conscious form of devi behind everything); therefore, one should undertake the chanting of this keelaka.

ऐश्वर्यं यत्प्रसादेन सौभाग्यारोग्यसम्पदः ॥
शत्रुहानिः परो मोक्षः स्तूयते सा न किं जनैः ॥१४॥

āiśvaryam ẏat-Prasādena Saubhāgya-[ā]arogya-Sampadah ॥
ṣatru-ḥānih Paro ṃokssah Stūyate Sā ṇa <u>kh</u>im Janaih ॥14॥

By whose grace divine qualities (aishwaryam) are awakened; by whose presence good fortune (saubhagya), health (freedom from disease) (arogya) and wealth (sampada) are manifested, by whose mercy enemies are eradicated; (and) by whose special grace one finally attains the highest liberation (moksha); why should'nt she be praised by the people (who is all-merciful)?

।। प्रथमोऽध्यायः ।।

मधु कैटभ वध

Śrī Durgāsaptaśatī—Prathamo'dhyāyaḥ (Madhukaiṭabhavadho Nāma Prathamo'dhyāyaḥ)

।। First Chapter ।।

The Slaying of Madhu and Kaiṭabha

।। विनियोगः ।।

।। Viniyogah ।।
(Statement of Purpose)

ॐ प्रथमचरित्रस्य ब्रह्मा ऋषिः, महाकाली देवता, गायत्री छन्दः,
नन्दा शक्तिः, रक्तदन्तिका बीजम्, अग्निस्तत्त्वम्,
ऋग्वेदः स्वरूपम्, श्रीमहाकालीप्रीत्यर्थे प्रथमचरित्रजपे विनियोगः ।

Oṃ prathamacaritrasya brahmā ṛṣiḥ,
mahākālī devatā, gāyatrī chandaḥ,

nandā śaktiḥ, raktadantikā bījam, agnistattvam,
ṛgvedaḥ svarūpam, śrīmahākālīprītyarthe
prathamacaritrajape vinayogaḥ ।

"Om. In the first Charitra (episode), the Rishi (seer) is Brahmā; the deity is Mahākālī; the meter is Gāyatrī; the Śakti is Nandā; the seed (bīja) is Raktadantikā; the elemental principle is Agni (fire); and the essence is of the Ṛgveda. This is the viniyoga (dedicatory statement) for the recitation of the first Charitra, intended for the propitiation of Śrī Mahākālī."

॥ ध्यानम् ॥

॥ Dhyānam ॥
(Meditation Verse)

ॐ खड्गं चक्रगदेषुचापपरिघाञ्छूलं भुशुण्डीं शिर:
शङ्खं संदधतीं करैस्त्रिनयनां सर्वाङ्गभूषावृताम् ।
नीलाश्मद्युतिमास्यपाददशकां सेवे महाकालिकां
यामस्तौत्स्वपिते हरौ कमलजो हन्तुं मधुं कैटभम् ॥१॥

Oṃ khaḍgaṃ cakragadeṣu cāpaparighāñ
chūlaṃ bhuśuṇḍīṃ śiraḥ
śaṅkhaṃ saṃdadhatīṃ karais trinayanāṃ
sarvāṅgabhūṣāvṛtām ।
Nīlāśmadyutim āsyapādadaśakāṃ
seve mahākālikāṃ

Yām astaut svapite harau kamalajo
hantuṃ madhuṃ kaiṭabham ||1||

"Om. I meditate on Mahākālikā,
who holds sword, discus, mace, bow, iron club,
spear, slingshot, and severed head,
who bears the conch in her hands, who has three eyes,
who is adorned with all ornaments on her entire body,
whose ten faces and feet shine like blue-black sapphires.
She is the one whom the lotus-born (Brahmā)
praised while Lord Hari (Viṣṇu) was asleep,
in order to slay Madhu and Kaiṭabha."

ॐ नमश्चण्डिकायै

Oṃ namaś caṇḍikāyai

OM Salutation to Chanḍika

"ॐ ऐं" मार्कण्डेय उवाच ॥१॥

"Oṃ aiṃ" Mārkaṇḍeya uvāca ||1||

OM aim. Markanḍeya said

सावर्णिः सूर्यतनयो यो मनुः कथ्यतेऽष्टमः ।
निशामय तदुत्पत्तिं विस्तराद् गदतो मम ॥२॥

Sāvarṇiḥ sūryatanayo yo manuḥ kathyate'ṣṭamaḥ ।
Niśāmaya tad utpattiṃ vistarād gadato mama ।।2।।

Savarṇi, who is Surya's son, is called the eighth manu.
Listen while I relate the story of his birth

ஃ

महामायानुभावेन यथा मन्वन्तराधिपः।
स बभूव महाभागः सावर्णिस्तनयो रवेः ।।३।।

Mahāmāyānubhāvena yathā manvantarādhipaḥ ।
Sa babhūva mahābhāgaḥ sāvarṇis tanayo raveḥ ।।3।।

And of how, by Mahāmāyā's authority, he—the illustrious son of the sun god came to be the lord of an age.

ஃ

स्वारोचिषेऽन्तरे पूर्वं चैत्रवंशसमुद्भवः ।
सुरथो नाम राजाभूत्समस्ते क्षितिमण्डले ।।४।।

Svārociṣe'ntare pūrvaṃ caitravaṃśasamudbhavaḥ ।
suratho nāma rājābhūt samaste kṣitimaṇḍale ।।4।।

Long ago in the age of the manu Svarociṣba, there arose from the line of Caitra a king named Suratha, who ruled over the whole earth.

ஃ

तस्य पालयतः सम्यक् प्रजाः पुत्रानिवौरसान् ।
बभूवुः शत्रवो भूपाः कोलाविध्वंसिनस्तदा ॥५॥

Tasya pālayataḥ samyak prajāḥ putrān ivaurasān ।
Babhūvuḥ śatravo bhūpāḥ kolāvidhvaṃsinas tadā ॥5॥

He looked after his subjects justly, as if they were his own children. But there were princes at that time who attacked the native hill tribes and became his enemies.

तस्य तैरभवद् युद्धमतिप्रबलदण्डिनः ।
न्यूनैरपि स तैर्युद्धे कोलाविध्वंसिभिर्जितः ॥६॥

Tasya tair abhavad yuddham atiprabala daṇḍinaḥ ।
Nyūnair api sa tair yuddhe kolāvidhvaṃsibhir jitaḥ ॥6॥

Though mightily armed and resolved to fight against them, he suffered defeat in battle, despite his enemies' inferior forces.

ततः स्वपुरमायातो निजदेशाधिपोऽभवत् ।
आक्रान्तः स महाभागस्तैस्तदा प्रबलारिभिः ॥७॥

Tataḥ svapuram āyāto nijadeśādhipo'bhavat ।
ākṛāntaḥ sa mahābhāgas tais tadā prabalāribhiḥ ॥7॥

And so, with only his native province left to rule, he returned to his own city. There, powerful adversaries set upon him, the illustrious Suratha.

अमात्यैर्बलिभिर्दुष्टैर्दुर्बलस्य दुरात्मभिः ।
कोशो बलं चापहृतं तत्रापि स्वपुरे ततः ॥८॥

Amātyair balibhis duṣṭair durbalasya durātmabhiḥ ।
Kośo balaṃ cāpahṛtaṃ tatrāpi svapure tataḥ ॥8॥

Now bereft of strength. His ministers, mighty, corrupted, and disposed to evil, seized power and plundered the treasury, even there in his own city.

ततो मृगयाव्याजेन हृतस्वाम्यः स भूपतिः ।
एकाकी हयमारुह्य जगाम गहनं वनम् ॥९॥

Tato mṛgayāvyājena hṛtasvātmyaḥ sa bhūpatiḥ ।
Ekākī hayam āruhya jagāma gahanaṃ vanam ॥9॥

Thus robbed of his dominion, the king mounted his horse on the pretext of hunting and rode off alone into the dense forest.

स तत्राश्रममद्राक्षीद् द्विजवर्यस्य मेधसः ।
प्रशान्तश्वापदाकीर्णं मुनिशिष्योपशोभितम् ॥१०॥

Sa tatrāśramam adrākṣīd dvijavaryasya medhasaḥ ।
Praśāntaśvāpadākīrṇaṃ muniśiṣyopaśobhitam ।।10।।

He came upon the hermitage of Medhas, chief among the twice-born, and beheld a forest retreat, graced by the sage's disciples. There he saw beasts once wild now peacefully abiding.

तस्थौ कंचित्स कालं च मुनिना तेन सत्कृतः ।
इतश्चेतश्च विचरंस्तस्मिन्मुनिवराश्रमे ।।११।।

Tasthau kaṃcit sa kālaṃ ca muninā tena satkṛtaḥ ।
Itaś cetaś ca vicaran tasmin munivarāśrame ।।11।।

Welcomed by the sage, he remained at the hermitage for some time, wandering here and there about the enclosure.

सोऽचिन्तयत्तदा तत्र ममत्वाकृष्टचेतनः ।
मत्पूर्वैः पालितं पूर्वं मया हीनं पुरं हि तत् ।।१२।।

So'cintayat tadā tatra mamatvākṛṣṭacetanaḥ ।
Matpūrvaiḥ pālitaṃ pūrvaṃ mayā hīnaṃ puraṃ hi tat ।।12।।

Then he (the king) thought there, with his mind drawn by attachment (mamattva): 'This city, formerly protected by my ancestors, has now been taken away from me.

मद्भृत्यैस्तैरसद्वृत्तैर्धर्मतः पाल्यते न वा ।
न जाने स प्रधानो मे शूरहस्ती सदामदः ॥१३॥

Madbhṛtyais tair asadvṛttair dharmataḥ pālyate na vā ।
Na jāne sa pradhāno me śūrahastī sadā madaḥ ॥13॥

By those servants of mine, who are of evil conduct, is it being governed righteously or not—I do not know. That chief among them, my war-elephant, is always intoxicated with pride.

~

मम वैरिवशं यातः कान् भोगानुपलप्स्यते।
ये ममानुगता नित्यं प्रसादधनभोजनैः ॥१४॥

Mama vairivaśaṃ yātaḥ kān bhogān upalapsyate ।
Ye mamānugatā nityaṃ prasādadhanabhojanaiḥ ॥14॥

My prized elephant, valiant and of unceasing prowess, has fallen into the hands of my enemies. I know not what comforts he'll now enjoy.

~

अनुवृत्तिं ध्रुवं तेऽद्य कुर्वन्त्यन्यमहीभृताम्।
असम्यग्व्यशीलैस्तैः कुर्वद्भिः सततं व्ययम् ॥१५॥

Anuvṛttiṃ dhruvaṃ te'dya kurvanty anyamahībhṛtām ।
Asamyaṅ vyāśīlaiḥ taiḥ kurvadbhiḥ satataṃ vyayam ॥15॥

Those retainers of mine, constantly eager for favor, wealth, and feasting, now surely submit to other lords.

संचितः सोऽतिदुःखेन क्षयं कोशो गमिष्यति।
एतच्चान्यच्च सततं चिन्तयामास पार्थिवः ॥१६॥

Saṃcitaḥ so'tiduḥkhena kṣayaṃ kośo gamiṣyati ।
Etac cānyac ca satataṃ cintayāmāsa pārthivaḥ ॥16॥

Their habitual squandering will soon deplete the wealth I so laboriously amassed.

तत्र विप्राश्रमाभ्याशे वैश्यमेकं ददर्श सः।
स पृष्टस्तेन कस्त्वं भो हेतुश्चागमनेऽत्र कः ॥१७॥

Tatra viprāśramābhyāśe vaiśyam ekaṃ dadarśa saḥ ॥
Sa pṛṣṭas tena kastvaṃ bho hetuś cāgamane'tra kaḥ ॥17॥

While pondering those and other questions, the king caught sight of a lone merchant approaching the sage's hermitage.

सशोक इव कस्मात्त्वं दुर्मना इव लक्ष्यसे।
इत्याकर्ण्य वचस्तस्य भूपतेः प्रणयोदितम् ॥१८॥

Śaśoka iva kasmāt tvaṃ durmanā iva lakṣyase ॥
Ity ākarṇya vacas tasya bhūpateḥ praṇayoditam ॥18॥

"Who are you," he asked, "and what brings you here? Why do you look so sorrowful and dejected?"

प्रत्युवाच स तं वैश्यः प्रश्रयावनतो नृपम् ॥१९॥

Pratyuvāca sa taṃ vaiśyaḥ praśrayāvanato nṛpam ॥19॥

Hearing the king speak in friendship, the merchant bowed respectfully and replied.

वैश्य उवाच ॥२०॥

Vaiśya uvāca ॥20॥

The merchant said:

समाधिर्नाम वैश्योऽहमुत्पन्नो धनिनां कुले ॥२१॥

Samādhir nāma vaiśyo'ham utpanno dhaninām kule ॥21॥

I am a merchant named Samādhi, born in a wealthy family.

पुत्रदारैर्निरस्तश्च धनलोभादसाधुभिः ।
विहीनश्च धनैर्दारैः पुत्रैरादाय मे धनम् ॥२२॥

Putradārair nirastaś ca dhanalobhād asādhubhiḥ ।
Vihīnaś ca dhanair dāraiḥ putrair ādāya me dhanam ॥22॥

My wife and children grew wicked through avarice and cast me out. Destitute of riches, wife, and children, my wealth taken from me.

वनमभ्यागतो दुःखी निरस्तश्चाप्तबन्धुभिः ।
सोऽहं न वेद्मि पुत्राणां कुशलाकुशलात्मिकाम् ॥२३॥

Vanam abhyāgato duḥkhī nirastaś cāptabandhubhiḥ ॥
So'haṃ na vedmi putrāṇāṃ kuśalākuśalātmikām ॥23॥

I have arrived in the forest, distressed and forsaken by trusted kinsmen. Being here, I know not whether good fortune or ill has befallen my children, wife, and family.

प्रवृत्तिं स्वजनानां च दाराणां चात्र संस्थितः ।
किं नु तेषां गृहे क्षेममक्षेमं किं नु साम्प्रतम् ॥२४॥

Pravṛttiṃ svajanānāṃ ca dārāṇāṃ cātra saṃsthitaḥ ॥
Kiṃ nu teṣāṃ gṛhe kṣemam akṣemaṃ kiṃ nu sāmpratam ॥24॥

Being here, I know not whether good fortune or ill has befallen my children, wife, and family. At present is well-being or misfortune theirs at home?

कथं ते किं नु सद्वृत्ता दुर्वृत्ताः किं नु मे सुताः ॥२५॥

Kathaṃ te kiṃ nu sadvṛttā durvṛttāḥ kiṃ nu me sutāḥ ॥25॥

How are my children? Is their behavior virtuous or vile?

राजोवाच ॥२६॥

Rājovāca ॥26॥

The king said:

यैर्निरस्तो भवाँल्लुब्धैः पुत्रदारादिभिर्धनैः ॥२७॥

Yair nirasto bhavān lubdhaiḥ putradārādibhir dhanair ॥27॥

Those greedy sons, wife, and others who
dispossessed you of your wealth—

तेषु किं भवतः स्नेहमनुबध्नाति मानसम् ॥२८॥

Teṣu kiṃ bhavataḥ sneham anubadhnāti mānasam ॥28॥

Why does your mind still cherish them?

वैश्य उवाच ॥२९॥

Vaiśya uvāca ॥29॥

The merchant said

एवमेतद्यथा प्राह भवानस्मद्गतं वचः ॥३०॥

Evam etad yathā prāha bhavān asmadgataṃ vacaḥ ॥30॥

Even as you say it, this very thought occurs to me.

किं करोमि न बध्नाति मम निष्ठुरतां मनः ।
यैः संत्यज्य पितृस्नेहं धनलुब्धैर्निराकृतः ॥३१॥

Kiṃ karomi na badhnāti mama niṣṭhuratāṃ manaḥ ।
Yaiḥ saṃtyajya pitṛsnehaṃ dhanalubdhair nirākṛtaḥ ॥31॥

But what can I do? My heart is not inclined to rancor,
but still turns with affection to those who drove me away.

पतिस्वजनहार्दं च हार्दि तेष्वेव मे मनः ।
किमेतन्नाभिजानामि जानन्नपि महामते ॥३२॥

Patisvajanahārdaṃ ca hārdi teṣv eva me manaḥ ।
Kim etan nābhijānāmi jānann api mahāmate ॥32॥

Scorning love for father, husband, and kinsman,
out of lust for wealth. I recognize this, O wise one.

यत्प्रेमप्रवणं चित्तं विगुणेष्वपि बन्धुषु ।
तेषां कृते मे निःश्वासो दौर्मनस्यं च जायते ॥३३॥

Yat premapravaṇaṃ cittaṃ viguṇeṣv api bandhuṣu ।
Teṣāṃ kṛte me niḥśvāso daurmanasyaṃ ca jāyate ॥33॥

Still, I do not understand how my thoughts are drawn
in love to my unworthy kinsfolk. Because of them
I sigh, overcome with despair.

करोमि किं यन्न मनस्तेष्वप्रीतिषु निष्ठुरम् ॥३४॥

Karomi kiṃ yan na manas teṣv aprītiṣu niṣṭhuram ॥34॥

What can I do, since the pain has failed to harden my heart?

मार्कण्डेय उवाच ॥३५॥

Mārkaṇḍeya uvāca ॥35॥

Mārkaṇḍeya said:

ततस्तौ सहितौ विप्र तं मुनिं समुपस्थितौ ॥३६॥

Tataḥ tau sahitau vipra taṁ muniṁ samupasthitau ॥36॥

Then together they approached the sage.

समाधिर्नाम वैश्योऽसौ स च पार्थिवसत्तमः ।
कृत्वा तु तौ यथान्यायं यथार्हं तेन संविदम् ॥३७॥

Samādhir nāma vaiśyo'sau sa ca pārthiva-sattamaḥ
Kṛtvā tu tau yathānyāyaṁ yathārhaṁ tena saṁ vidam ॥37॥

That merchant named Samādhi and Suratha, the best of kings. Having observed the respect that was the sage's due.

उपविष्टौ कथाः काश्चिच्चक्रतुर्वैश्यपार्थिवौ ॥३८॥

Upaviṣṭau kathāḥ kāścit cakratur vaiśya-pārthivau ॥38॥

The merchant and the king sat down to tell their stories.

राजोवाच ॥३९॥

Rājovāca ॥39॥

The king said:

भगवंस्त्वामहं प्रष्टुमिच्छाम्येकं वदस्व तत् ॥४०॥

Bhagavaṁstvāmahaṁ praṣṭumicchāmyekaṁ vadasva tat ॥40॥

Revered sir, I wish to ask you one thing. Please reply.

दुःखाय यन्मे मनसः स्वचित्तायत्ततां विना।
ममत्वं गतराज्यस्य राज्याङ्गेष्वखिलेष्वपि ॥४१॥

Duḥkhāya yanme manasaḥ svacittāyattatāṁ vinā ।
Mamatvaṁ gatarājyasya rājyāṅgeṣvakhileṣvapi ॥41॥

Without control of my thoughts, my mind is coming to grief. I remain possessive toward my lost kingdom and all parts of the realm as if unaware that they are no longer mine.

जानतोऽपि यथाज्ञस्य किमेतन्मुनिसत्तम ।
अयं च निकृतः पुत्रैर्दारैर्भृत्यैस्तथोज्झितः ॥४२॥

Jānato'pi yathājñasya kimetanmunisattama ।
Ayaṁ ca nikṛtaḥ putrairdārairbhṛtyaistathojjhitaḥ ॥42॥

Venerable sage, how can this be? And this fellow has been humiliated by his children and wife, deserted by his servants, and forsaken by his own people.

स्वजनेन च संत्यक्तस्तेषु हार्दी तथाप्यति ।
एवमेष तथाहं च द्वावप्यत्यन्तदु:खितौ ।।४३।।

Svajanena ca saṁtyaktasteṣu hārdī tathāpyati ।
Evameṣa tathāhaṁ ca dvāvapyatyantaduḥkhitau ।।43।।

Still he feels exceeding affection for them, It is the same with me. We both are distressed to the utmost.

दृष्टदोषेऽपि विषये ममत्वाकृष्टमानसौ ।
तत्किमेतन्महाभाग यन्मोहो ज्ञानिनोरपि ।।४४।।

Dṛṣṭadoṣe'pi viṣaye mamatvākṛṣṭamānasau ।
Tatkimetanmahābhāga yanmoho jñāninorapi ।।44।।

Held by attachment to things, even though we see their faults. Venerable sir, how is it that we who should know better can be so deluded?

ममास्य च भवत्येषा विवेकान्धस्य मूढता ।।४५।।

Mamāsya ca bhavaty eṣā vivekāndhasya mūḍhatā ।।45।।

Ours is the perplexity of those who are blind to right understanding.

ऋषिरुवाच ।।४६।।

Ṛṣiruvāca ।।46।।

The seer said:

ज्ञानमस्ति समस्तस्य जन्तोर्विषयगोचरे ।।४७।।

Jñānamasti samastasya jantorviṣayagocare ।।47।।

Illustrious king, through the perceptions of the senses, every living being has knowledge of the manifest universe.

विषयश्च महाभागयाति चौवं पृथक्-पृथक् ।
दिवान्धाः प्राणिनः केचिद्रात्रावन्धास्तथापरे ।।४८।।

Viṣayaśca mahābhāgayāti caivaṁ pṛthak pṛthak ।
Divāndhāḥ prāṇinaḥ kecidrātrāvandhāstathāpare ।।48।।

The objects of sense-perception reveal themselves in various ways. Some creatures are blind by day, and others are blind by night.

केचिद्दिवा तथा रात्रौ प्राणिनस्तुल्यदृष्टयः।
ज्ञानिनो मनुजाः सत्यं किं तु ते न हि केवलम् ।।४९।।

Keciddivā tathā rātrau prāṇinastulyadṛṣṭayaḥ ।
Jñānino manujāḥ satyaṁ kiṁ tu te na hi kevalam ॥49॥

Some creatures see equally by day and night.
Truly, humans are endowed with the power of perception,
but they are not alone.

यतो हि ज्ञानिनः सर्वे पशुपक्षिमृगादयः।
ज्ञानं च तन्मनुष्याणां यत्तेषां मृगपक्षिणाम् ॥५०॥

Yato hi jñāninaḥ sarve paśupakṣimṛgādayaḥ ।
Jñānaṁ ca tanmanuṣyāṇāṁ yatteṣāṁ mṛgapakṣiṇām ॥50॥

For cattle, birds, wild animals, and all other living creatures
also perceive. That awareness which humans have, birds
and beasts possess also.

मनुष्याणां च यत्तेषां तुल्यमन्यत्तथोभयोः।
ज्ञानेऽपि सति पश्यैतान् पतङ्गाञ्छावचञ्चुषु ॥५१॥

Manuṣyāṇāṁ ca yatteṣāṁ tulyamanya ttathobhayau ।
Jñāne'pi sati paśyaitān pataṅgāñchāvacañcuṣu ॥51॥

And their awareness, humans have, too. In other ways
also the two are similar. Look at these birds. Though
feeling the pangs of hunger.

कणमोक्षादृतान्मोहात्पीड्यमानानपि क्षुधा।
मानुषा मनुजव्याघ्र साभिलाषाः सुतान् प्रति ।।५२।।

Kaṇamokṣādṛtānmohātpīḍyamānānapi kṣudhā ।
Mānuṣā manujavyāghra sābhilāṣāḥ sutān prati ।।52।।

Out of delusion they still busy themselves by
dropping food into the beaks of their young.
Illustrious sir, humans long for offspring.

लोभात्प्रत्युपकाराय नन्वेता*न् किं न पश्यसि।
तथापि ममतावर्त्ते मोहगर्ते निपातिताः ।।५३।।

Lobhātpratyupakārāya nanvetān kiṁ na paśyasi ।
Tathāpi mamatāvartte mohagarte nipātitāḥ ।।53।।

Surely expecting gratitude in return. Do you not see this?
In this very manner they are hurled into the whirlpool of
attachment, the pit of delusion.

महामायाप्रभावेण संसारस्थितिकारिणा।
तन्नात्र विस्मयः कार्यो योगनिद्रा जगत्पतेः ।।५४।।

Mahāmāyāprabhāveṇa saṁsārasthitikāriṇā ।
Tannātra vismayaḥ kāryo yoganidrā jagatpateḥ ।।54।।

By the power of Mahāmāyā, Who produces the continuing cycle of this transitory world. Do not be astonished. This same Mahāmāyā is Yoganidrā, the meditative sleep of Viṣṇu, the lord of the world.

महामाया हरेश्चैषा तया सम्मोह्यते जगत्।
ज्ञानिनामपि चेतांसि देवी भगवती हि सा ॥५५॥

Mahāmāyā hareścaivā tayā sammohyate jagat ।
Jñānināmapi cetāṁsi devī bhagavatī hi sā ॥55॥

This is the great Māyā of Hari, by whom the entire world is deluded. Even the minds of the wise are bewitched—she, the Goddess, is Bhagavatī herself.

बलादाकृष्य मोहाय महामाया प्रयच्छति।
तया विसृज्यते विश्वं जगदेतच्चराचरम् ॥५६॥

Balādākṛṣya mohāya mahāmāyā prayacchati ।
Tayā visṛjyate viśvaṁ jagadeta ccarācaram ॥56॥

Seizes the minds of even the wise and draws them into delusion. She creates all this universe, moving and unmoving.

सैषा प्रसन्ना वरदा नृणां भवति मुक्तये।
सा विद्या परमा मुक्तेर्हेतुभूता सनातनी ॥५७॥

Saiṣā prasannā varadā nṛṇāṁ bhavati muktaye ।
Sā vidyā paramā mukterhetubhūtā sanātanī ॥57॥

And it is She Who graciously bestows liberation on humanity. She is the supreme knowledge and the eternal cause of liberation.

संसारबन्धहेतुश्च सैव सर्वेश्वरेश्वरी ॥५८॥

Saṁsārabandhahetuśca saiva sarveśvareśvarī ॥58॥

Even as She is the cause of bondage to this transitory existence. She is the sovereign of all lords.

राजोवाच ॥५९॥

Rājovāca ॥59॥

The king said:

भगवन् का हि सा देवी महामायेति यां भवान् ॥६०॥

Bhagavan kā hi sā devī mahāmāyeti yāṁ bhavān ॥60॥

“Revered sir, Who is that Goddess
whom you call Mahāmāyā?

ब्रवीति कथमुत्पन्ना सा कर्मास्याश्च किं द्विज।
यत्प्रभावा च सा देवी यत्स्वरूपा यदुद्भवा ।।६१।।

Bravīti kathamutpannā sā karmāsyāśca kiṁ dvija ।
Yatprabhāvā ca sā devī yatsvarūpā yadudbhavā ।।61।।

How did She originate, and in what ways does She Act?
And whatever Her Glory, this Goddess, whatever
Her Form and Origin.

तत्सर्वं श्रोतुमिच्छामि त्वत्तो ब्रह्मविदां वर ।।६२।।

Tatsarvaṁ śrotumicchāmi tvatto brahmavidāṁ vara ।।62।।

All that I wish to learn from you, who are supreme
among the knowers of Brahman.”

ऋषिरुवाच ।।६३।।

Ṛṣiruvāca ।।63।।

The seer said:

नित्यैव सा जगन्मूर्तिस्तया सर्वमिदं ततम् ।।६४।।

Nityaiva sā jaganmūrtistayā sarvamidaṁ tatam ।।64।।

She Is Eternal, having the world as Her Form.
She Pervades All This.

तथापि तत्समुत्पत्तिर्बहुधा श्रूयतां मम।
देवानां कार्यसिद्ध्यर्थमाविर्भवति सा यदा ।।६५।।

Tathāpi tatsamutpattirbahudhā śrūyatāṁ mama ।
Devānāṁ kāryasiddhyarthamāvirbhavati sā yadā ।।65।।

Yet She Emerges in various ways. Hear it from me.
Although She Is Eternal, when She Manifests to
accomplish
the purpose of the Gods.

उत्पन्नेति तदा लोके सा नित्याप्यभिधीयते।
योगनिद्रां यदा विष्णुर्जगत्येकार्णवीकृते ।।६६।।

Utpanneti tadā loke sā nityāpyabhidhīyate ।
Yoganidrāṁ yadā viṣṇurjagatyekārṇavīkṛte ।।66।।

She is said to be born in the world. At the end of the cosmic day, when the universe dissolved into the primordial ocean.

आस्तीर्य शेषमभजत्कल्पान्ते भगवान् प्रभुः।
तदा द्वावसुरौ घोरौ विख्यातौ मधुकैटभौ ॥६७॥

Āstīrya śeṣamabhajatkalpānte bhagavān prabhuḥ ।
Tadā dvāvasurau ghorau vikhyātau madhukaiṭabhau ॥67॥

The blessed lord Viṣṇu stretched out on the serpent Śeṣa and entered into meditative sleep. Then two fearsome asuras, the notorious Madhu and Kaiṭabha.

विष्णुकर्णमलोद्भूतो हन्तुं ब्रह्माणमुद्यतौ।
स नाभिकमले विष्णोः स्थितो ब्रह्मा प्रजापतिः ॥६८॥

Viṣṇukarṇamalodbhūto hantuṁ brahmāṇamudyatau ।
Sa nābhikamale viṣṇoḥ sthito brahmā prajāpatiḥ ॥68॥

Issued forth from the wax in Viṣṇu's ears, intent on slaying Brahmā, who was seated on the lotus that grew from Viṣṇu's navel.

दृष्ट्वा तावसुरौ चोग्रौ प्रसुप्तं च जनार्दनम्।
तुष्टाव योगनिद्रां तामेकाग्रहृदयस्थितः ॥६९॥

Dṛṣṭvā tāvasurau cograu prasuptaṁ ca janārdanam ।
Tuṣṭāva yoganidrāṁ tāmekāgrahṛdayasthitaḥ ॥69॥

When he saw the raging asuras and the sleeping Viṣṇu,
Brahmā could think of nothing but to awaken him.

विबोधनार्थाय हरेर्हरिनेत्रकृतालयाम्*।
विश्वेश्वरीं जगद्धात्रीं स्थितिसंहारकारिणीम् ॥७०॥

Vibodhanārthāya harerharinetra-kṛtālayām ।
Viśveśvarīṁ jagaddhātrīṁ sthitisaṁhārakāriṇīm ॥70॥

And to that end he extolled Yoganidrā, Who had settled over Viṣṇu's eyes as his blessed sleep. The resplendent lord Brahmā extolled Her Who rules the universe.

निद्रां भगवतीं विष्णोरतुलां तेजसः प्रभुः ॥७१॥

Nidrāṁ bhagavatīṁ viṣṇoratulāṁ tejasaḥ prabhuḥ ॥71॥

Who Sustains and Dissolves it. He extolled
Her Who Is Incomparable.

ब्रह्मोवाच ॥७२॥

Brahmovāca ॥72॥

Brahmā said:

त्वं स्वाहा त्वं स्वधां त्वं हि वषट्कार:स्वरात्मिका ।।७३।।

Tvaṁ svāhā tvaṁ svadhāṁ tvaṁ hi vaṣaṭkāraḥ svarātmikā ।।73।।

You Are the Mantras of Consecration to the Gods and the ancestors. At Your Bidding They Are uttered, and They Are your very embodiment.

सुधा त्वमक्षरे नित्ये त्रिधा मात्रात्मिका स्थिता।
अर्धमात्रास्थिता नित्या यानुच्चार्या विशेषत: ।।७४।।

Sudhā tvamakṣare nitye tridhā mātrātmikā sthitā ।
Ardhamātrāsthitā nityā yānucchāryā viśeṣataḥ ।।74।।

You Are The Nectar of Immortality, O Imperishable, Eternal One. Truly, You Abide As The Transcendent Being, yet in every moment You Abide, inseparable and inexpressible, as the eternal source of all becoming. Indeed you are that.

त्वमेव संध्या सावित्री त्वं देवि जननी परा।
त्वयैतद्धार्यते विश्वं त्वयैतत्सृज्यते जगत् ।।७५।।

Tvameva saṁdhyā sāvitrī tvaṁ devī jananī parā ।
Tvayaitaddhāryate viśvaṁ tvayaitatsṛjyate jagat ।।75।।

You Are Sāvitrī, the Source of All Purity and Protection; You Are the Supreme Mother of The Gods. By You is this universe supported, of You is this world born, by You is it protected.

त्वयैतत्पाल्यते देवि त्वमत्स्यन्ते च सर्वदा।
विसृष्टौ सृष्टिरूपा त्वं स्थितिरूपा च पालने ।।७६।।

Tvayaitatpālyate devī tvamatsyante ca sarvadā ।
Visṛṣṭau sṛṣṭirūpā tvaṁ sthitirūpā ca pālane ।।76।।

O Devī, and You always Consume it at the end. You Are the Creative Force at the World's Birth and Its Sustenance for as long as it endures.

तथा संहृतिरूपान्ते जगतोऽस्य जगन्मये।
महाविद्या महामाया महामेधा महास्मृतिः ।।७७।।

Tathā saṁhṛtirūpānte jagato'sya jaganmayi ।
Mahāvidyā mahāmāyā mahāmedhā mahāsmṛtiḥ ।।77।।

So even at the end of this world, You Appear as Its Dissolution, You Who Encompass it all. You Are The Great Knowledge and The Great Illusion, The Great Intelligence.

महामोहा च भवती महादेवी महासुरी*।
प्रकृतिस्त्वं च सर्वस्य गुणत्रयविभाविनी ।।७८।।

Mahāmoha ca bhavatī mahādevī mahāsurī ।
Prakṛtistvaṁ ca sarvasya guṇatrayavibhāvinī ।।78।।

The Great Memory and the Great Delusion, The Great Goddess and The Great Demoness. You Are Primordial Matter, Differentiating into the Threefold Qualities of Everything.

कालरात्रिर्महारात्रिर्मोहरात्रिश्च दारुणा।
त्वं श्रीस्त्वमीश्वरी त्वं ह्रीस्त्वं बुद्धिर्बोधलक्षणा ।।७९।।

Kālarātrirmahārātrirmoharātriśca dāruṇā ।।
Tvaṁ śrīstvamīśvarī tvaṁ hrīstvaṁ buddhirbodhalakṣaṇā ।।79।।

You Are The Dark Night Of Periodic Dissolution, The Great Night of Final Dissolution, and The Terrifying Night Of Delusion. You Are Radiant Splendor; You Reign Supreme Yet Are Unassuming; You Are The Light Of Understanding.

लज्जा पुष्टिस्तथा तुष्टिस्त्वं शान्तिः क्षान्तिरेव च।
खड्गिनी शूलिनी घोरा गदिनी चक्रिणी तथा ।।८०।।

Lajjā puṣṭistathā tuṣṭistvaṁ śāntiḥ kṣāntireva ca ।
Khaḍginī śūlinī ghorā gadinī cakriṇī tathā ॥80॥

Modesty are You, and Prosperity, Contentment, Tranquility and Forbearance. Armed with Sword and Spear, and with Club And Discus.

शङ्खिनी चापिनी बाणभुशुण्डीपरिघायुधा।
सौम्या सौम्यतराशेषसौम्येभ्यस्त्वतिसुन्दरी ॥८१॥

Śaṅkhinī cāpinī bāṇabhuśuṇḍīparighāyudhā ।
Saumyā saumyatarāśeṣasaumyebhyastvatisundarī ॥81॥

Waging War with Conch, Bow and Arrows, Sling and Iron Mace, You Inspire Dread. Yet, You Are Pleasing, More Pleasing Than All Else That Is Pleasing, and Exceedingly Beautiful.

परापराणां परमा त्वमेव परमेश्वरी।
यच्च किंचित्क्वचिद्वस्तु सदसद्वाखिलात्मिके ॥८२॥

Parāparāṇāṁ paramā tvameva parameśvarī ।
Yacca kiñcitkvacidvastu sadasadvākhilātmike ॥82॥

Transcending Both Highest and Lowest, You Are Indeed The Supreme Sovereign. Whatever exists, true or untrue, and wherever it may be, O Soul of Everything.

तस्य सर्वस्य या शक्तिः सा त्वं किं स्तूयसे तदा।
यया त्वया जगत्स्रष्टा जगत्पात्यत्ति* यो जगत् ॥८३॥

Tasya sarvasya yā śaktiḥ sā tvaṁ kiṁ stūyase tadā ।
Yayā tvayā jagatsraṣṭā jagatpātyatti yo jagat ॥83॥

You Are the Power of All That. How can I praise you?
By you, even he Who Creates, Protects, and Devours
the world is Subdued with Sleep.

सोऽपि निद्रावशं नीतः कस्त्वां स्तोतुमिहेश्वरः।
विष्णुः शरीरग्रहणमहमीशान एव च ॥८४॥

So'pi nidrāvaśaṁ nītaḥ kastvāṁ stotum iheśvaraḥ ।
Viṣṇuḥ śarīragrahaṇamahamīśāna eva ca ॥84॥

Who here can praise you? You have caused even Viṣṇu,
Śiva, and Me to assume Our embodied forms.

कारितास्ते यतोऽतस्त्वां कः स्तोतुं शक्तिमान् भवेत्।
सा त्वमित्थं प्रभावैः स्वैरुदारैर्देवि संस्तुता ॥८५॥

Kāritāste yato'tastvāṁ kaḥ stotuṁ śaktimān bhavet ।
Sā tvamitthaṁ prabhāvaiḥ svairudārairdevī saṁstutā ॥85॥

Who then can truly praise you? Thus Extolled, O Devī, may you with Your Exalted Powers Confound.

मोहयैतौ दुराधर्षावसुरौ मधुकैटभौ।
प्रबोधं च जगत्स्वामी नीयतामच्युतो लघु ॥८६॥

Mohayaitau durādharṣāvasurau madhukaiṭabhau ।
Prabodhaṁ ca jagatsvāmī nīyatāmacyuto laghu ॥86॥

Those Unassailable asuras, Madhu and Kaiṭabha. Let Viṣṇu, the lord of the world, be quickly awakened from his slumber.

बोधश्च क्रियतामस्य हन्तुमेतौ महासुरौ ॥८७॥

Bodhaśca kriyatāmasya hantumetau mahāsurau ॥87॥

And be roused to slay the two great asuras.

ऋषिरुवाच ॥८८॥

Ṛṣiruvāca ॥88॥

The seer said:

एवं स्तुता तदा देवी तामसी तत्र वेधसा ॥८९॥

Evaṁ stutā tadā devī tāmasī tatra vedhasā ।।89।।

Praised thus by the creator to rouse.

विष्णोः प्रबोधनार्थाय निहन्तुं मधुकैटभौ।
नेत्रास्यनासिकाबाहुहृदयेभ्यस्तथोरसः ।।९०।।

Viṣṇoḥ prabodhanārthāya nihantuṁ madhukaiṭabhau ।
Netrāsya nāsikābāhuhṛdayebhyastathorasaḥ ।।90।।

Viṣṇu into slaying Madhu and Kaiṭabha, then and there The Dark Goddess, Emerged from his eyes, mouth, nostrils, arms, heart, and chest, and appeared before Brahmā.

निर्गम्य दर्शने तस्थौ ब्रह्मणोऽव्यक्तजन्मनः।
उत्तस्थौ च जगन्नाथस्तया मुक्तो जनार्दनः ।।९१।।

Nirgamyadarśane tasthau brahmaṇo'vyaktajanmanaḥ ।
Uttasthau ca jagannāthastayā mukto janārdanaḥ ।।91।।

Who is born from the Unmanifest. And released by Her, Viṣṇu, the Lord of the world.

एकार्णवेऽहिशयनात्ततः स ददृशे च तौ।
मधुकैटभो दुरात्मानावतिवीर्यपराक्रमौ ।।९२।।

Ekārṇave'hiśayanāttataḥ sa dadṛśe ca tau ।
Madhukaiṭabho durātmānāvativīryaparākramau ।।92।।

Arose from his serpent couch on the undifferentiated ocean and beheld, the evil-natured Madhu and Kaiṭabha, exceedingly strong and courageous.

क्रोधरक्तेक्षणावत्तुं' ब्रह्माणं जनितोद्यमौ।
समुत्थाय ततस्ताभ्यां युयुधे भगवान् हरिः ।।९३।।

Krodharaktekṣaṇāvattuṁ brahmāṇaṁ janitodyamau ।
Samutthāya tatastābhyāṁ yuyudhe bhagavān hariḥ ।।93।।

Seeing red with anger and determined to devour Brahmā. Then the blessed, all-pervading Viṣṇu rose up and fought.

पञ्चवर्षसहस्राणि बाहुप्रहरणो विभुः।
तावप्यतिबलोन्मत्तौ महामायाविमोहितौ ।।९४।।

Pañcavarṣasahasrāṇi bāhu-praharaṇo vibhuḥ ।
Tāvapyatibalonmattau mahāmāyāvimohitau ।।94।।

With them in hand-to-hand combat for five thousand years. And they, mad with the arrogance of power and confounded by Mahāmāyā.

उक्तवन्तौ वरोऽस्मत्तो व्रियतामिति केशवम् ।।९५।।

Uktavantau varo'smatto vriyatāmiti keśavam ।।95।।

Exclaimed to him, 'Ask a boon from us!

श्रीभगवानुवाच ।।९६।।

Śrībhagavānuvāca ।।96।।

The blessed lord Viṣṇu said:

भवेतामद्य मे तुष्टौ मम वध्यावुभावपि ।।९७।।

Bhavetāmadya me tuṣṭau mama vadhyāvubhāvapi ।।97।।

'Since you are pleased with me, so be it.
I will surely slay both of you now.

किमन्येन वरेणात्र एतावद्धि वृतं मम ।।९८।।

Kimanyena vareṇātra etāvaddhi vṛtaṁ mama ।।98।।

What other boon is there to ask?''

ऋषिरुवाच ॥९९॥

Ṛṣiruvāca ॥99॥

The seer said:

वञ्चिताभ्यामिति तदा सर्वमापोमयं जगत् ॥१००॥

Vañcitābhyāmiti tadā sarvamāpomayaṁ jagat ॥100॥

Thus deceived, and beholding that the world.

विलोक्य ताभ्यां गदितो भगवान् कमलेक्षणः*।
आवां जहि न यत्रोर्वी सलिलेन परिप्लुता ॥१०१॥

Vilokya tābhyāṁ gadito bhagavān kamalekṣaṇaḥ ।
Āvāṁ jahi na yatrorvī salilena pariplutā ॥101॥

Consisted entirely of water, they addressed the lotus-eyed Viṣṇu, saying: 'Slay us where water does not flood the earth.

ऋषिरुवाच ॥१०२॥

Ṛṣiruvāca ॥102॥

The seer said:

तथेत्युक्त्वा भगवता शङ्खचक्रगदाभृता।
कृत्वा चक्रेण वै च्छिन्ने जघने शिरसी तयोः ॥१०३॥

Tathetyuktvā bhagavatā śaṅkhacakragadābhṛtā ।
Kṛtvā cakreṇa vai chinne jaghane śirasī tayoḥ ॥103॥

So be it, said Viṣṇu, the wielder of conch, discus, and mace. Taking the two of them onto his lap, he cut off their heads with his discus.

एवमेषा समुत्पन्ना ब्रह्मणा संस्तुता स्वयम्।
प्रभावमस्या देव्यास्तु भूयः श्रृणु वदामि ते ॥ ऐं ॐ ॥१०४॥

Evameṣā samutpannā brahmaṇā
saṁstutā svayam ॥
Prabhāvamasyā devyāstu bhūyaḥ
śṛṇu vadāmi te॥ aiṁ oṁ ॥104॥

Thus did The Devī Herself appear when praised by Brahmā. Hear still more of Her Glory, which I will tell you.

इति श्रीमार्कण्डेयपुराणे सावर्णिके मन्वन्तरे देवीमाहात्म्ये मधुकैटभवधो नाम प्रथमोऽध्याय: ॥१॥

Iti śrī-mārkaṇḍeyapurāṇe sāvarnike manvantare devīmāhātmye madhukaiṭabhavadho nāma prathamo'dhyāyaḥ ॥1॥

Thus ends the first chapter, called 'The Slaying of Madhu and Kaiṭabha', of the Devī Māhātmya in the Mārkaṇḍeya Purāṇa, in the period of the Sāvarṇi Manu. (1)

।। द्वितीयोऽध्यायः ।।

महिषासुरसेना का संहार

।। Second Chapter ।।

The Slaughter of the Armies of Mahishasura

Meditation of Mahalakshmi: I resort to Mahalakshmi, the destroyer of Mahishasura, who is seated on the lotus, is of the complexion of coral and who holds in her (eighteen) hands rosary, axe, mace, arrow, thunderbolt, lotus, bow, pitcher, rod, sakti, sword, shield, conch, bell, wine-cup, trident, noose and the discus Sudarsana.

।। śrīdur̥gāsaptaśatī – dvitīyo'dhyāyaḥ ।।

देवताओं के तेज से देवी का प्रादुर्भाव
और महिषासुर की सेना का वध

devatāoṁ ke tejas se devī kā prādurbhāva
aura mahiṣāsura kī senā kā vadha

The Emergence of the Goddess from the Energies of the Gods and the Slaying of Mahiṣāsura's Army

॥ विनियोगः ॥

ॐ मध्यमचरित्रस्य विष्णुर्ऋषिः, महालक्ष्मीर्देवता, उष्णिक् छन्दः, शाकम्भरी शक्तिः, दुर्गा बीजम्, वायुस्तत्त्वम्, यजुर्वेदः स्वरूपम्, श्रीमहालक्ष्मीप्रीत्यर्थं मध्यमचरित्रजपे विनियोगः ।

॥ vinayogaḥ ॥

oṁ madhyamacaritrasya viṣṇur ṛṣiḥ,
mahālakṣmīr devatā, uṣṇik chandaḥ,
śākambharī śaktiḥ, durgā bījam,
vāyus tattvam, yajurvedaḥ svarūpam,
śrīmahālakṣmīprītyarthaṁ madhyamacaritrajape viniyogaḥ
।

Invocation (Viniyogaḥ)

Om. In this middle section of the text—the Madhyama Caritra—the sage is Viṣṇu, and the divine form we invoke is Mahālakṣmī. The verse meter is Uṣṇik, the goddess's power here is Śākambharī, and her seed syllable is Durgā. This part of the scripture is aligned with the energy of the air element and reflects the essence of the Yajurveda. With devotion, this recitation is offered for the grace and pleasure of Śrī Mahālakṣmī.

॥ ध्यानम् ॥

ॐ अक्षस्रक्परशुं गदेषुकुलिशं पद्मं धनुष्कुण्डिकां
दण्डं शक्तिमसिं च चर्म जलजं घण्टां सुराभाजनम् ।
शूलं पाशसुदर्शने च दधतीं हस्तैः प्रसन्नाननां
सेवे सैरिभमर्दिनीमिह महालक्ष्मीं सरोजस्थिताम् ॥

॥ dhyānam ॥

oṁ akṣasrak-paraśuṁ gadeṣu-kuliśaṁ padmaṁ dhanuḥ-kuṇḍikāṁ
daṇḍaṁ śaktim asiṁ ca carma jalajaṁ ghaṇṭāṁ surābhājanam ।
śūlaṁ pāśa-sudarśane ca dadhatīṁ hastaiḥ prasannānanāṁ
seve sairibhamardinīm iha mahālakṣmīṁ sarojasthitām ॥

Meditation Verse (Dhyānam)

Om. I meditate on the radiant Mahālakṣmī, seated gracefully upon a lotus. Her serene face shines with compassion. In her many hands, she holds sacred weapons and symbols—a rosary, axe, mace, arrows, thunderbolt, lotus, bow, water vessel, staff, spear, sword, shield, water lily, bell, and a cup of celestial nectar. She also carries a trident, noose, and the divine discus. I bow to this powerful goddess, the fierce slayer of the buffalo demon, who protects the cosmos with her boundless strength and beauty.

"ॐ ह्रीं" ऋषिरुवाच ॥१॥

OṀ hṛīm ṛṣir uvāca ॥1॥

OṀ hrīṁ. The seer said: ॥1॥

देवासुरमभूद्युद्धं पूर्णमब्दशतं पुरा ।
महिषेऽसुराणामधिपे देवानां च पुरन्दरे ॥२॥

devāsuram abhūd yuddhaṁ pūrṇamabdaśataṁ purā। ।
mahiṣe 'surāṇām adhipe devānāṁ ca purandare ॥2॥

तत्रासुरैर्महावीर्यैर्देवसैन्यं पराजितम् ।
जित्वा च सकलान् देवानिन्द्रोऽभून्महिषासुरः ॥३॥

tatrāsurair mahāvīryair devasainyaṁ parājitam ।
jitvā ca sakalān devān indro 'bhūn mahiṣāsuraḥ ॥3॥

Of yore when Mahisasura was the lord of asuras and Indra the lord of devas, there was a war between the devas and asuras for a full hundred years. In that the army of the devas was vanquished by the valorous asuras. After conquering all the devas, Mahisasura became the lord of heaven (Indra).

ततः पराजिता देवाः पद्मयोनिं प्रजापतिम् ।
पुरस्कृत्य गतास्तत्र यत्रेशगरुडध्वजौ ॥४॥

tataḥ parājitā devāḥ padmayonim prajāpatim ||
puraskṛtya gatās tatra yatreśagaruḍadhvajau ||4||

यथावृत्तं तयोस्तद्वन्महिषासुरचेष्टितम् ॥
त्रिदशाः कथयामासुर्देवाभिभवविस्तरम् ॥५॥

yathāvṛttaṁ tayos tadvan mahiṣāsuraceṣṭitam ||
tridaśāḥ kathayāmāsur devābhibhavavistaram ||5||

Then the vanquished devas headed by Brahma, the lord of beings, went to the place where Siva and Vishnu were. The devas described to them in detail, as it had happened, the story of their defeat wrought by Mahisasura.

सूर्येन्द्राग्न्यनिलेन्दूनां यमस्य वरुणस्य च ॥
अन्येषां चाधिकारान् स स्वयमेवाधितिष्ठति ॥६॥

sūryendrāgnyanilendūnāṁ yamasya vanmasya ca ||
anyeṣām cādhikārān sa svayam evādhitiṣṭhati ||6||

स्वर्गान्निराकृताः सर्वे तेन देवगणा भुवि ॥
विचरन्ति यथा मर्त्या महिषेण दुरात्मना ॥७॥

svargān nirākṛtāḥ sarve tena devagaṇā bhuvi ||
vicaranti yathā martyā mahiseṇa durātmanā ||7||

एतद्वः कथितं सर्वममरारिविचेष्टितम् ॥
शरणं वः प्रपन्नाः स्मो वधस्तस्य विचिन्त्यताम् ॥८॥

etad vaḥ kathitaṁ sarvam amarāriviceṣṭitam ||
śaraṇaṁ vaḥ prapannāḥ smo vadhastasya vicintyatām ||8||

'He (Mahisasura) himself has assumed the jurisdictions of Surya, Indra, Agni, Vayu, Candra, Yama and Varuna and other (devas). Thrown out from heaven by that evil-natured Mahisa, the hosts of devas wander on the earth like mortals. All that has been done by the enemy of the devas, has been related to you both, and we have sought shelter under you both. May both of you be pleased to think out the means of his destruction.'

इत्थं निशम्य देवानां वचांसि मधुसूदनः॥
चकार कोपं शम्भुश्च भ्रुकुटीकुटिलाननौ ॥९॥

itthaṁ niśamya devānāṁ vacāṁsi madhusūdanaḥ ||
cakāra kopāṁ śambhuś ca bhrukuṭīkuṭilānanau ||9||

Having thus heard the words of the devas, Vishnu was angry and also Siva, and their faces became fierce with frowns.

ततोऽतिकोपपूर्णस्य चक्रिणो वदनात्ततः ॥
निश्चक्राम महत्तेजो ब्रह्मणः शंकरस्य च ॥१०॥

tato 'tikopapūrṇasya cakriṇo vadanāt tataḥ ||
niścakrāma mahat tejo brahmaṇaḥ śaṅkarasya ca ||10||

अन्येषां चैव देवानां शक्रादीनां शरीरतः ॥
निर्गतं सुमहत्तेजस्तच्चैक्यं समगच्छत ॥११॥

anyeṣāṁ caiva devānāṁ śakrādīnāṁ śarīrataḥ ॥
nirgataṁ sumahat tejas tac caikyaṁ samagacchata ॥11॥

It issued forth a great light from the face of Vishnu who was full of intense anger, and from that of Brahma and Siva too. From the bodies of Indra and other devas also sprang forth a very great light. And (all) this light united together.

अतीव तेजसः कूटं ज्वलन्तमिव पर्वतम् ॥
ददृशुस्ते सुरास्तत्र ज्वालाव्याप्तदिगन्तरम् ॥१२॥

atīva tejasaḥ kūṭaṁ jvalantam iva parvatam ॥
dadṛśus te sūrās tatra jvālāvyāptadigantaram ॥12॥

अतुलं तत्र तत्तेजः सर्वदेवशरीरजम् ॥
एकस्थं तदभून्नारी व्याप्तलोकत्रयं त्विषा ॥१३॥

atulaṁ tatra tat tejaḥ sarvadevaśarīrajam ॥
ekasthaṁ tadabhūn nārī vyāptalokatrayaṁ tviṣā ॥13॥

The Devas saw there a concentration of light like a mountain blazing excessively, pervading all the quarters with its flames. Then that unique light, produced from the bodies of all the Devas, pervading the three worlds with its lustre, combined into one and became a female form.

यदभूच्छाम्भवं तेजस्तेनाजायत तन्मुखम् ।।
याम्येन चाभवन् केशा बाहवो विष्णुतेजसा ।।१४।।

yad abhūc chāmbhavaṁ tejas tenājāyata tan mukham ॥
yāmyena cābhavan keśā bāhavo viṣṇutejasā ॥14॥

सौम्येन स्तनयोर्युग्मं मध्यं चौन्द्रेण चाभवत् ।।
वारुणेन च जङ्घोरू नितम्बस्तेजसा भुवः ।।१५।।

saumyena stanayor yugmaṁ
madhyaṁ caindreṇa cābhavat ॥
vāruṇena ca jaṅghorū nitambas
tejasā bhuvaḥ ॥15॥

By that which was Siva's light, her face came into being; by Yama's (light) her hair, by Vishnu's light her arms; and by Candra's (light) her two breasts. By Indra's light her waist, by Varuna's (light) her shanks and thighs and by earth's light her hips.

ब्रह्मणस्तेजसा पादौ तदङ्गुल्योऽर्कतेजसा ।।
वसूनां च कराङ्गुल्यः कौबेरेण च नासिका ।।१६।।

brahmaṇas tejasā pādau tad aṅgulyo 'rkatejasā ॥
vasūnāṁ ca karāṅgulyaḥ kaubereṇa ca nāsikā ॥16॥

तस्यास्तु दन्ताः सम्भूताः प्राजापत्येन तेजसा ।।
नयनत्रितयं जज्ञे तथा पावकतेजसा ।।१७।।

tasyāstu dantāḥ sambhūtāḥ prājāpatyena tejasā ।।
nayanatritayaṁ jajñe tathā pāvakatejasā ।।17।।

भ्रुवौ च संध्ययोस्तेजः श्रवणावनिलस्य च ।।
अन्येषां चौव देवानां सम्भवस्तेजसां शिवा ।।१८।।

bhruvau ca sandhyayos tejah śravaṇāv anilasya ca ।।
anyeṣāṁ caiva devānāṁ sambhavas tejasāṁ śivā ।।18।।

By Brahma's light her feet came into being; by Surya's light
her toes, by Vasus (light) her fingers, by Kubera's (light) her nose; by Prajapati's light her teeth came into being and similarly by Agni's light her three eyes were formed. The light of the two sandhyas became her eye-brows, the light of Vayu her ears; the manifestation of the lights of other devas too (contributed to the being of the) auspicious Devi.

ततः समस्तदेवानां तेजोराशिसमुद्भवाम् ।।
तां विलोक्य मुदं प्रापुरमरा महिषार्दिताः* ।।१९।।

tataḥ samastadevānāṁ tejorāśisamudbhavām ।।
tāṁ vilokya mudaṁ prāpur amarā mahiṣārditāḥ ।।19।।

Then looking at her, who had come into being from the assembled lights of all the devas, the immortals who were oppressed by Maḥisasura experienced joy.

शूलं शूलाद्विनिष्कृष्य ददौ तस्यै पिनाकधृक् ॥
चक्रं च दत्तवान् कृष्णः समुत्पाद्य स्वचक्रतः ॥२०॥

śūlaṁ śūlād viniṣkṛṣya dadau tasyai pinākadhṛk ॥
cakraṁ ca dattavān kṛṣṇaḥ samutpādya svacakrataḥ ॥20॥

शङ्खं च वरुणः शक्तिं ददौ तस्यै हुताशनः ॥
मारुतो दत्तवांश्चापं बाणपूर्णे तथेषुधी ॥२१॥

śaṅkhaṁ ca varuṇaḥ śaktiṁ dadau tasyai hutāṣanaḥ ॥
māruto dattavāṁś cāpaṁ bāṇapūrṇe tatheṣudhī ॥21॥

The bearer of Pinaka (Siva) drawing forth a trident from his own trident presented it to her; and Vishnu bringing forth a discus out of his own discus gave her. Varuna gave her a conch, Agni a spear; and Maruta gave a bow as well as two quivers full of arrows.

वज्रमिन्द्रः समुत्पाद्य* कुलिशादमराधिपः ॥
ददौ तस्यै सहस्राक्षो घण्टामैरावताद् गजात् ॥२२॥

vajram indraḥ samutpāṭya kuliśād amarādhipaḥ ॥
dadau tasyai sahasrākṣo ghaṇṭām airāvatād gājāt ॥22॥

कालदण्डाद्यमो दण्डं पाशं चाम्बुपतिर्ददौ ।।
प्रजापतिश्चाक्षमालां ददौ ब्रह्मा कमण्डलुम् ।।२३।।

kāladaṇḍād yamo daṇḍaṁ pāśaṁ cāmbupatir dadau ।।
prajāpatiś cākṣamālāṁ dadau brahmā kamaṇḍalum ।।23।।

Indra, lord of the Devas, brought forth a thunderbolt from his own, and a bell from that of his elephant Airavata, and gave them to her Yama gave a staff from his own staff of Death and Varuna, the lord of waters, a noose; and Brahma, the lord of beings, gave a string of beads and a water-pot.

समस्तरोमकूपेषु निजरश्मीन् दिवाकरः ।।
कालश्च दत्तवान् खड्गं तस्याश्चर्म* च निर्मलम् ।।२४।।

samastaromakūpeṣu nijaraśmīn divākarah ।।
kālaś ca dattavān khaḍgaṁ tasyāś carma ca nirmalam ।।24।।

Surya bestowed his own rays on all the pores of her skin and Kala (Time) gave a spotless sword and a shield.

क्षीरोदश्चामलं हारमजरे च तथाम्बरे ।।
चूडामणिं तथा दिव्यं कुण्डले कटकानि च ।।२५।।

kṣīrodaś cāmalaṁ hāram ajare ca tathāmbare ।।
cūḍāmaṇiṁ tathā divyaṁ kuṇḍale kaṭakāni ca ।।25।।

अर्धचन्द्रं तथा शुभ्रं केयूरान् सर्वबाहुषु ॥
नूपुरौ विमलौ तद्वद् ग्रैवेयकमनुत्तमम् ॥२६॥

ardhacandram tathā śubhraṁ keyūrān sarvabāhuṣu ॥
nūpurau vimalau tadvad graiveyakam anuttamam ॥26॥

अङ्गुलीयकरत्नानि समस्तास्वङ्गुलीषु च ॥
विश्वकर्मा ददौ तस्यै परशुं चातिनिर्मलम् ॥२७॥

aṅgullyakaratnāni samastāsvangulīṣu ca ॥
viśvakarmā dadau tasyai paraśuṁ cātinirmalam ॥27॥

अस्त्राण्यनेकरूपाणि तथाभेद्यं च दंशनम् ॥
अम्लानपङ्कजां मालां शिरस्युरसि चापराम् ॥२८॥

astrāṇy anekarūpāṇi tathā 'bhedyaṁ ca daṁśanam ॥
amlānapankajāṁ mālāṁ śirasy urasi cāparām ॥28॥

अददज्जलधिस्तस्यै पङ्कजं चातिशोभनम् ॥
हिमवान् वाहनं सिंहं रत्नानि विविधानि च ॥२९॥

adadaj jaladhis tasyai pankajaṁ cātiśobhanam ॥
himavān vāhanam siṁhaṁ ratnāni vividhāni ca ॥29॥

The milk-ocean gave a pure necklace, a pair of un-decaying garments, a divine crest-jewel, a pair of ear-rings, bracelets, a brilliant half-moon(ornament), armlets on all arms, a pair of shining anklets, a unique necklace and excellent rings on all the fingers. Visvakarman gave her a very brilliant axe, weapons of various forms and also an impenetrable armour. The ocean gave her a garland of unfading lotuses for her head and another for her breast, besides a very beautiful lotus in her hand. The (mountain) Himavat gave her a lion to ride on a various jewels.

ददावशून्यं सुरया पानपात्रं धनाधिपः ॥
शेषश्च सर्वनागेशो महामणिविभूषितम् ॥३०॥

dadāv asūnyaṁ surayā pānapātraṁ dhanādhipaḥ ॥
śeṣaś ca sarvanāgeśo mahāmaṇivibhūṣitam ॥30॥

नागहारं ददौ तस्यै धत्ते यः पृथिवीमिमाम् ॥
अन्यैरपि सुरैर्देवी भूषणैरायुधैस्तथा ॥३१॥

nāgahāraṁ dadau tasyai dhatte yaḥ pṛthivīmimām ॥
anyair api surair devī bhūsaṇair āyudhais tathā ॥31॥

सम्मानिता ननादोच्चैः साट्टहासं मुहुर्मुहुः ॥
तस्या नादेन घोरेण कृत्स्नमापूरितं नभः ॥३२॥

sammānitā nanādoccaiḥ sāṭṭahāsaṁ muhur muhuḥ ॥
tasyā nādena ghoreṇa kṛtsnam āpūritaṁ nabhaḥ ॥32॥

अमायतातिमहता प्रतिशब्दो महानभूत् ॥
चुक्षुभुः सकला लोकाः समुद्राश्च चकम्पिरे ॥३३॥

amāyatātimahatā pratiśabdo mahānabhūt ॥
cukṣubhuh sakala lokāḥ samudraś ca cakampire ॥33॥

The lord of wealth (Kubera) gave her a drinking cup, ever full of wine. Sesa, the lord of all serpents, who supports this earth, gave her a serpent-necklace bedecked with best jewels. Honoured likewise by other devas also with ornaments and weapons, she (the Devi) gave out a loud roar with a decrying laugh again and again. By her unending, exceedingly great, terrible roar the entire sky was filled, and there was great reverberation. All worlds shook, the seas trembled.

चचाल वसुधा चेलुः सकलाश्च महीधराः ॥
जयेति देवाश्च मुदा तामूचुः सिंहवाहिनीम् ॥३४॥

cacāla vasudhā celuḥ sakalāś ca mahldharāḥ ॥
jayeti devās ca mudā tām ūcuḥ simhavāhinīm ॥34॥

तुष्टुवुर्मुनयश्चैनां भक्तिनम्रात्ममूर्तयः ॥
दृष्ट्वा समस्तं संक्षुब्धं त्रैलोक्यममरारयः ॥३५॥

tuṣṭuvur munayaś cainām bhaktinamrātmamūrtayaḥ ॥
dṛṣṭvā samastaṁ saṁkṣubdhaṁ trailokyam amarārayaḥ ॥35॥

सन्नद्धाखिलसैन्यास्ते समुत्तस्थुरुदायुधाः ।।
आः किमेतदिति क्रोधादाभाष्य महिषासुरः ।।३६।।

sannaddhākhilasainyāste samuttasthur udāyudhāḥ ।।
āḥ kim etad iti krodhād ābhāṣya mahiṣāsuraḥ ।।36।।

अभ्यधावत तं शब्दमशेषैरसुरैर्वृतः ।।
स ददर्श ततो देवीं व्याप्तलोकत्रयां त्विषा ।।३७।।

abhyadhāvata taṁ śabdam aśeṣair asurair vṛtaḥ ।।
sa dadarśa tato devīṁ vyāptalokatrayāṁ tviṣā ।।37।।

पादाक्रान्त्या नतभुवं किरीटोल्लिखिताम्बराम् ।।
क्षोभिताशेषपातालां धनुर्ज्यानिःस्वनेन ताम् ।।३८।।

pādākrāntyā natabhuvaṁ kirīṭollikhitāmbarām ।।
kṣobhitāśeṣapātālāṁ dhanurjyāniḥsvanena tām ।।38।।

दिशो भुजसहस्रेण समन्ताद् व्याप्य संस्थिताम् ।।
ततः प्रववृते युद्धं तया देव्या सुरद्विषाम् ।।३९।।

diśo bhujasahasreṇa samantād vyāpya saṁsthitām ।।
tataḥ pravavṛte yuddhaṁ tayā devyā suradviṣām ।।39।।

शस्त्रास्त्रैर्बहुधा मुक्तैरादीपितदिगन्तरम् ।।
महिषासुरसेनानीश्चिक्षुराख्यो महासुरः ।।४०।।

śastrāstrair bahudhā muktair ādīpitadigantaram ।।
mahiṣāsurasenānīś cikṣurākhyo mahāsurah ।।40।।

युयुधे चामरश्चान्यैश्चतुरङ्गबलान्वितः ॥
रथानामयुतैः षड्भिरुदग्राख्यो महासुरः ॥४१॥

yuyudhe cāmaraś cānyaiś caturangabalānvitaḥ ॥
rathānāmayutaiḥ ṣaḍbhir udagrākhyo mahāsuraḥ ॥41॥

अयुध्यतायुतानां च सहस्रेण महाहनुः ॥
पञ्चाशद्भिश्च नियुतैरसिलोमा महासुरः ॥४२॥

ayudhyatāyutānāṁ ca sahasreṇa mahāhanuḥ ॥
pañcāśadbhiś ca niyutair asilomā mahāsuraḥ ॥42॥

अयुतानां शतैः षड्भिर्बाष्कलो युयुधे रणे ॥
गजवाजिसहस्रौघैरनेकैः परिवारितः ॥४३॥

ayutānāṁ śataiḥ ṣaḍbhir bāṣkalo yuyudhe raṇe ॥
gajavājisahasraughair anekaiḥ parivāritaḥ ॥43॥

वृतो रथानां कोट्या च युद्धे तस्मिन्नयुध्यत ॥
बिडालाख्योऽयुतानां च पञ्चाशद्भिरथायुतैः ॥४४॥

vṛto rathānāṁ koṭyā ca yuddhe tasminn ayudhyat ॥
biḍālākhyo 'yutānāṁ ca pañcāśadbhir athāyutaiḥ ॥44॥

युयुधे संयुगे तत्र रथानां परिवारितः ॥
अन्ये च तत्रायुतशो रथनागहयैर्वृताः ॥४५॥

yuyudhe saṁyuge tatra rathānāṁ parivāritaḥ ॥
anye ca tatrāyutaso rathanāgahayair vṛtāḥ ॥45॥

युयुधुः संयुगे देव्या सह तत्र महासुराः ॥
कोटिकोटिसहस्रैस्तु रथानां दन्तिनां तथा ॥४६॥

yuyudhuḥ samyuge devyā saha tatra mahāsurāḥ ॥
koṭikoṭisahasrais tu rathānām dantināṁ tathā ॥46॥

The earth quaked and all the mountains rocked. 'Victory to you,' exclaimed the devas in joy to her, the lion-rider. the sages, who bowed their bodies in devotion, extolled her. Seeing the three worlds agitated the foes of devas, mobilized all their armies and rose up together with uplifted weapons. Mahisasura, exclaiming in wrath, 'Ha! What is this?' rushed towards that roar, surrounded by innumerable asuras. Then he saw the Devi pervading the three worlds with her lustre. Making the earth bend with her footstep, scraping the sky with her diadem, shaking the nether worlds with the twang of the bowstring, and standing there pervading all the quarters around with her thousand arms. Then began a battle between that Devi and the enemies of the devas, in which the quarters of the sky were illumined by the weapons and arms hurled diversely. Mahisasura's general, a great asura named Ciksura and Camara, attended by forces comprising four parts, and other (asuras) fought. A great asura named Udagra with sixty thousand chariots, and Mahahanu with ten millions (of chariots) gave battle. Asiloman, another great asura, with fifteen millions (of chariots), and Baskala with six millions fought in that battle. Privarita with many thousands of elephants and horses, and surrounded by ten millions of chariots, fought in that battle. An asura named Bidala fought in that battle surrounded with five hundred crores of chariots. And other great asuras, thousands in number, surrounded with chariots, elephants and horses fought with the Devi in that battle.

हयानां च वृतो युद्धे तत्राभून्महिषासुरः ॥
तोमरैर्भिन्दिपालैश्च शक्तिभिर्मुसलैस्तथा ॥४७॥

hayānāṁ ca vṛto yuddhe tatrābhūn mahiṣāsuraḥ ॥
tomarair bhindipālaiś ca śaktibhir musalais tathā ॥47॥

युयुधुः संयुगे देव्या खड्गैः परशुपट्टिशैः ॥
केचिच्च चिक्षिपुः शक्तीः केचित्पाशांस्तथापरे ॥४८॥

yuyudhuḥ samyuge devyā khaḍgaiḥ paraśupaṭṭiśaiḥ ॥
kecic ca cikṣipuḥ śaktīḥ kecit pāśāṁs tathāpare ॥48॥

Mahisasura was surrounded in that battle with thousands of crores of horses, elephants and chariots. Others (asuras) fought in the battle against the Devi with iron maces and javelins, with spears and clubs, with swords, axes and halberds. Some hurled spears and others nooses.

देवीं खड्गप्रहारैस्तु ते तां हन्तुं प्रचक्रमुः ॥
सापि देवी ततस्तानि शस्त्राण्यस्त्राणि चण्डिका ॥४९॥

Devīṁ khaḍgaprahārais tu te tāṁ hantuṁ pracakramuḥ ॥
sāpi Devī tatas tāni śastrāṇy astrāṇi Caṇḍikā ॥49॥

लीलयैव प्रचिच्छेद निजशस्त्रास्त्रवर्षिणी ॥
अनायस्तानना देवी स्तूयमाना सुरर्षिभिः ॥५०॥

Lilayaiva praciccheda nijaśastrāstravarṣiṇī ॥
anāyastānanā Devī stūyamānā surarṣibhiḥ ॥50॥

मुमोचासुरदेहेषु शस्त्राण्यस्त्राणि चेश्वरी ॥
सोऽपि क्रुद्धो धुतसटो देव्या वाहनकेशरी ॥५१॥

mumocāsuradeheṣu śastrāṇyastrāṇi ceśvarī ॥
so'pi kruddho dhutasaṭo Devyā vāhanakesarī ॥51॥

चचारासुरसैन्येषु वनेष्विव हुताशनः ॥
निःश्वासान् मुमुचे यांश्च युध्यमाना रणेऽम्बिका ॥५२॥

cacārāsurasainyeṣu vanesv iva hutāśanaḥ ॥
niḥśvāsān mumuce yāṁś ca yudhyamānā
raṇe 'mbikā ॥52॥

त एव सद्यः सम्भूता गणाः शतसहस्रशः ॥
युयुधुस्ते परशुभिर्भिन्दिपालासिपट्टिशैः ॥५३॥

ta eva sadyaḥ sambhūtā gaṇāḥ śatasahasraśaḥ ।।
yuyudhus te paraśubhir bhindipālāsipaṭṭiśaiḥ ।।53।।

नाशयन्तोऽसुरगणान् देवीशक्त्युपबृंहिताः ।।
अवादयन्त पटहान् गणाः शङ्खांस्तथापरे ।।५४।।

nāsayanto 'suragaṇān Devīsaktyupabṛmhitāḥ ।।
avādayanta paṭahān gaṇāḥ śankhāms tathāpare ।।54।।

मृदङ्गांश्च तथैवान्ये तस्मिन् युद्धमहोत्सवे ।।
ततो देवी त्रिशूलेन गदया शक्तिवृष्टिभिः ।।५५।।

mṛdaṅgāṁś ca tathaivānye tasmin yuddhamahotsave ।।
tato Devī triśūlena gadayā śaktivṛṣṭibhiḥ ।।55।।

खड्गादिभिश्च शतशो निजघान महासुरान् ।।
पातयामास चौवान्यान् घण्टास्वनविमोहितान् ।।५६।।

khaḍgādibhiś ca śataśo nijaghāna mahāsurān ।।
pātayāmāsa caivānyān ghaṇṭāsvanavimohitān ।।56।।

असुरान् भुवि पाशेन बद्ध्वा चान्यानकर्षयत् ।।
केचिद् द्विधा कृतास्तीक्ष्णैः खड्गपातैस्तथापरे ।।५७।।

asurān bhuvi pāśena baddhvā cānyān akarṣayat ।।
kecid dvidhākṛtās tīkṣṇaiḥ khaḍgapātais tathāpare ।।57।।

विपोथिता निपातेन गदया भुवि शेरते ।।
वेमुश्च केचिद्रुधिरं मुसलेन भृशं हताः ।।५८।।

vipothitā nipātena gadayā bhuvi serate ||
vemuś ca kecid rudhiraṁ musalena bhṛśaṁ hatāḥ ||58||

They struck at her with swords, seeking to kill her. But Devi Chandika, showering forth her own weapons, effortlessly shattered all their arms into pieces. Without the slightest strain upon her face, and as gods and sages extolled her glory, the Isvari hurled her weapons at the bodies of the asuras. The lion that carried her, its mane bristling in rage, stalked through the demon hosts like a raging conflagration through a forest.

The very sighs of Ambika, engaged in battle, became at once battalions by the hundreds and thousands. Empowered by the Devi's own strength, these battalions fought with axes, javelins, swords, and halberds, laying waste to the asuras. Some beat drums, some blew conches, and others played tabors in that great festival of war.

Then the Devi slew hundreds of asuras with her trident, her club, and showers of spears and swords. Others, stupefied by the deafening roar of her bell, she cast down. Still others she bound with her noose and dragged along the ground. Some were cleaved in two by the sharp strokes of her sword, while others lay smashed upon the earth by the crushing blows of her mace. Many, struck hard by her club, spewed forth blood as they perished.

केचिन्निपतिता भूमौ भिन्नाः शूलेन वक्षसि ॥
निरन्तराः शरौघेण कृताः केचिद्रणाजिरे ॥५९॥

kecin nipatitā bhūmau bhinnāḥ śūlena vakṣasi ॥
nirantarāḥ śaraugheṇa kṛtāḥ kecidraṇājire ॥59॥

श्येनानुकारिणः प्राणान् मुमुचुस्त्रिदशार्दनाः ॥
केषांचिद् बाहवश्छिन्नाश्छिन्नग्रीवास्तथापरे ॥६०॥

śaynānukāriṇaḥ prāṇān mumucus tridaśārdanāḥ ॥
keṣāñcid bāhavaś chinnāś chinnagrīvās tathāpare ॥60॥

शिरांसि पेतुरन्येषामन्ये मध्ये विदारिताः ॥
विच्छिन्नजङ्घास्त्वपरे पेतुरुर्व्यां महासुराः ॥६१॥

śirāmsi petur anyeṣām anye madhye vidāritāḥ ॥
vicchinnajanghās tv apare petur urvyāṁ mahāsurāḥ ॥61॥

Pierced in the breast by her trident, some fell on the ground. Pierced all over by her arrows and resembling porcupines, some of the enemies of devas gave up their lives on that field of battle. Some had their arms cut off, some, their necks broken, the heads of others rolled down; some others were torn asunder in the middle of their trunks, and some great asuras fell on the ground with their legs severed.

एकबाह्वक्षिचरणाः केचिद्देव्या द्विधा कृताः ।।
छिन्नेऽपि चान्ये शिरसि पतिताः पुनरुत्थिताः ।।६२।।

ekabāhvakṣicaraṇāḥ kecid Devyā dvidhākṛtāḥ ।।
chinne 'pi cānye śirasi patitāḥ punar utthitāḥ ।।62।।

Some rendered one-armed, one-eyed, and one-legged were again clove in twain by the Devi. And others, though rendered headless, fell and rose again.

कबन्धा युयुधुर्देव्या गृहीतपरमायुधाः ।।
ननृतुश्चापरे तत्र युद्धे तूर्यलयाश्रिताः ।।६३।।

kabandhā yuyudhūr devyā gṛhīta-paramāyudhāḥ ।।
nanṛtuś cāpare tatra yuddhe tūryalayāśritāḥ ।।63।।

Headless trunks fought with the Devi with best weapons in their hands. Some of these headless trunks danced there in the battle to the rhythm of the musical instruments.

कबन्धाश्छिन्नशिरसः खड्गशक्त्यृष्टिपाणयः ।।
तिष्ठ तिष्ठेति भाषन्तो देवीमन्ये महासुराः ।।६४।।

kabandhāś chinnaśirasaḥ khaḍga-śakty-ṛṣṭi-pāṇayaḥ ।।
tiṣṭha tiṣṭheti bhāṣanto devīm anye mahāsurāḥ ।।64।।

पातितै रथनागाश्वैरसुरैश्च वसुन्धरा ॥
अगम्या साभवत्तत्र यत्राभूत्स महारणः ॥६५॥

pātitai ratha-nāgāśvair asuraiś ca vasundharā ॥
agamya sābhavat tatra yatrābhūtsa mahāraṇaḥ ॥65॥

The trunks of some other great asuras, with their swords, spears and lances still in their hands, shouted at the Devi with their just severed heads, 'Stop, stop'. That part of earth where the battle was fought became impassable with the asuras, elephants and horses and chariots that had been felled.

शोणितौघा महानद्यः सद्यस्तत्र प्रसुस्रुवुः ॥
मध्ये चासुरसैन्यस्य वारणासुरवाजिनाम् ॥६६॥

śoṇitaughā mahānadyaḥ sadyas tatra prasusruvuḥ ॥
madhye cāsura-sainyasya vāraṇāsura-vājinām ॥66॥

क्षणेन तन्महासैन्यमसुराणां तथाम्बिका ॥
निन्ये क्षयं यथा वह्निस्तृणदारुमहाचयम् ॥६७॥

kṣaṇena tanmahāsainyam asurāṇāṁ tathāmbikā ॥
ninye kṣayaṁ yathā vahnis tṛṇa-dāru-mahācayam ॥67॥

66-67. The profuse blood from the asuras, elephants and horses flowed immediately like large rivers amidst that army of the asuras. As fire consumes a huge heap of straw and wood, so did Ambika destroy that vast army of asuras in no time.

स च सिंहो महानादमुत्सृजन्धुतकेसरः ।।
शरीरेभ्योऽमरारीणामसूनिव विचिन्वति ।।६८।।

sa ca siṁho mahānādam utsṛjan dhuta-keśaraḥ ।।
śarīrebhyo 'marārīṇām asūn iva vicinvati ।।68।।

देव्या गणैश्च तैस्तत्र कृतं युद्धं महासुरैः ।।
यथैषां' तुतुषुर्देवाः' पुष्पवृष्टिमुचो दिवि ।।ॐ ।।६९।।

devyā gaṇaiś ca tais tatra kṛtaṁ yuddhaṁ mahāsuraiḥ ।।
yathaiṣāṁ tutuṣur devāḥ puṣpavṛṣṭim uco divi ।।69।।

68-69. And her carrier-lion, thundering aloud with quivering mane, prowled about in the battlefield, appearing to search out the vital breaths from the bodies of the enemies of devas.

In that battlefield the battalions of the Devi fought in such a manner with the asuras that the devas in heaven, showering flowers, extolled them.

इति श्रीमार्कण्डेयपुराणे सावर्णिके मन्वन्तरे देवीमाहात्म्ये ।।
महिषासुरसैन्यवधो नाम द्वितीयोऽध्यायः ।।२।।
उवाच १, श्लोकाः ६८, एवम् ६९,
एवमादितः ।।१७३।।

iti śrī-mārkaṇḍeya-purāṇe sāvarnike
manvantare devīmāhātmye
mahiṣāsura-sainya-vadho nāma dvitīyo 'dhyāyaḥ ||2||
uvāca – 1, ślokāḥ – 68, evam – 69,
evam-āditaḥ – 173

Here ends the second chapter called 'Slaughter of the armies of Mahisasura' of Devi-mahatmya in Markandeya-purana, during the period of Savarni, the Manu.

॥ तृतीयोऽध्यायः ॥

महिषासुर का वध

॥ Third Chapter ॥

The Slaying of Mahishasura

॥ ध्यानम् ॥

ॐ उद्यद्भानुसहस्रकान्तिमरुणक्षौमां शिरोमालिकां
रक्तालिप्तपयोधरां जपवटीं विद्यामभीतिं वरम्।
हस्ताब्जैर्दधतीं त्रिनेत्रविलसद्वक्त्रारविन्दश्रियं
देवीं बद्धहिमांशुरत्नमुकुटां वन्देऽरविन्दस्थिताम् ॥

॥ dhyānam ॥

om udyadabhānusahasrakāntimaruṇakṣaumāṁ śiromālikāṁ
raktāliptapayodharāṁ japavaṭīṁ vidyāmbhītiṁ varam |
hastābjairdadhatīṁ trinetra vilasadvaktrāravindaśriyaṁ
devīṁ baddhahimāṁśuratanamukuṭāṁ
vande'ravindasthitām ॥

Meditation

I bow to the Goddess who wears a garland resembling the rising sun with the brilliance of a thousand rays, whose hair is reddish and fiery like flames. She is adorned with a crimson, water-stained chest, and a sacred thread for chanting (japavāṭī). She is the embodiment of supreme knowledge and fearlessness. With lotus-like hands and three radiant eyes, her face shines brilliantly like a lotus flower. This Goddess, crowned with a snowy-mountain-like jewel-studded crown, I respectfully worship, who is seated on the lotus.

"ॐ" ऋषिरुवाच ॥१॥

Om ṛṣir uvāca

निहन्यमानं तत्सैन्यमवलोक्य महासुरः ॥
सेनानीश्चिक्षुरः कोपाद्ययौ योद्धुमथाम्बिकाम् ॥२॥

nihanyamānaṁ tat sainyam avalokya mahāsuraḥ ॥
senānīś cikṣuraḥ kopād yayau yoddhum athāmbikām ॥2॥

Then Ciksura, the great asura general, seeing that army being slain (by the Devi), advanced in anger to fight with Ambika.

स देवीं शरवर्षेण ववर्ष समरेऽसुरः ॥
यथा मेरुगिरेः श्रृङ्गं तोयवर्षेण तोयदः ॥३॥

Sa Devīṁ śaravarṣeṇa vavarṣa samara 'suraḥ ॥
yathā merugireḥ śṛṅgaṁ toyavarṣeṇa toyadaḥ ॥3॥

That asura rained showers of arrows on the Devi in the battle, even as a cloud (showers) rain on the summit of Mount Meru.

तस्यच्छित्त्वा ततो देवी लीलयैव शरोत्करान् ॥
जघान तुरगान् बाणैर्यन्तारं चौव वाजिनाम् ॥४॥

Tasya chitvā tato Devī līlayaiva śarotkarān ॥
jaghāna turagān bāṇair yantāraṁ caiva vājinām ॥4॥

Then the Devi, easily cutting asunder the masses of his arrows, killed his horses and their controller with her arrows.

चिच्छेद च धनुः सद्यो ध्वजं चातिसमुच्छ्रितम् ॥
विव्याध चौव गात्रेषु छिन्नधन्वानमाशुगैः ॥५॥

Ciccheda ca dhanuḥ sadyo dhvajaṁ cātisamucchritam ॥
vivyādha caiva gātreṣu chinnadhanvānam āśugaiḥ ॥5॥

Forthwith she split his bow and lofty banner, and with her arrows pierced the body of that (asura) whose bow had been cut.

सच्छिन्नधन्वा विरथो हताश्वो हतसारथिः ।।
अभ्यधावत तां देवीं खड्गचर्मधरोऽसुरः ।।६।।

Sa chinnadhanvā viratho hatāśvo hatasārathiḥ ।।
abhyadhāvata tāṁ Devīṁ khaḍgacarmadharo 'surah ।।6।।

His bow shattered, his chariot broken, his horses killed and his charioteer slain, the asura armed with sword and shield rushed at the Devi.

सिंहमाहत्य खड्गेन तीक्ष्णधारेण मूर्धनि ।।
आजघान भुजे सव्ये देवीमप्यतिवेगवान् ।।७।।

Siṁham āhatya khaḍgena tīkṣṇadhāreṇa mūrdhani ।।
ājaghāna bhuje savye Devīm apyativegavān ।।7।।

Swiftly he smote the lion on the head with his sharp-edged sword and struck the Devi also on her left arm.

तस्याः खड्गो भुजं प्राप्य पफाल नृपनन्दन ।।
ततो जग्राह शूलं स कोपादरुणलोचनः ।।८।।

Tasyāḥ khadgo bhujaṁ prāpya paphāla nṛpanandana ||
tato jagrāha śūlaṁ sa kopād aruṇalocanaḥ ||8||

O king, his sword broke into pieces as it touched her arm. Thereon his eyes turning red with anger, he grasped his pike.

चिक्षेप च ततस्तत्तु भद्रकाल्यां महासुरः ॥
जाज्वल्यमानं तेजोभी रविबिम्बमिवाम्बरात् ॥९॥

cikṣepa ca tatas tat tu bhadrakālyāṁ mahāsuraḥ ||
jājvalyamānaṁ tejobhī ravibimbam ivāmbarāt ||9||

Then the great asura flung at Bhandrakali the pike, blazing with lustre, as if he was hurling the very sun from the skies.

दृष्ट्वा तदापतच्छूलं देवी शूलममुञ्चत ॥
तच्छूलं शतधा तेन नीतं स च महासुरः ॥१०॥

Dṛṣṭvā tad āpatac chūlaṁ Devī śūlam amuñcata ||
tac chūlaṁ śatadhā tena nītaṁ sa ca mahāsuraḥ ||10||

Seeing that pike coming upon her, the Devi hurled her pike that shattered his pike into a hundred fragments and the great asura himself.

हते तस्मिन्महावीर्ये महिषस्य चमूपतौ ॥
आजगाम गजारूढश्चामरस्त्रिदशार्दनः ॥११॥

Hate tasmin mahāvīrye mahiṣasya camūpatau ॥
ājagāma gajārūḍhaś cāmaras tridaśārdanaḥ ॥11॥

Mahisasura's very valiant general having been killed, Camara, the afflictor of devas, mounted on an elephant, advanced.

सोऽपि शक्तिं मुमोचाथ देव्यास्तामम्बिका द्रुतम् ॥
हुंकाराभिहतां भूमौ पातयामास निष्प्रभाम् ॥१२॥

So 'pi śaktiṁ mumocātha devyās tām ambikā drutam ॥
hunkārābhihatāṁ bhūmau pātayāmāsa niṣprabhām ॥12॥

He also hurled his spear at the Devi. Ambika quickly assailed it with a whoop, made it lustreless and fall to the ground.

भग्नां शक्तिं निपतितां दृष्ट्वा क्रोधसमन्वितः ॥
चिक्षेप चामरः शूलं बाणैस्तदपि साच्छिनत् ॥१३॥

Bhagnāṁ śaktiṁ nipatitāṁ dṛṣṭvā krodhasamanvitaḥ ॥
cikṣepa cāmaraḥ śūlaṁ bāṇais tad api sācchinat ॥13॥

Seeing his spear broken and fallen, Camara, full of rage, flung a pike, and she split that also with her arrows.

ततः सिंहः समुत्पत्य गजकुम्भान्तरे स्थितः ।।
बाहुयुद्धेन युयुधे तेनोच्चैस्त्रिदशारिणा ।।१४।।

Tataḥ siṁhaḥ samutpatya gajakumbhāntarasthitaḥ ।।
bāhuyuddhena yuyudhe tenocchais tridaśāriṇā ।।14।।

Then the lion, leaping up and seating itself at the centre of the elephant's forehead, engaged itself in a hand to hand fight with that foe of the devas.

युद्ध्यमानौ ततस्तौ तु तस्मान्नागान्महीं गतौ ।।
युयुधातेऽतिसंरब्धौ प्रहारैरतिदारुणैः ।।१५।।

Yudhyamānau tatas tau tu tasmān nāgān mahīṁ gatau ।।
yuyudhāte 'tisaṁrabdhau prahārair atidāruṇaiḥ ।।15।।

The two then came down to the earth from the back of the elephant, and fought very impetuously, dealing the most terrible blows at each other.

ततो वेगात् खमुत्पत्य निपत्य च मृगारिणा ।।
करप्रहारेण शिरश्चामरस्य पृथक्कृतम् ।।१६।।

Tato vegāt kham utpatya nipatya ca mṛgāriṇā ।।
karaprahāreṇa śiraś cāmarasya pṛthak kṛtam ।।16।।

Then the lion, springing up quickly to the sky, and descending, severed Camara's head with a blow from its paw.

उदग्रश्च रणे देव्या शिलावृक्षादिभिर्हत: ।।
दन्तमुष्टितलैश्चौव करालश्च निपातित: ।।१७।।

Udagraś ca raṇe Devyā śilāvṛkṣādibhir hataḥ ।।
dantamuṣṭitalaiś caiva karālaś ca nipātitaḥ ।।17।।

And Udagra was killed in the battle by the Devi with stones, trees and the like, and Karala also stricken down by her teeth and fists and slaps.

देवी क्रुद्धा गदापातैश्चूर्णयामास चोद्धतम् ।।
बाष्कलं भिन्दिपालेन बाणैस्ताम्रं तथान्धकम् ।।१८।।

Devī kruddhā gadāpātaiś cūrṇayāmāsa coddhatam ।।
bāṣkalaṁ bhindipālena bāṇais tāmraṁ tathāndhakam ।।18।।

Enraged, the Devi ground Uddhata to powder with the blows of her club, and killed Baskala with a dart and destroyed Tamra and Andhaka with arrows.

उग्रास्यमुग्रवीर्यं च तथैव च महाहनुम् ।।
त्रिनेत्रा च त्रिशूलेन जघान परमेश्वरी ।।१९।।

ugrāsyam ugravīryaṁ ca tathaiva ca mahāhanum ||
trinetrā ca triśūlena jaghāna parameśvarī ||19||

The three-eyed Supreme Isvari killed Ugrasya and Ugravirya and Mahahanu also with her trident.

बिडालस्यासिना कायात्पातयामास वै शिरः ||
दुर्धरं दुर्मुखं चोभौ शरैर्निन्ये यमक्षयम् ||२०||

Biḍālasyāsinā kāyāt pātayāmāsa vai śiraḥ ||
durdharaṁ durmukhaṁ cobhau
śarair ninye yamakṣayam ||20||

With her sword she struck down Bidala's head from his body, and dispatched both Durdhara and Durmudha to the abode of Death with her arrows.

एवं संक्षीयमाणे तु स्वसैन्ये महिषासुरः ||
माहिषेण स्वरूपेण त्रासयामास तान् गणान् ||२१||

Evaṁ samkṣīyamāṇe tu svasainye mahiṣāsuraḥ ||
māhiṣeṇa svarūpeṇa trāsayāmāsa tān gaṇān ||21||

As his army was thus being destroyed, Mahisasura terrified the troops of the Devi with his own buffalo form.

कांश्चित्तुण्डप्रहारेण खुरक्षेपैस्तथापरान् ।।
लाङ्गूलताडितांश्चान्याञ्छृङ्गाभ्यां च विदारितान् ।।२२।।

kāṁścit tuṇḍaprahāreṇa khurakṣepais tathāparān ।।
lāṅgūlatāḍitāṁś cānyān śṛngābhyāṁ ca vidāritān ।।22।।

Some (he laid low) by a blow of his muzzle, some by stamping with his hooves, some by the lashes of his tail, and others by the pokes of his horns.

वेगेन कांश्चिदपरान्नादेन भ्रमणेन च ।।
निःश्वासपवनेनान्यान् पातयामास भूतले ।।२३।।

Vegena kāṁścid aparān nādena bhramaṇena ca ।।
niḥśvāsapavanenānyān pātayāmāsa bhūtale ।।23।।

Some he laid low on the face of the earth by his impetuous speed, some by his bellowing and wheeling movement, and others by the blast of his breath.

निपात्य प्रमथानीकमभ्यधावत सोऽसुरः ।।
सिंहं हन्तुं महादेव्याः कोपं चक्रे ततोऽम्बिका ।।२४।।

Nipātya pramathānīkam abhyadhāvata so 'suraḥ ।।
siṁhaṁ hantuṁ mahādevyāḥ kopaṁ cakre
tato 'mbikā ।।24।।

Having laid low her army, Mahisasura rushed to slay the lion of the Mahadevi. This enraged Ambika.

सोऽपि कोपान्महावीर्यः खुरक्षुण्णमहीतलः ॥
श्रृङ्गाभ्यां पर्वतानुच्चांश्चिक्षेप च ननाद च ॥२५॥

So 'pi kopān mahāvīryaḥ khurakṣuṇṇamahītalaḥ ॥
śṛṅgābhyāṁ parvatān uccāṁś cikṣepa ca nanāda ca ॥25॥

Mahisasura, great in valour, pounded the surface of the earth with his hooves in rage, tossed up the high mountains with his horns, and bellowed terribly.

वेगभ्रमणविक्षुण्णा मही तस्य व्यशीर्यत ॥
लाङ्गूलेनाहतश्चाब्धिः प्लावयामास सर्वतः ॥२६॥

Vegabhramaṇavikṣuṇṇā mahī tasya vyaśīryata ॥
lāṅgūlenāhataś cābdhiḥ plāvayāmāsa sarvataḥ ॥26॥

Crushed by the velocity of his wheeling, the earth disintegrated, and lashed by his tail, the sea overflowed all around.

धुतश्रृङ्गविभिन्नाश्च खण्डं* खण्डं ययुर्घनाः ॥
श्वासानिलास्ताः शतशो निपेतुर्नभसोऽचलाः ॥२७॥

Dhutaśṛṅgavibhinnāś ca khaṇḍaṁ khaṇḍarh yayur ghanāḥ ।।
śvāsānilāstāḥ śataśo nipetur nabhaso 'calāḥ ।।27।।

Pierced by his swaying horns, the clouds went into fragments. Cast up by the blast of his breath, mountains fell down from the sky in hundreds.

इति क्रोधसमाध्मातमापतन्तं महासुरम् ।।
दृष्ट्वा सा चण्डिका कोपं तद्वधाय तदाकरोत् ।।२८।।

Iti krodhasamādhmātam āpatantaṁ mahāsuram ।।
dṛṣṭvā sā Caṇḍikā kopāṁ tad vadhāya tadākarot ।।28।।

Seeing the great asura swollen with rage and advancing towards her, Chandika displayed her wrath in order to slay him.

सा क्षिप्त्वा तस्य वै पाशं तं बबन्ध महासुरम् ।।
तत्याज माहिषं रूपं सोऽपि बद्धो महामृधे ।।२९।।

Sā ksiptvā tasya vai pāśaṁ taṁ babandha mahāsuraṁ ।।
tatyāja māhiṣaṁ rūpaṁ so 'pi baddho mahāmṛdhe ।।29।।

She flung her noose over him and bound the great asura. Thus bound in the great battle, he quitted his buffalo form.

ततः सिंहोऽभवत्सद्यो यावत्तस्याम्बिका शिरः ॥
छिनत्ति तावत्पुरुषः खड्गपाणिरदृश्यत ॥३०॥

tataḥ siṁho 'bhavat sadyo yāvat tasyāmbikā śiraḥ ॥
chinatti tāvat puruṣaḥ khadgapāṇir adṛśyata ॥30॥

Then he became a lion suddenly. While Ambika cut off the head (of his lion form), he took the appearance of a man with sword in hand.

ततः एवाशु पुरुषं देवी चिच्छेद सायकैः ॥
तं खड्गचर्मणा सार्धं ततः सोऽभून्महागजः ॥३१॥

Tata evāśu puruṣaṁ Devī ciccheda sāyakaiḥ ॥
taṁ khaḍgacarmaṇā sārdhaṁ tataḥ
so 'bhūn mahāgajaḥ ॥31॥

31. Immediately then the Devi with her arrows chopped off the man together with his sword and shield. Then he became a big elephant.

करेण च महासिंहं तं चकर्ष जगर्ज च ॥
कर्षतस्तु करं देवी खड्गेन निरकृन्तत ॥३२॥

kareṇa ca mahāsiṁhaṁ taṁ cakarṣa jagarja ca ॥
karṣatas tu karaṁ Devī khaḍgena nirakṛntata ॥32॥

(The elephant) tugged at her great lion with his trunk and roared loudly, but as he was dragging, the Devi cut off his trunk with her sword.

ततो महासुरो भूयो माहिषं वपुरास्थितः ॥
तथैव क्षोभयामास त्रैलोक्यं सचराचरम् ॥३३॥

Tato mahāsuro bhūyo māhiṣaṁ vapurāsthitaḥ ॥
tathaiva kṣobhayāmāsa trailokyaṁ sacarācaram ॥33॥

The great asura then resumed his buffalo shape and shook the three worlds with their movable and immovable objects.

ततः क्रुद्धा जगन्माता चण्डिका पानमुत्तमम् ॥
पपौ पुनः पुनश्चौव जहासारुणलोचना ॥३४॥

Tataḥ kruddhā jaganmātā Caṇḍikā pānam uttamam ॥
papau punaḥ punaś caiva jahāsāruṇalocanā ॥34॥

Enraged threat, Chandika, the Mother of the worlds, quaffed a divine drink again and again, and laughed, her eyes becoming red.

ननर्द चासुरः सोऽपि बलवीर्यमदोद्धतः ॥
विषाणाभ्यां च चिक्षेप चण्डिकां प्रति भूधरान् ॥३५॥

Nanarda cāsuraḥ so 'pi balavīryamadoddhataḥ ।।
viṣāṇābhyāṁ ca cikṣepa Caṇḍikāṁ prati bhūdharān ।।35।।

And the asura, also roared intoxicated with his strength and valour, and hurled mountains against Chandika with his horns.

सा च तान् प्रहितांस्तेन चूर्णयन्ती शरोत्करैः ।।
उवाच तं मदोद्धूतमुखरागाकुलाक्षरम् ।।३६।।

Sā ca tān prahitāṁs tena cūrṇayantī śarotkaraiḥ ।।
uvāca taṁ madoddhūtamukharāgākulākṣaram ।।36।।

And she with showers of arrows pulverized (those mountains) hurled at her, and spoke to him in flurried words, the colour of her face accentuated with the intoxication of the divine drink. The Devi said:

देव्युवाच ।।३७।।

Devy uvāca ।।37।।

The Devī said

गर्ज गर्ज क्षणं मूढ मधु यावत्पिबाम्यहम् ।।
मया त्वयि हतेऽत्रैव गर्जिष्यन्त्याशु देवताः ।।३८।।

garja garja kṣaṇaṁ mūḍha madhu yāvat pibāmy aham ।।
mayā tvayi hate 'traiva garjiṣyanty āśu devatāḥ ।।38।।

'Roar, roar, O fool, for a moment while I drink this wine. When you will be slain by me, the devas will soon roar in this very place.' The Rishi said:

ऋषिरुवाच ।।३९।।

Ṛṣir uvāca ।।39।।

The seer said:

एवमुक्त्वा समुत्पत्य साऽऽरूढा तं महासुरम् ।।
पादेनाक्रम्य कण्ठे च शूलेनैनमताडयत् ।।४०।।

evam uktvā samutpatya sārūḍhā taṁ mahāsuram ।।
pādenākramya kaṇṭhe ca śulenainam atāḍayat ।।40।।

Having exclaimed thus, she jumped and landed herself on that great asura, pressed him on the neck with her foot and struck him with her spear.

ततः सोऽपि पदाऽऽक्रान्तस्तया निजमुखात्ततः ।।
अर्धनिष्क्रान्त एवासीद्' देव्या वीर्येण संवृतः ।।४१।।

Tataḥ so 'pi padākrāntas tayā nijamukhāt tataḥ ||
ardhaniṣkrānta evāsīd Devyā vīryeṇa saṁvṛtaḥ ||41||

And thereupon, caught up under her foot. Mahisasura half issued forth (in his real form) from his own (buffalo) mouth, being completely overcome by the valour of the Devi.

अर्धनिष्क्रान्त एवासौ युध्यमानो महासुरः ।।
तया महासिना देव्या शिरश्छित्त्वा निपातितः ।।४२।।

Ardhaniṣkrānta evāsau yudhyamāno mahāsuraḥ ||
tayā mahāsinā Devyā śiraśchittvā nipātitaḥ ||42||

Fighting thus with his half-revealed form, the great asura was laid by the Devi who struck off his head with her great sword.

ततो हाहाकृतं सर्वं दैत्यसैन्यं ननाश तत् ।।
प्रहर्षं च परं जग्मुः सकला देवतागणाः ।।४३।।

Tato hāhākṛtaṁ sarvaṁ daityasainyaṁ nanāśa tat ||
praharṣaṁ ca paraṁ jagmuḥ sakalā devatāgaṇāḥ ||43||

Then, crying in consternation, the whole asura army perished; and all the hosts of deva were in exultation.

तुष्टुवुस्तां सुरा देवीं सह दिव्यैर्महर्षिभिः ।।
जगुर्गन्धर्वपतयो ननृतुश्चाप्सरोगणाः ।।ॐ ।।४४।।

Tuṣṭuvus tāṁ surā Devīṁ saha divyair maharṣibhiḥ ।।
jagur gandharvapatayo nanṛtuś cāpsarogaṇāḥ ।।44।।

With the great sages of heaven, the devas praised the Devi. The Gandharva chiefs sang and the bevies of apsaras danced. Here ends the third chapter called 'The Slaying of Mahisasura' of Devi-mahatmya in Markandeya-purana during the period of Savarni, the Manu.

इति श्रीमार्कण्डेयपुराणे सावर्णिके मन्वन्तरे देवीमाहात्म्ये
महिषासुरवधो नाम तृतीयोऽध्यायः ।।३ ।।
उवाच ३, श्लोकाः ४१, एवम् ४४,
एवमादितः ।।२१७ ।।

iti śrī-mārkaṇḍeya-purāṇe sāvarṇike
manvantare devī-māhātmye
mahiṣāsura-vadho nāma tṛtīyo'dhyāyaḥ ।।3।।
uvāca 3, ślokaḥ 41, evam 44, evam-āditaḥ 217

Thus ends the third chapter called 'The Slaying of Mahishasura' in the Devi Mahatmya, from the Savarni Manvantara of the sacred Markandeya Purana.

॥ चतुर्थोऽध्यायः ॥

इन्द्रादि देवताओं द्वारा देवी की स्तुतिः

॥ Fourth Chapter ॥

Praise by Indra and the Other Gods

॥ ध्यानम् ॥

ॐ कालाभ्राभां कटाक्षैररिकुलभयदां मौलिबद्धेन्दुरेखां
शङ्खं चक्रं कृपाणं त्रिशिखमपि करैरुद्वहन्तीं त्रिनेत्राम्।
सिंहस्कन्धाधिरूढां त्रिभुवनमखिलं तेजसा पूरयन्तीं
ध्यायेद् दुर्गां जयाख्यां त्रिदशपरिवृतां सेवितां सिद्धिकामैः ॥

॥ Dhyānam ॥

oṁ kālābhrābhāṁ kaṭākṣair arikulabhayadāṁ
maulibaddhendurekhāṁ
śaṅkhaṁ cakraṁ kṛpāṇaṁ triśikham
api karair udvahantīṁ trinetrām |

siṁhaskandhādhirūḍhāṁ tribhuvanam
akhilaṁ tejasā pūrayantīṁ
dhyāyed durgāṁ jayākhyāṁ tridaśaparivṛtāṁ
sevitāṁ siddhikāmaiḥ ||

Meditation (Dhyānam):

One should meditate upon Durgā, known as Jaya (the Victorious), who is surrounded by the host of gods and served by those desiring success. She has the complexion of a dark storm cloud, and with her sidelong glances, she dispels the fear of enemy hordes. The crescent moon adorns her crown. With her hands, she holds a conch, discus, sword, and trident. She is three-eyed, seated upon the shoulder of a lion, and she fills the three worlds entirely with her brilliance.

"ॐ" ऋषिरुवाच ।।१।।

Om the seer said:

शक्रादयः सुरगणा निहतेऽतिवीर्ये
तस्मिन्दुरात्मनि सुरारिबले च देव्या ।।
तां तुष्टुवुः प्रणतिनम्रशिरोधरांसा
वाग्भिः प्रहर्षपुलकोद्गमचारुदेहाः ।।२।।

śakrādayaḥ suragaṇā nihate 'tivīrye
tasmin durātmani surāribale ca Devyā ॥
tāṁ tuṣṭuvuḥ praṇatinamraśirodharāṁsā
vāgbhiḥ praharṣapulakodgamacārudehāḥ ॥2॥

"When the Devī had struck down the brave but wicked Mahiṣāsura and his army of the Gods' foes, Indra and the hosts of Gods lifted their voices to Her in praise, their heads bowed in reverence, their bodies made beautiful by the thrill of rapture.

देव्या यया ततमिदं जगदात्मशक्त्या
निश्शेषदेवगणशक्तिसमूहमूर्त्या ॥
तामम्बिकामखिलदेवमहर्षिपूज्यां
भक्तया नताः स्म विदधातु शुभानि सा नः ॥३॥

Devyā yayā tatam idaṁ jagad ātmaśaktyā
niḥśeṣadevagaṇaśaktisamūhamūrtyā ॥
tāṁ Ambikām akhiladevamaharṣipūjyāṁ
bhaktyā natāḥ sma vidadhātu śubhāni sā naḥ ॥3॥

'To the Devī, Who spreads out this world through Her own power and Who embodies Herself as all the powers of the hosts of Gods; to Ambikā, Who is worthy of worship by all the Gods and great seers, we bow down in devotion. May She grant us that which is auspicious.

यस्याः प्रभावमतुलं भगवाननन्तो
ब्रह्मा हरश्च न हि वक्तुमलं बलं च ।।
सा चण्डिकाखिलजगत्परिपालनाय
नाशाय चाशुभभयस्य मतिं करोतु ।।४।।

yasyāḥ prabhāvam atulaṁ bhagavān ananto
brahmā haraś ca na hi vaktum alaṁ balaṁ ca ।।
sā caṇḍikākhilajagat paripālanāya
nāśāya cāśubhabhayasya matiṁ karotu ।।4।।

May She whose unequalled might and splendor even the blessed Viṣṇu, Brahmā, and Śiva are powerless to describe, may She, Caṇḍikā, be intent on protecting all the world and on destroying the fear of misfortune.

❧

या श्रीः स्वयं सुकृतिनां भवनेष्वलक्ष्मीः
पापात्मनां कृतधियां हृदयेषु बुद्धिः ।।
श्रद्धा सतां कुलजनप्रभवस्य लज्जा
तां त्वां नताः स्म परिपालय देवि विश्वम् ।।५।।

yā śrīḥ svayaṁ sukṛtināṁ bhavaneṣvalakṣmīḥ
pāpātmanāṁ kṛtadhiyāṁ hṛdayeṣu buddhiḥ ।।
śraddhā satāṁ kulajanaprabhavasya lajjā
tāṁ tvāṁ natāḥ sma paripālaya Devi viśvam ।।5।।

O Devī, we bow before You—fortune in the homes of the virtuous, misfortune in the abodes of the wicked; wisdom in the hearts of the learned, faith in the hearts of the righteous, and modesty in the hearts of the noble. May You, O Mother, protect the universe!

किं वर्णयाम तव रूपमचिन्त्यमेतत्
किं चातिवीर्यमसुरक्षयकारि भूरि ॥
किं चाहवेषु चरितानि तवाद्भुतानि
सर्वेषु देव्यसुरदेवगणादिकेषु ॥६॥

kiṁ varṇayāma tava rūpam acintyam etat
kiñ cātivīryam asurakṣayakāri bhūri ॥
kiṁ cāhaveṣu caritāni tavāti yāni
sarveṣu Devy asuradevagaṇādikeṣu ॥6॥

How can we describe this form of yours, which surpasses thought? And Your abundant, exceeding valor that destroys evil? And Your deeds in battle, O Devī, among all the throngs of Gods and demons?

हेतुः समस्तजगतां त्रिगुणापि दोषैर्न
ज्ञायसे हरिहरादिभिरप्यपारा ॥
सर्वाश्रयाखिलमिदं जगदंशभूत-
मव्याकृता हि परमा प्रकृतिस्त्वमाद्या ॥७॥

hetuḥ samastajagatāṁ triguṇāpi doṣair
na jñāyase hariharādibhir apyapārā ॥

sarvāśrayākhilam idam jagad aṁśabhūtam
avyākṛtā hi paramā prakṛtis tvam ādyā ॥7॥

You are the cause of all the worlds. Though containing the triple forces of creation within yourself, You are untouched by any imperfection. You are unfathomable even to Viṣṇu, Śiva, and the other Gods. You are the resort of all. You are this entire, manifold world and You are primordial matter, supreme and untransformed.

ॐ

यस्याः समस्तसुरता समुदीरणेन
तृप्तिं प्रयाति सकलेषु मखेषु देवि ॥
स्वाहासि वै पितृगणस्य च तृप्तिहेतु-
रुच्चार्यसे त्वमत एव जनैः स्वधा च ॥८॥

yasyāḥ samastasuratā samudīraṇena
tṛptiṁ prayāti sakaleṣu makheṣu Devi ॥
svāhāsi vai pitṛgaṇasya ca tṛptihetur
uccāryase tvam ata eva janaiḥ svadhā ca ॥8॥

O Devī, You are the mantra of consecration whose utterance in all sacrifices brings satisfaction to the whole assemblage of Gods, and You are the mantra which humans proclaim as the cause of satisfaction to the hosts of ancestral spirits.

ॐ

या मुक्तिहेतुरविचिन्त्यमहाव्रता त्व*-
मभ्यस्यसे सुनियतेन्द्रियतत्त्वसारैः ।।
मोक्षार्थिभिर्मुनिभिरस्तसमस्तदोषै-
र्विद्यासि सा भगवती परमा हि देवि ।।९।।

yā muktihetur avicintyamahāvratā tvaṁ
abhyasyase suniyatendriyatattvasāraiḥ ।।
mokṣārthibhir munibhir astasamastadoṣair
vidyāsi sā bhagavatī paramā hi Devi ।।9।।

O Devī, Who are the cause of liberation and great, inconceivable austerities: sages yearning for liberation contemplate You with senses restrained, intent upon truth, with all faults cast off, for You are the blessed, supreme knowledge.

~

शब्दात्मिका सुविमलर्ग्यजुषां निधान-
मुद्गीथरम्यपदपाठवतां च साम्नाम् ।।
देवी त्रयी भगवती भवभावनाय
वार्ता च सर्वजगतां परमार्तिहन्त्री ।।१०।।

śabdātmikā suvimalargyajuṣām nidhānam
udgītharamyapadapāṭhavatāṁ ca sāmnām ।।
Devī trayī Bhagavatī bhavabhāvanāya
vārtā ca sarvajagatāṁ paramārtihantrī ।।10।।

With sound as Your essence, You are the treasury that holds the taintless Vedic hymns, sung to resound joyfully with

Your holy name. You are the blessed Devī, Who embodies the three Vedas. Intent on conferring well-being, You are the supreme destroyer of pain in all the worlds.

मेधासि देवि विदिताखिलशास्त्रसारा
दुर्गासि दुर्गभवसागरनौरसङ्गा ॥
श्रीः कैटभारिहृदयैककृताधिवासा
गौरी त्वमेव शशिमौलिकृतप्रतिष्ठा ॥११॥

medhāsi Devi viditākhilaśāstrasārā
Durgāsi durgabhavasāgaranaur asaṅgā ॥
śrīḥ kaiṭabhārihṛdayaikakṛtādhivāsā
Gaurī tvaṁ eva śaśimaulikṛtapratiṣṭhā ॥11॥

O Devī, You are the intelligence by which the essence of all scriptures is understood. You are Durgā, the vessel free of attachments that takes one across life's difficult ocean. You are Srī, the radiant splendor that abides in the heart of Viṣṇu. You are Gaurī, the shining goddess Who abides with the moon-crowned Śiva.

ईषत्सहासममलं परिपूर्णचन्द्र-
बिम्बानुकारि कनकोत्तमकान्तिकान्तम् ॥
अत्यद्भुतं प्रहृतमात्तरुषा तथापि
वक्त्रं विलोक्य सहसा महिषासुरेण ॥१२॥

īṣatsahāsam amalaṁ paripūrṇacandra-
bimbānukāri kanakottamakāntikāntam ||
atyadbhutaṁ prahṛtam āttaruṣā tathāpi
vaktraṁ vilokya sahasā mahiṣāsureṇa ||12||

Gently smiling, Your shining face resembles the full moon's orb and is as pleasing as the lustre of the finest gold. Beholding It, how could Mahiṣāsura, even though enraged, be moved to strike it?

दृष्ट्वा तु देवि कुपितं भ्रुकुटीकराल-
मुद्यच्छशाङ्कसदृशच्छवि यन्न सद्यः ॥
प्राणान्मुमोच महिषस्तदतीव चित्रं
कैर्जीव्यते हि कुपितान्तकदर्शनेन ॥१३॥

dṛṣṭvā tu Devi kupitaṁ bhrukuṭīkarālam
udyacchaśāṅkasadṛśacchavi yan na sadyaḥ ||
prāṇān mumoca mahiṣas tad atīva citraṁ
kair jīvyate hi kupitāntakadarśanena ||13||

Still stranger was it, O Devī, that Mahiṣa did not perish the instant he beheld Your wrathful face, reddened like the rising moon and scowling frightfully. For who can behold the enraged face of death and still live?

देवि प्रसीद परमा भवती भवाय
सद्यो विनाशयसि कोपवती कुलानि ।।
विज्ञातमेतदधुनैव यदस्तमेत-
न्नीतं बलं सुविपुलं महिषासुरस्य ।।१४।।

Devi prasīda paramā bhavatī bhavāya
sadyo vināśayasi kopavatī kulāni ।।
vijñātam etad adhunaiva yad astam etan
nnītaṁ balaṁ suvipulaṁ mahiṣāsurasya ।।14।।

O Devī, Who are supreme, be gracious to all creation, for when angered You can annihilate multitudes. We saw this the moment You brought Mahiṣāsura's vast power to an end.

❧

ते सम्मता जनपदेषु धनानि तेषां
तेषां यशांसि न च सीदति धर्मवर्गः ।।
धन्यास्त एव निभृतात्मजभृत्यदारा
येषां सदाभ्युदयदा भवती प्रसन्ना ।।१५।।

te sammatā janapadeṣu dhanāni teṣāṁ
teṣāṁ yaśāṁsi na ca sīdati dharmavargaḥ ।।
dhanyāsta eva nibhṛtatmajabhṛtyadārā
yeṣāṁ sadābhyudayadā bhavatī prasannā ।।15।।

Those to whom You are bounteous are honored among peoples, theirs are riches, theirs are glories, and their righteous acts know no limit. They indeed are blessed with devoted children, attendants, and wives.

धर्म्याणि देवि सकलानि सदैव कर्मा-
ण्यत्यादृतः प्रतिदिनं सुकृती करोति ॥
स्वर्गं प्रयाति च ततो भवतीप्रसादा-
ल्लोकत्रयेऽपि फलदा ननु देवि तेन ॥१६॥

dharmyāṇi Devi sakalāni sadaiva karmāṇy
atyādṛtaḥ pratidinaṁ sukṛtī karoti ॥
svargaṁ prayāti ca tato bhavatlī prasādā
llokatraye 'pi phaladā nanu Devi tena ॥16॥

One who is virtuous and ever mindful performs daily all righteous deeds, O Devī, and by Your grace attains to heaven. Are You not, then, the giver of rewards in all the three worlds?

दुर्गे स्मृता हरसि भीतिमशेषजन्तोः
स्वस्थैः स्मृता मतिमतीव शुभां ददासि॥
दारिद्र्यदुःखभयहारिणि का त्वदन्या
सर्वोपकारकरणाय सदाऽऽर्द्रचित्ता ॥१७॥

Durge smṛtā harasi bhītim aśeṣajantoḥ
svasthaiḥ smṛtā matim atīva śubhāṁ dadāsi ॥
dāridryaduḥkhabhayahāriṇi kā tvad anyā
sarvopakārakaraṇāya sadārdracittā ॥17॥

Remembered in distress, You remove fear from every creature. Remembered by the untroubled, You confer even greater serenity of mind. Dispeller of poverty, suffering, and fear, Who other than You is ever intent on benevolence toward all?

एभिर्हतैर्जगदुपैति सुखं तथैते
कुर्वन्तु नाम नरकाय चिराय पापम् ।।
संग्राममृत्युमधिगम्य दिवं प्रयान्तु
मत्वेति नूनमहितान् विनिहंसि देवि ।।१८।।

ebhir hatair jagad upaiti sukhaṁ tathaite
kurvantu nāma narakāya cirāya pāpam ।।
saṁgrāma mṛtyum adhigamya divaṁ prayāntu
matveti nūnam ahitān vinihaṁsi Devi ।।18।।

The world attains happiness when You slay its foes, and though they may have committed enough evil to keep them long in torment, even as You strike down our enemies, O Devī, You think, May they reach heaven through death in battle with Me.

दृष्ट्वैव किं न भवती प्रकरोति भस्म
सर्वासुरानरिषु यत्प्रहिणोषि शस्त्रम् ।।
लोकान् प्रयान्तु रिपवोऽपि हि शस्त्रपूता
इत्थं मतिर्भवति तेष्वपि तेऽतिसाध्वी ।।१९।।

dṛṣṭvaiva kiṁ na bhavatī prakaroti bhasma
sarvāsurān ariṣu yat prahiṇoṣi śastram ।।
lokān prayāntu ripavo ’pi hi śastrapūtā
itthaṁ matir bhavati teṣv api te ’tisādhvī ।।19।।

Why does Your mere glance not reduce all asuras to ashes? Because when assailed by Your weapons and thus purified, even those adversaries may attain the higher worlds.

खड्गप्रभानिकरविस्फुरणैस्तथोग्रैः
शूलाग्रकान्तिनिवहेन दृशोऽसुराणाम् ।।
यन्नागता विलयमंशुमदिन्दुखण्ड-
योग्याननं तव विलोकयतां तदेतत् ।।२०।।

khaḍgaprabhānikaravisphuraṇais tathograiḥ
śūlāgrakāntinivahena dṛśo ’surāṇām ।।
yan nāgatā vilayam aṁśumad indukhaṇḍa
yogyānanam tava vilokayatāṁ tad etat ।।20।।

If the intense light flashing frightfully from Your sword or the glaring brilliance of Your spearpoint did not blind the asuras’ eyes, it was because You made them behold the moonlike radiance beaming from Your face.

दुर्वृत्तवृत्तशमनं तव देवि शीलं
रूपं तथैतदविचिन्त्यमतुल्यमन्यैः ।।
वीर्यं च हन्तृ हृतदेवपराक्रमाणां
वैरिष्वपि प्रकटितैव दया त्वयेत्थम् ।।२१।।

durvṛttavṛttaśamanaṁ tava Devi śīlaṁ
rūpaṁ tathaitad avicintyam atulyam anyaiḥ ।।
vīryaṁ ca hantṛ hṛtadevaparākramāṇāṁ
vairiṣv api prakṭitaiva dayā tvayettham ।।21।।

Even toward them Your intentions are most gracious. O Devī, Your nature is to subdue the misconduct of the wicked. Others cannot equal Your inconceivable grace, for even while Your might destroys those Who have wrested power from the Gods, You show compassion toward those very foes.

केनोपमा भवतु तेऽस्य पराक्रमस्य
रूपं च शत्रुभयकार्यतिहारि कुत्र ।।
चित्ते कृपा समरनिष्ठुरता च दृष्टा
त्वय्येव देवि वरदे भुवनत्रयेऽपि ।।२२।।

kenopamā bhavatu te ’sya parākramasya
rūpaṁ ca śatrubhayakāry atihāri kutra ।।
citte kṛpā samaranişṭhuratā ca dṛṣṭā
tvayy eva Devi varade bhuvanatraye ’pi ।।22।।

To what may Your prowess be compared? Where else is there beauty so ravishing, yet striking fear into enemies? Where in the three worlds are compassion in heart and resolve in battle seen as they are in You, O beneficent Devī?

त्रैलोक्यमेतदखिलं रिपुनाशनेन
त्रातं त्वया समरमूर्धनि तेऽपि हत्वा ।।
नीता दिवं रिपुगणा भयमप्यपास्त-
मस्माकमुन्मदसुरारिभवं नमस्ते ।।२३।।

trailokyam etad akhilaṁ ripunāśanena
trātam tvayā samaramūrdhani te 'pi hatvā ।।
nītā divaṁ ripugaṇā bhayam apy apāstam
asmākam unmada surāribhavam namaste ।।23।।

Destroying all foes, You have saved the three worlds. Slaying them at the battle-front, You led even those frenzied, hostile throngs to heaven, even while dispelling our fear of them. Salutations to You!

शूलेन पाहि नो देवि पाहि खड्गेन चाम्बिके ।।
घण्टास्वनेन नः पाहि चापज्यानिःस्वनेन च ।।२४।।

śūlena pāhi no Devi pāhi khaḍgena cāmbike ।।
ghaṇṭāsvanena naḥ pāhi cāpajyānissvanena ca ।।24।।

Protect us with Your spear, O Devī, and protect us with Your sword, O Ambikā. Protect us with the clangor of Your bell and the resonance of Your bowstring.

प्राच्यां रक्ष प्रतीच्यां च चण्डिके रक्ष दक्षिणे ॥
भ्रामणेनात्मशूलस्य उत्तरस्यां तथेश्वरि ॥२५॥

prācyāṁ rakṣa pratīcyāṁ ca caṇḍike rakṣa dakṣine ॥
bhrāmaṇenātmaśūlasya uttarasyāṁ tatheśvari ॥25॥

Guard us in the east and in the west, O Caṇḍikā. Guard us in the south and also in the north, O Īśvarī, by brandishing Your spear.

सौम्यानि यानि रूपाणि त्रैलोक्ये विचरन्ति ते ॥
यानि चात्यर्थघोराणि तै रक्षास्मांस्तथा भुवम् ॥२६॥

saumyāni yāni rūpāṇi trailokye vicaranti te ॥
yāni cātyantaghorāṇi tai rakṣāsmāṁs tathā bhuvam ॥26॥

With Your gentle forms that move through the three worlds and with Your surpassingly terrible ones, protect us and also the Earth.

खड्गशूलगदादीनि यानि चास्त्राणी तेऽम्बिके ।।
करपल्लवसङ्गीनि तैरस्मान् रक्ष सर्वतः ।।२७।।

khaḍgaśūlagadādīni yāni cāstrāṇi te 'mbike ।।
karapallavasaṅgīni tair asmān rakṣa sarvataḥ ।।27।।

O Ambikā, with sword, spear, mace, and whatever other weapons Your tender hands have touched, protect us on all sides.

ऋषिरुवाच ।।२८।।

ṛṣir uvāca ।।28।।

The seer said:

एवं स्तुता सुरैर्दिव्यैः कुसुमैर्नन्दनोद्भवैः ।।
अर्चिता जगतां धात्री तथा गन्धानुलेपनैः ।।२९।।

evaṁ stutā surair divyaiḥ kusumair nandanodbhavaiḥ ।।
arcitā jagatām dhātrī tathā gandhānulepanaiḥ ।।29।।

In that way the Gods praised Her Who supports the worlds, honoring Her with flowers that bloom in Indra's paradise and anointing Her with perfumes.

भक्त्या समस्तैस्त्रिदशैर्दिव्यैर्धूपैस्तु धूपिता ॥
प्राह प्रसादसुमुखी समस्तान् प्रणतान् सुरान् ॥३०॥

bhaktyā samastais tridaśair divyair dhūpaiḥ sudhūpitā ॥
prāha prasādasumukhī samastān praṇatān surān ॥30॥

Devotedly the assembled Gods offered heavenly incense to Her. Serene of countenance, She spoke to all the Gods, who were bowed down in reverence.

देव्युवाच ॥३१॥

Devy uvāca ॥31॥

The Devī said:

व्रियतां त्रिदशाः सर्वे यदस्मत्तोऽभिवाञ्छितम् ॥३२॥

vriyatām tridaśāḥ sarve yad asmatto 'bhivāñchitam ॥32॥

'All You Gods, ask whatever You wish of Me. Well pleased with Your hymns, I will gladly grant it.'

देवा ऊचुः ॥३३॥

Devā ūcuḥ ॥33॥

The Gods said:

भगवत्या कृतं सर्वं न किंचिदवशिष्यते ॥३४॥

Bhagavatyā kṛtaṁ sarvaṁ na kiñcid avasiṣyate ॥34॥

'Since You, the glorious one, have slain our enemy.

यदयं निहतः शत्रुरस्माकं महिषासुरः ॥
यदि चापि वरो देयस्त्वयास्माकं महेश्वरि ॥३५॥

yad ayaṁ nihataḥ śatrur asmākam mahiṣāsuraḥ ॥
yadi cāpi varo deyas tvayā 'smākaṁ Maheśvari ॥35॥

This Mahiṣāsura, all has been accomplished; nothing remains to be done. But if You are to grant a blessing, O great sovereign,...

संस्मृता संस्मृता त्वं नो हिंसेथाः परमापदः ॥
यश्च मर्त्यः स्तवैरेभिस्त्वां स्तोष्यत्यमलानने ॥३६॥

saṁsmṛtā saṁsmṛtā tvaṁ no hiṁsethāḥ paramāpadaḥ ॥
yaś ca martyaḥ stavair ebhis tvāṁ stoṣyaty amalānane ॥36॥

When remembered again and again, O stainless-faced (pure-faced) Goddess, you destroy for us the greatest dangers. And any mortal who praises you with these hymns shall also be protected.

तस्य वित्तर्द्धिविभवैर्धनदारादिसम्पदाम् ॥
वृद्धयेऽस्मत्प्रसन्ना त्वं भवेथाः सर्वदाम्बिके ॥३७॥

tasya vittarddhivibhavair dhanadārādisampadām ॥
vṛddhaye 'smat prasannā tvam bhavethāḥ sarvadāmbike ॥37॥

O Mother Ambikā, may you always look upon us with favor and bless him (the devotee) with ever-growing wealth, prosperity, power, and all forms of abundance—including riches, a good spouse, and other worldly blessings.

ऋषिरुवाच ॥३८॥

ṛṣir uvāca ॥38॥

The seer said:

इति प्रसादिता देवैर्जगतोऽर्थे तथाऽऽत्मनः ॥
तथेत्युक्त्वा भद्रकाली बभूवान्तर्हिता नृप ॥३९॥

iti prasāditā de vair jagato 'rthe tathātmanaḥ ।।
tathety uktvā Bhadrakālī babhuvāntarhitā nṛpa ।।39।।

"O king, thus propitiated by the Gods for the world's sake and for their own, Bhadrakālī said, 'So let it be,' and vanished from sight.

इत्येतत्कथितं भूप सम्भूता सा यथा पुरा ।।
देवी देवशरीरेभ्यो जगत्त्रयहितैषिणी ।।४०।।

ity etat kathitaṁ bhūpa sambhūtā sā yathā purā ।।
Devī devaśarīrebhyo jagattrayahitaiṣinī ।।40।।

So is it told, O king, how She came forth long ago from the bodies of the Gods, the Devī Who desires the wellbeing of the three worlds.

पुनश्च गौरीदेहात्सा समुद्भूता यथाभवत् ।।
वधाय दुष्टदैत्यानां तथा शुम्भनिशुम्भयोः ।।४१।।

punaś ca Gaurīdehāt sā samudbhūtā yathābhavat ।।
vadhāya duṣṭadaityānām tathā śumbhaniśumbhayoḥ ।।41।।

I shall relate further how, for the destruction of Śumbha and Niśumbha and other wicked daityas, She appeared from the body of Gaurī.

रक्षणाय च लोकानां देवानामुपकारिणी ।।
तच्छृणुष्व मयाऽऽख्यातं यथावत्कथयामि ते ।।ह्रीं ॐ ।।४२।।

rakṣanāya ca lokānāṁ devānām upakāriṇī ॥
tac chṛṇuṣva mayā''khyātaṁ yathāvat
kathayāmi te॥hrīṁ oṁ॥42॥

The benefactor of the Gods, for the protection of the three worlds. Hear me tell it. I shall relate it to you as it happened."

इति श्रीमार्कण्डेयपुराणे सावर्णिके मन्वन्तरे देवीमाहात्म्ये
शक्रादिस्तुतिर्नाम चतुर्थोऽध्यायः ।।४।।
उवाच ५, अर्धश्लोकौ: २, श्लोका: ३५,
एवम् ४२, एवमादित: ।।२५९।।

iti śrīmārkaṇḍeyapurāṇe sāvarnike manvantare
devīmāhātmye
śakrādistutir nāma caturtho'dhyāyaḥ ॥4॥
uvāca 5, ardhaślokauḥ 2, ślokāḥ 35,
evam 42, evamāditaḥ ॥259॥

Thus ends the fourth chapter, called 'The Praise by Indra and the Other Gods' (Śakrādi-stutiḥ), in the Devī Māhātmya, which occurs in the Mārkaṇḍeya Purāṇa, during the Sāvārṇika Manvantara.

|| पञ्चमोऽध्यायः ||

देव्याः दूतसंवाद

|| Fifth Chapter ||

Devi's conversation with the messenger

देवताओं द्वारा देवी की स्तुति, चण्ड-मुण्डके मुख से अम्बिका के रूप की प्रशंसा सुनकर शुम्भ का उनके पास दूत भेजना और दूत का निराश लौटना।

The gods praise the Goddess; upon hearing Chanda and Munda's praise of Ambika's form, Shumbha sends a messenger to her, and the messenger returns disappointed.

॥ विनियोगः ॥

ॐ अस्य श्रीउत्तरचरित्रस्य रूद्र ऋषिः, महासरस्वती देवता, अनुष्टुप् छन्दः, भीमा शक्तिः, भ्रामरी बीजम्, सूर्यस्तत्त्वम्, सामवेदः स्वरूपम्, महासरस्वतीप्रीत्यर्थे उत्तरचरित्रपाठे विनियोगः ।

॥ Vinayogaḥ ॥

oṁ asya śrī-uttaracaritrasya rūdra ṛṣiḥ, mahāsarasvatī devatā, anuṣṭup chandaḥ, bhīmā śaktiḥ, bhrāmarī bījam, sūryas tattvam, sāmavedaḥ svarūpam, mahāsarasvatī-prītyarthe uttaracaritrapāṭhe vinayogaḥ ।

॥ Statement of purpose for the recitation or ritual ॥

"Om. This is the invocation for the recitation of the Śrī Uttaracaritra (the final episode of the Devī Māhātmya). The sage (ṛṣi) associated with this text is Rudra. The presiding deity is the Goddess Mahāsarasvatī. The metre used is Anuṣṭubh. The power or energy (śakti) invoked is Bhīmā. The seed syllable (bīja) is Bhrāmarī. The guiding principle (tattva) is the Sun, and its essential nature (svarūpa) is the Sāma Veda. This recitation is undertaken for the pleasure and propitiation of Mahāsarasvatī."

॥ ध्यानम् ॥

ॐ घण्टाशूलहलानि शङ्खमुसले चक्रं धनुः सायकं
हस्ताब्जैर्दधतीं घनान्तविलसच्छीतांशुतुल्यप्रभाम् ।
गौरीदेहसमुद्भवां त्रिजगतामाधारभूतां महा-
पूर्वामत्र सरस्वतीमनुभजे शुम्भादिदैत्यार्दिनीम् ॥

॥ Dhyānam ॥

oṁ ghaṇṭāśūlahalāni śaṅkhamusale
cakraṁ dhanuḥ sāyakaṁ

hastābjairdadhatīṁ ghanāntavilasacchītāṁśutulyaprabhām ।
gaurīdehasamudbhavāṁ trijagatām ādhārabhūtāṁ mahā-
pūrvām atra sarasvatīṁ anubhaje śumbhādi-daityārdinīm ॥

Meditation Verse

"Om. I meditate upon that form of Sarasvatī, who holds in her lotus-like hands a bell, trident, plough, conch, mace, discus, bow, and arrows; whose radiance is like the cool light of the moon shining at the end of the rainy season; who was born from the body of Gaurī; who is the foundation of the three worlds; who is the primordial great Goddess; and who is the destroyer of demons like Śumbha and others."

"ॐ क्लीं" ऋषिरुवाच ॥१॥

OṀ klīm ṛṣir uvāca ॥1॥

OṀ klīm. The seer said:

पुरा शुम्भनिशुम्भाभ्यामसुराभ्यां शचीपतेः ॥
त्रैलोक्यं यज्ञभागाश्च हृता मदबलाश्रयात् ॥२॥

purā śumbhanisumbhābhyām asurābhyāṁ śacīpateḥ ॥
trailokyaṁ yajñabhāgāś ca hṛtā madabalāśrayāt ॥2॥

"Long ago, grown arrogant with power, the asuras Śumbha and Niśumbha seized Indra's sovereignty over the three worlds and his share of the sacrifices.

❧

तावेव सूर्यतां तद्वदधिकारं तथैन्दवम् ॥
कौबेरमथ याम्यं च चक्राते वरुणस्य च ॥३॥

tāv eva sūryatām tadvad adhikāraṁ tathaindavam ॥
kauberam atha yāmyaṁ ca cakrāte varuṇasya ca ॥3॥

In like manner they usurped the authority of the sun and the moon, and that of Kubera, Yama, and Varuṇa—the lords of wealth, death, and the ocean.

❧

तावेव पवनर्द्धिं च चक्रतुर्वह्निकर्म च ॥
ततो देवा विनिर्धूता भ्रष्टराज्याः पराजिताः ॥४॥

tāv eva pavanarddhiṁ ca cakratur vahnikarma ca ॥
tato devā vinirdhūtā bhraṣṭarājyāḥ parājitāḥ ॥4॥

They seized the wind god's power and Agni's functions. The gods were defeated, deposed, and driven out.

❧

हताधिकारास्त्रिदशास्ताभ्यां सर्वे निराकृताः ॥
महासुराभ्यां तां देवीं संस्मरन्त्यपराजिताम् ॥५॥

hṛtādhikārās tridaśās tābhyāṁ sarve nirākṛtāḥ ॥
mahāsurābhyāṁ tāṁ Devīṁ saṁsmaranty aparājitāṁ ॥5॥

Stripped of their powers and cast out by those two great asuras, all the gods remembered the invincible Devī.

तयास्माकं वरो दत्तो यथाऽऽपत्सु स्मृताखिलाः ॥
भवतां नाशयिष्यामि तत्क्षणात्परमापदः ॥६॥

tayāsmākaṁ varo datto yathāpatsu smṛtākhilāḥ ॥
bhavatāṁ nāśayiṣyāmi tatkṣaṇāt paramāpadaḥ ॥6॥

'She granted us a boon, saying, "Whenever you remember Me in times of distress, from that very moment I will put an end to all your worst calamities."'

इति कृत्वा मतिं देवा हिमवन्तं नगेश्वरम् ॥
जग्मुस्तत्र ततो देवीं विष्णुमायां प्रतुष्टुवुः ॥७॥

iti kṛtvā matiṁ devā himavantaṁ nageśvaram ॥
jagmus tatra tato Devīm viṣṇumāyām pratuṣṭuvuḥ ॥7॥

With that in mind, the gods went to Himālaya, the lord of mountains, and there praised the Devī, Who is Viṣṇumāyā.

देवा ऊचुः ॥८॥

devā ūcuḥ ॥8॥

The gods said:

नमो देव्यै महादेव्यै शिवायै सततं नमः ॥
नमः प्रकृत्यै भद्रायै नियताः प्रणताः स्म ताम् ॥९॥

namo Devyai MahāDevyai śivāyai satataṁ namaḥ ॥
namaḥ prakṛtyai bhadrāyai niyatāḥ praṇatāḥ sma tām ॥9॥

'Salutation to the Devī, to the great Devī. Salutation always to Her Who is auspicious. Salutation to Her Who is the primordial cause, to Her Who is gracious. With minds intent, we bow down to Her.

रौद्रायै नमो नित्यायै गौर्यै धात्र्यै नमो नमः ॥
ज्योत्स्नायै चेन्दुरूपिण्यै सुखायै सततं नमः ॥१०॥

raudrāyai namo nityāyai Gauryai dhātryai namo namaḥ ॥
jyotsnāyai cendurūpiṇyai sukhāyai satataṁ namaḥ ॥10॥

Salutation to Her Who is terrible. To Gaurī, the eternal, shining one; to Her Who sustains the universe, salutations again and again. Salutation always to Her Who is moonlight, Who has the form of the moon and is blissful.

कल्याण्यै प्रणतां वृद्ध्यै सिद्ध्यै कुर्मो नमो नमः ।।
नैर्ऋत्यै भूभृतां लक्ष्म्यै शर्वाण्यै ते नमो नमः ।।११।।

kalyāṇyai praṇatā vṛddhyai siddhyai kurmo namo namaḥ ।।
nairṛtyai bhūbhṛtām lakṣmyai śarvāṇyai te namo namaḥ ।।11।।

We bow to Her Who is auspicious beauty. We make salutations again and again to Her Who is prosperity and attainment. Salutations again and again to Her Who is the fortune and misfortune of kings, to Śarvāṇī, the consort of Śiva.

दुर्गायै दुर्गपारायै सारायै सर्वकारिण्यै ।।
ख्यात्यै तथैव कृष्णायै धूम्रायै सततं नमः ।।१२।।

Durgāyai Durgapārāyai sārāyai sarvakāriṇyai ।।
khyātyai tathaiva kṛṣṇāyai dhūmrāyai satatam namaḥ ।।12।।

Salutation always to Durgā, Who takes us through difficulties, Who is the creator and indwelling essence of all, Who is right knowledge, and Who also appears dark as smoke.

अतिसौम्यातिरौद्रायै नतास्तस्यै नमो नमः ।।
नमो जगत्प्रतिष्ठायै देव्यै कृत्यै नमो नमः ।।१३।।

atisaumyātiraudrāyai natās taṣyai namo namaḥ ।।
namo jagatpratiṣṭhāyai Devyai kṛtyai namo namaḥ ।।13।।

We bow down to Her Who is at once most gentle and most fierce. Salutations to her again and again. Salutation to the support of the world. To the Devī, Who is creative action, salutations again and again.

या देवी सर्वभूतेषु विष्णुमायेति शब्दिता ।।
नमस्तस्यै ।।१४।।, नमस्तस्यै ।।१५।।, नमस्तस्यै नमो नमः ।।१६।।

yā Devī sarvabhūteṣu viṣṇumāyeti śabditā ।।
namas tasyai ।।14।।, namas tasyai। ।15।।,
namas tasyai namo namaḥ ।।16।।

To the Devī, Who in all beings is called Viṣṇumāyā, salutation to Her, salutation to Her, salutation to Her again and again.

या देवी सर्वभूतेषु चेतनेत्यभिधीयते ।।
नमस्तस्यै ।।१७।।, नमस्तस्यै ।।१८।।, नमस्तस्यै नमो नमः ।।१९।।

yā Devī sarvabhūteṣu cetanety abhidhīyate ।।
namas tasyai ।।17।।, namas tasyai ।।18।।,
namas tasyai namo namaḥ ।।19।।

To the Devī, Who in all beings is seen as consciousness, salutation to Her, salutation to Her, salutation to Her again and again.

या देवी सर्वभूतेषु बुद्धिरूपेण संस्थिता ।।
नमस्तस्यै ।।२०।।, नमस्तस्यै ।।२१।।, नमस्तस्यै नमो नमः ।।२२।।

yā Devī sarvabhūteṣu buddhirūpeṇa saṁsthitā ।।
namas tasyai ।।20।।, namas tasyai ।।21।।,
namas tasyai namo namaḥ ।।22।।

To the Devī, Who abides in all beings in the form of intelligence, salutation to Her, salutation to Her, salutation to Her again and again.

या देवी सर्वभूतेषु निद्रारूपेण संस्थिता ।।
नमस्तस्यै ।।२३।।, नमस्तस्यै ।।२४।।, नमस्तस्यै नमो नमः ।।२५।।

yā Devi sarvabhūteṣu nidrārūpeṇa saṁsthitā ।।
namas tasyai ।।23।।, namas tasyai ।।24।।,
namas tasyai namo namaḥ ।।25।।

To the Devī, Who abides in all beings in the form of sleep, salutation to Her, salutation to Her, salutation to Her again and again.

या देवी सर्वभूतेषु क्षुधारूपेण संस्थिता ।।
नमस्तस्यै ।।२६ ।।, नमस्तस्यै ।।२७।।, नमस्तस्यै नमो नमः ।।२८।।

yā Devī sarvabhūteṣu kṣudhārūpeṇa saṁsthitā ||
namas tasyai ||26||, namas tasyai ||27||,
namas tasyai namo namaḥ ||28||

To the Devī, Who abides in all beings in the form of hunger, salutation to Her, salutation to Her, salutation to Her again and again.

या देवी सर्वभूतेषुच्छायारूपेण संस्थिता ॥
नमस्तस्यै ॥२९॥, नमस्तस्यै ॥३०॥, नमस्तस्यै नमो नमः ॥३१॥

yā Devī sarvabhūteṣu chāyārūpeṇa saṁsthitā ||
namas tasyai ||29||, namas tasyai ||30||,
namas tasyai namo namaḥ ||31||

To the Devī, Who abides in all beings in the form of shadow, salutation to Her, salutation to Her, salutation to Her again and again.

या देवी सर्वभूतेषु शक्तिरूपेण संस्थिता ॥
नमस्तस्यै ॥३२॥, नमस्तस्यै ॥३३॥, नमस्तस्यै नमो नमः ॥३४॥

yā Devī sarvabhūteṣu śaktirūpeṇa saṁsthitā ||
namas tasyai ||32||, namas tasyai ||33||,
namas tasyai namo namaḥ ||34||

To the Devī, Who abides in all beings in the form of power, salutation to Her, salutation to Her, salutation to Her again and again.

या देवी सर्वभूतेषु तृष्णारूपेण संस्थिता ।।
नमस्तस्यै ।।३५।।, नमस्तस्यै ।।३६।।, नमस्तस्यै नमो नमः ।।३७।।

yā Devi sarvabhūteṣu tṛṣṇārūpeṇa saṁsthitā ।।
namas tasyai ।।35।।, namas tasyai ।।36।।,
namas tasyai namo namaḥ ।।37।।

To the Devī, Who abides in all beings in the form of thirst, salutation to Her, salutation to Her, salutation to Her again and again.

या देवी सर्वभूतेषु क्षान्तिरूपेण संस्थिता ।।
नमस्तस्यै ।।३८।।, नमस्तस्यै ।।३९।।, नमस्तस्यै नमो नमः ।।४०।।

yā Devi sarvabhūteṣu kṣāntirūpeṇa saṁsthitā ।।
namas tasyai ।।38।।, namas tasyai ।।39।।,
namas tasyai namo namaḥ ।।40।।

To the Devī, Who abides in all beings in the form of forgiveness, salutation to Her, salutation to Her, salutation to Her again and again.

या देवी सर्वभूतेषु जातिरूपेण संस्थिता ।।
नमस्तस्यै ।।४१।।, नमस्तस्यै ।।४२।।, नमस्तस्यै नमो नमः ।।४३।।

yā Devī sarvabhūteṣu jātirūpeṇa saṁsthitā ।।
namas tasyai ।।41।।, namas tasyai ।।42।।,
namas tasyai namo namaḥ ।।43।।

To the Devī, Who abides in all beings in the form of order, salutation to Her, salutation to Her, salutation to Her again and again.

या देवी सर्वभूतेषु लज्जारूपेण संस्थिता ।।
नमस्तस्यै ।।४४।।, नमस्तस्यै ।।४५।।, नमस्तस्यै नमो नमः ।।४६।।

yā Devī sarvabhūteṣu lajjārūpeṇa saṁsthitā ।।
namas tasyai ।।44।।, namas tasyai ।।25।।,
namas tasyai namo namaḥ ।।45।।

To the Devī, Who abides in all beings in the form of modesty, salutation to Her, salutation to Her, salutation to Her again and again.

या देवी सर्वभूतेषु शान्तिरूपेण संस्थिता ।।
नमस्तस्यै ।।४७।।, नमस्तस्यै ।।४८।।, नमस्तस्यै नमो नमः ।।४९।।

yā Devī sarvabhūteṣu śāntirūpeṇa saṁsthitā ।।
namas tasyai ।।47।।, namas tasyai ।।48।।,
namas tasyai namo namaḥ ।।49।।

To the Devī, Who abides in all beings in the form of peace, salutation to Her, salutation to Her, salutation to Her again and again.

❧

या देवी सर्वभूतेषु श्रद्धारूपेण संस्थिता ।।
नमस्तस्यै ।।५०।।, नमस्तस्यै ।।५१।।, नमस्तस्यै नमो नमः ।।५२।।

yā Devi sarvabhūteṣu śraddhārūpeṇa saṁsthitā ।।
namas tasyai ।।50।।, namas tasyai ।।51।।,
namas tasyai namo namaḥ ।।52।।

To the Devī, Who abides in all beings in the form of faith, salutation to Her, salutation to Her, salutation to Her again and again.

❧

या देवी सर्वभूतेषु कान्तिरूपेण संस्थिता ।।
नमस्तस्यै ।।५३।।, नमस्तस्यै ।।५४।।, नमस्तस्यै नमो नमः ।।५५।।

yā Devī sarvabhūteṣu kāntirūpeṇa saṁsthitā ।।
namas tasyai ।।53।।, namas tasyai ।।54।।,
namas tasyai namo namaḥ ।।55।।

To the Devī, Who abides in all beings in the form of loveliness, salutation to Her, salutation to Her, salutation to Her again and again.

❧

या देवी सर्वभूतेषु लक्ष्मीरूपेण संस्थिता ।।
नमस्तस्यै ।।५६।।, नमस्तस्यै ।।५७।।, नमस्तस्यै नमो नमः ।।५८।।

yā Devi sarvabhūteṣu lakṣmīrūpeṇa saṁsthitā ।।
namas tasyai ।।56।।, namas tasyai ।।57।।,
namas tasyai namo namaḥ ।।58।।

To the Devī, Who abides in all beings in the form of good fortune, salutation to Her, salutation to Her, salutation to Her again and again.

या देवी सर्वभूतेषु वृत्तिरूपेण संस्थिता ।।
नमस्तस्यै ।।५९।।, नमस्तस्यै ।।६०।।, नमस्तस्यै नमो नमः ।।६१।।

yā Devī sarvabhūteṣu vṛttirūpeṇa saṁsthitā ।।
namas tasyai ।।59।।, namas tasyai ।।60।।,
namas tasyai namo namaḥ ।।61।।

To the Devī, Who abides in all beings in the form of activity, salutation to Her, salutation to Her, salutation to Her again and again.

या देवी सर्वभूतेषु स्मृतिरूपेण संस्थिता ।।
नमस्तस्यै ।।६२।।, नमस्तस्यै ।।६३।।, नमस्तस्यै नमो नमः ।।६४।।

yā Devī sarvabhūteṣu smṛtirūpeṇa saṁsthitā ।।
namas tasyai ।।62।।, namas tasyai ।।63।।,
namas tasyai namo namaḥ ।।64।।

To the Devī, Who abides in all beings in the form of memory, salutation to Her, salutation to Her, salutation to Her again and again.

❧

या देवी सर्वभूतेषु दयारूपेण संस्थिता ।।
नमस्तस्यै ।।६५।।, नमस्तस्यै ।।६६।।, नमस्तस्यै नमो नमः ।।६७।।

yā Devi sarvabhūteṣu dayārūpeṇa saṁsthitā ।।
namas tasyai ।।65।।, namas tasyai ।।66।।,
namas tasyai namo namaḥ ।।67।।

To the Devī, Who abides in all beings in the form of compassion, salutation to Her, salutation to Her, salutation to Her again and again.

❧

या देवी सर्वभूतेषु तुष्टिरूपेण संस्थिता ।।
नमस्तस्यै ।।६८।।, नमस्तस्यै ।।६९।।, नमस्तस्यै नमो नमः ।।७०।।

yā Devī sarvabhūteṣu tuṣṭirūpeṇa saṁsthitā ।।
namas tasyai ।।68।।, namas tasyai ।।69।।,
namas tasyai namo namaḥ ।।70।।

To the Devī, Who abides in all beings in the form of contentment, salutation to Her, salutation to Her, salutation to Her again and again.

❧

या देवी सर्वभूतेषु मातृरूपेण संस्थिता ।।
नमस्तस्यै ।।७१।।, नमस्तस्यै ।।७२।।, नमस्तस्यै नमो नमः ।।७३।।

yā Devī sarvabhūteṣu mātṛrūpeṇa saṁsthitā ।।
namas tasyai ।।71।।, namas tasyai ।।72।।,
namas tasyai namo namaḥ ।।73।।

To the Devī, Who abides in all beings in the form of mother, salutation to Her, salutation to Her, salutation to Her again and again.

या देवी सर्वभूतेषु भ्रान्तिरूपेण संस्थिता ।।
नमस्तस्यै ।।७४।।, नमस्तस्यै ।।७५।।, नमस्तस्यै नमो नमः ।।७६।।

yā Devī sarvabhūteṣu bhrāntirūpeṇa saṁsthitā ।।
namas tasyai ।।74।।, namas tasyai ।।75।।,
namas tasyai namo namaḥ ।।76।।

To the Devī, Who abides in all beings in the form of error, salutation to Her, salutation to Her, salutation to Her again and again.

इन्द्रियाणामधिष्ठात्री भूतानां चाखिलेषु या ।।
भूतेषु सततं तस्यै व्याप्तिदेव्यै नमो नमः ।।७७।।

indriyāṇāṁ adhiṣṭhātrī bhūtānāṁ cākhileṣu yā ।।
bhūteṣu satataṁ tasyai vyāptidevyai namo namaḥ ।।77।।

To Her Who presides over the elements and the senses, and is ever present in all beings, to the all-pervading Devī, salutations again and again.

चितिरूपेण या कृत्स्नमेतद् व्याप्य स्थिता जगत् ।।
नमस्तस्यै ।।७८।।, नमस्तस्यै ।।७९।।, नमस्तस्यै नमो नमः ।।८०।।

citirūpeṇa yā kṛtsnam etad vyāpya sthitā jagat ।।
namas tasyai ।।78।।, namas tasyai ।।79।।,
namas tasyai namo namaḥ ।।80।।

To Her Who pervades this entire world and abides in the form of consciousness, salutation to Her, salutation to Her, salutation to Her again and again.

स्तुता सुरैः पूर्वमभीष्टसंश्रयात्तथा सुरेन्द्रेण दिनेषु सेविता ।।
करोतु सा नः शुभहेतुरीश्वतरी शुभानि भद्राण्यभिहन्तु चापदः ।।८१।।

stutā suraiḥ pūrvam abhīṣṭasaṁśrayāt
tathā surendreṇa dineṣu sevitā ।।
karotu sā naḥ śubhahetur īśvarī śubhāni
bhadrāṇy abhihantu cāpadaḥ ।।81।।

Praised long ago by the gods for fulfilling their desires and likewise honored daily by the lord of the gods, may Īśvarī, the source of all good, create happiness and prosperity for us, and may She destroy our misfortunes.

या साम्प्रतं चोद्धतदैत्यतापितैरस्माभिरीशा च सुरैर्नमस्यते ॥
या च स्मृता तत्क्षणमेव हन्ति नः सर्वापदो भक्तिविनम्रमूर्तिभिः ॥८२॥

yā sāmpratam̐ coddhatadaityatāpitair
asmābhir īsā ca surair namasyate ॥
yā ca smṛtā tat kṣaṇam eva hanti naḥ sarvāpado
bhaktivinamramūrtibhiḥ ॥82॥

Tormented by arrogant daityas, we Gods now honor Her, the supreme power. With bodies bowed down in devotion, at this moment we remember Her Who destroys all afflictions.

ऋषिरुवाच ॥८३॥

ṛṣir uvāca ॥83॥

The seer said:

एवं स्तवादियुक्तानां देवानां तत्र पार्वती ॥
स्नातुमभ्याययौ तोये जाह्नव्या नृपनन्दन ॥८४॥

evam̐ stavādiyuktānām̐ devānām̐ tatra Pārvatī ॥
snātum abhyāyayau toye jāhnavyā nṛpanandana ॥84॥

O king, while the gods were thus engaged in praise and adoration, Pārvatī came to bathe in the waters of the Gaṇgā.

साब्रवीत्तान् सुरान् सुभ्रूर्भवद्भिः स्तूयतेऽत्र का ॥
शरीरकोशतश्चास्याः समुद्भूताब्रवीच्छिवा ॥८५॥

sābravīt tān surān subhrūr bhavadbhiḥ stūyate 'tra kā ॥
śarīrakośataś cāsyāḥ samudbhūtā 'bravīc chivā ॥85॥

She Who is fair of countenance asked the gods, 'Whom are you praising?' From Her own body an auspicious form emerged and replied:

स्तोत्रं ममैतत् क्रियते शुम्भदैत्यनिराकृतैः ॥
देवैः समेतैः' समरे निशुम्भेन पराजितैः ॥८६॥

stotraṁ mamaitat kriyate śumbhadaityanirākṛtaiḥ ॥
Devaiḥ sametaiḥ samare niśumbhena parājitaiḥ ॥86॥

'This hymn is an appeal to Me by those whom the daitya Śumbha cast out, by the assembled gods whom Niśumbha defeated in battle.'

शरीर कोशाद्यत्तस्याः पार्वत्या निःसृताम्बिका ॥
कौशिकीति समस्तेषु ततो लोकेषु गीयते ॥८७॥

śarīrakośād yat tasyāḥ Pārvatyā niḥsṛtāmbikā ॥
kauśikīti samasteṣu tato lokeṣu gīyate ॥87॥

And since Ambikā came forth from Pārvatī's bodily form,
She is glorified in all the worlds as Kauśikī.

तस्यां विनिर्गतायां तु कृष्णाभूत्सापि पार्वती ॥
कालिकेति समाख्याता हिमाचलकृताश्रया ॥८८॥

tasyāṁ vinirgatāyāṁ tu kṛṣṇābhūt sāpi Pārvatī ॥
Kāliketi samākhyātā himācalakṛtāśrayā ॥88॥

Thereupon, Pārvatī became black. Thus known as Kālīkā,
She makes Her abode in the Himālayas.

ततोऽम्बिकां परं रूपं बिभ्राणां सुमनोहरम् ॥
ददर्श चण्डो मुण्डश्च भृत्यौ शुम्भनिशुम्भयोः ॥८९॥

tato 'mbikāṁ paraṁ rūpaṁ bibhrāṇāṁ sumanoharam ॥
dadarśa caṇḍo muṇḍaś ca bhṛtyau śumbhaniśumbhayoḥ ॥89॥

Then Caṇḍa and Muṇḍa, two servants of Śumbha and
Niśumbha, beheld Ambikā's captivating beauty.

ताभ्यां शुम्भाय चाख्याता अतीव सुमनोहरा ।।
काप्यास्ते स्त्री महाराज भासयन्ती हिमाचलम् ।।९०।।

tābhyāṁ śumbhāya cākhyātā sātīva sumanoharā ।।
kāpyāste strī maharaja bhāsayantī himācalam ।।90।।

And they told Śumbha, 'O great king, an unknown woman, surpassingly beautiful, dwells illuminating the Himālayas.

नैव तादृक् क्वचिद्रूपं दृष्टं केनचिदुत्तमम् ।।
ज्ञायतां काप्यसौ देवी गृह्यतां चासुरेश्वर ।।९१।।

naiva tādṛk kvacid rūpaṁ dṛṣṭaṁ kenacid uttamam ।।
jñāyatāṁ kāpy asau devī gṛhyatāṁ cāsureśvara ।।91।।

Nowhere has anyone ever seen such supreme beauty. May you learn Who that goddess is and take possession of Her, O lord of asuras!

स्त्रीरत्नंमतिचार्वङ्गी द्योतयन्ती दिशस्त्विषा ।।
सा तु तिष्ठति दैत्येन्द्र तां भवान् द्रष्टुमर्हति ।।९२।।

stnīratnam aticārvaṅgī dyotayantī diśas tviṣā ।।
sā tu tiṣṭhati daityendra tāṁ bhavān draṣṭum arhati ।।92।।

She abides there, a jewel among Women, fairest of limb, casting Her radiance in all directions. O chief of daityas, surely you must behold Her!

यानि रत्नामनि मणयो गजाश्वा्दीनि वै प्रभो ।।
त्रैलोक्ये तु समस्तानि साम्प्रतं भान्ति ते गृहे ।।९३।।

yāni ratnāni maṇayo gajāśvādīni vai prabho ।।
trailokye tu samastāni sāmpratam bhānti te gṛhe ।।93।।

Master, whatever gems and jewels, elephants, horses, and other riches exist in the three worlds, all those now enhance your dwelling

ऐरावत: समानीतो गजरत्नं पुरन्दरात् ।।
पारिजाततरुश्चा्यं तथैवोच्चै:श्रवा हय: ।।९४।।

airāvataḥ samānīto gajaratnam purandarāt ।।
pārijātataruś cāyam tathaivoccaiḥśravā hayaḥ ।।94।।

From Indra you have taken Airāvata, the jewel among elephants, and also the celestial coral tree and the horse Uccaiḥśravas.

विमानं हंससंयुक्तमेतत्तिष्ठति तेऽङ्गणे ।।
रत्नभूतमिहानीतं यदासीद्वेधसोऽद्भुतम् ।।९५।।

vimānam haṁsasaṁyuktam etat tiṣṭhati te 'ṅgaṇe ।।
ratnabhūtam ihānītam yadāsīd vedhaso 'dbhutam ।।95।।

Taken from Brahmā, this wondrous jewel among chariots, yoked with swans, stands here in your courtyard.

निधिरेष महापद्मः समानीतो धनेश्वरात् ।।
किञ्जल्किनीं ददौ चाब्धिर्मालामम्लानपङ्कजाम् ।।९६।।

nidhir eṣa mahāpadmaḥ samānīto dhaneśvarāt ।।
kiñjalkinīṁ dadau cābdhir mālām amlānapaṅkajām ।।96।।

Seized from Kubera, the lord of wealth, is his treasure. And the lord of the ocean has relinquished his garland of unfading lotuses.

छत्रं ते वारुणं गेहे काञ्चनस्रावि तिष्ठति ।।
तथायं स्यन्दनवरो यः पुराऽऽसीत्प्रजापतेः ।।९७।।

chatraṁ te vāruṇaṁ gehe kāñcanasrāvi tiṣṭhati ।।
tathā 'yaṁ syandanavaro yaḥ purāsīt prajāpateḥ ।।97।।

Varuṇa's umbrella, which showers down gold, now stands in your house along with this best of chariots, which once was Prajāpati's.

मृत्योरुत्क्रान्तिदा नाम शक्तिरीश त्वया हृता ।।
पाशः सलिलराजस्य भ्रातुस्तव परिग्रहे ।।९८।।

mṛtyor utkrāntidā nāma śaktir īśa tvayā hṛtā ||
pāśaḥ salilarājasya bhrātus tava parigrahe ||98||

Master, you have taken Yama's spear, which grants departure from this life. Varuṇa's noose is among your brother's possessions.

निशुम्भस्याब्धिजाताश्च समस्ता रत्नजातयः ।।
वह्निरपि ददौ तुभ्यमग्निशौचे च वाससी ।।९९।।

niśumbhasyābdhijātāś ca samastā ratnajātayaḥ ||
vahniścāpi dadau tubhyam agniśauce ca vāsasī ||99||

To Niśumbha belong all manner of gems born of the sea. And to the two of you, Agni has given garments purified by his own fire.

एवं दैत्येन्द्र रत्नामनि समस्तान्याहृतानि ते।।
स्त्रीरत्नामेषा कल्याणी त्वया कस्मान्न गृह्यते ।।१००।।

evaṁ daityendra ratnāni samastany āhṛtāni te ||
strīratnam eṣā kalyāṇi tvayā kasmān na gṛhyate ||100||

Thus, O chief of daityas, you have appropriated all things of value. Why then do you not seize this jewel among Women for yourself?'"

ऋषिरुवाच ॥१०१॥

ṛṣir uvāca ॥101॥

The seer said:

निशम्येति वचः शुम्भः स तदा चण्डमुण्डयोः ॥
प्रेषयामास सुग्रीवं दूतं देव्या महासुरम् ॥१०२॥

niśamyeti vacaḥ śumbhaḥ sa tadā caṇḍamuṇḍayoḥ ॥
preṣayāmāsa sugrīvaṁ dūtaṁ devyā mahāsuram ॥102॥

"On hearing these words of Caṇḍa and Muṇḍa, Śumbha sent the great asura Sugrīva as a messenger to the Devī.

इति चेति च वक्तव्या सा गत्वा वचनान्मम ॥
यथा चाभ्येति सम्प्रीत्या तथा कार्यं त्वया लघु ॥१०३॥

iti ceti ca vaktavyā sā gatvā vacanān mama ॥
yathā cābhyeti samprītyā tathā kāryaṁ tvayā laghu ॥103॥

Instructing him, he said: 'Go to Her and speak such words on my behalf that She will be delighted and will quickly come to me.'

स तत्र गत्वा यत्रास्ते शैलोद्देशेऽतिशोभने ।।
सा देवी तां ततः प्राहश्लिक्ष्णं मधुरया गिरा ।।१०४।।

sa tatra gatvā yatrāste śailoddeśe 'tiśobhane ।।
sā Devī tāṁ tataḥ prāha ślakṣṇam madhurayā girā ।।104।।

Sugrīva went there to the resplendent, craggy place where the Devī dwelt and spoke honeyed words to Her in unctuous tones.

दूत उवाच ।।१०५।।

dūta uvāca ।।105।।

The messenger said:

देवि दैत्येश्वरः शुम्भस्त्रैलोक्ये परमेश्वषरः ।।
दूतोऽहं प्रेषितस्तेन त्वत्सकाशमिहागतः ।।१०६।।

Devi daityeśvaraḥ śumbhas trailokye parameśvaraḥ ।।
duto 'haṁ preṣitas tena tvat sakāśam ihāgataḥ ।।106।।

'O Devī, in the three worlds Śumbha, the lord of daityas, is the supreme sovereign. I am his messenger. I have come here to your presence, sent by him

अव्याहताज्ञः सर्वासु यः सदा देवयोनिषु ।।
निर्जिताखिलदैत्यारिः स यदाह श्रृणुष्व तत् ।।१०७।।

avyāhatājñaḥ sarvāsu yaḥ sadā devayoniṣu ।।
nirjitākhiladaityāriḥ sa yadāha śṛṇuṣva tat ।।107।।

Who has conquered all the enemies of the daityas and whose command is never resisted in the dwellings of the gods. Hear what he says:

मम त्रैलोक्यमखिलं मम देवा वशानुगाः ।।
यज्ञभागानहं सर्वानुपाश्नातमि पृथक्-पृथक् ।।१०८।।

mama trailokyam akhilaṁ mama devā vaśānugāḥ ।।
yajñabhāgān ahaṁ sarvān upāśnāmi pṛthak pṛthak ।।108।।

"All the three worlds are mine, and the gods submit to my will. I enjoy each one's share of the sacrifices, every one of them.

त्रैलोक्ये वररत्नापनि मम वश्याशन्यशेषतः ।।
तथैव गजरत्नं च हृत्वा' देवेन्द्रवाहनम् ।।१०९।।

trailokye vararatnāni mama vaśyāny aśeṣataḥ ।।
tathaiva gajaratnaṁ ca hṛtaṁ devendravāhanam ।।109।।

Indeed I possess all the finest gems in the three worlds, and I have taken Airāvata, the jewel among elephants and Indra's mount.

क्षीरोदमथनोद्भूतमश्वरत्नं ममामरैः ॥
उच्चैःश्रवससंज्ञं तत्प्रणिपत्य समर्पितम् ॥११०॥

kṣīrodamathanodbhūtam aśvaratnaṁ mamāmaraiḥ ॥
uccaiḥśravasasaṁmjñam tat praṇipatya samarpitam ॥110॥

The immortal gods, bowed down in reverence, offered me Uccaihśravas, the jewel among horses, born from the churning of the milk ocean.

यानि चान्यानि देवेषु गन्धर्वेषूरगेषु च ॥
रत्नैभूतानि भूतानि तानि मय्येव शोभने ॥१११॥

yāni cānyāni deveṣu gandharveṣūrageṣu ca ॥
ratnabhūtāni bhūtāni tāni mayy eva śobhane ॥111॥

And whatever else is precious among the gods and celestial beings, all that is mine, O fair one.

स्त्रीरत्नसभूतां त्वां देवि लोके मन्यामहे वयम् ॥
सा त्वमस्मानुपागच्छ यतो रत्न भुजो वयम् ॥११२ ॥

strīratnabhūtāṁ tvāṁ Devi loke manyāmahe vayam ||
sā tvam asmān upāgaccha yato ratnabhujo vayam ||112||

We think of you, O Goddess, as the jewel among Women in the world, which indeed You are. Come to us, for we take pleasure in all the finest things.

मां वा ममानुजं वापि निशुम्भमुरुविक्रमम् ॥
भज त्वं च चञ्चलापाङ्गि रत्नमभूतासि वै यतः ॥११३॥

māṁ vā mamānujaṁ vāpi niśumbham uruvikramam ||
bhaja tvam cañcalāpāṅgi ratnabhūtāsi vai yataḥ ||113||

Choose either me or my valiant younger brother, Niśumbha, for with our flashing eyes You are truly a jewel.

परमैश्वतर्यमतुलं प्राप्स्यसे मत्परिग्रहात् ॥
एतद् बुद्ध्या समालोच्य मत्परिग्रहतां व्रज ॥११४॥

paramaiśvaryam atulam prāpsyase matparigrahāt ||
etad buddhyā samālocya matparigrahatām vraja ||114||

By taking me you will obtain dominion beyond compare. With reasoning mind, consider this well and become my wife.

ऋषिरुवाच ॥११५॥

ṛṣir uvāca ॥115॥

The seer said:

इत्युक्ता सा तदा देवी गम्भीरान्तःस्मिता जगौ ।
दुर्गा भगवती भद्रा ययेदं धार्यते जगत् ॥११६॥

ity uktā sā tadā Devī gambhīrāntaḥsmitā jagau ।
Durgā Bhagavatī Bhadrā yayedaṁ dhāryate jagat ॥116॥

Thus addressed, the Devī smiled inscrutably. The blessed, auspicious Durgā, Who supports the universe, spoke.

देव्युवाच ॥११७॥

Devy uvāca ॥117॥

The Devī said:

सत्यमुक्तं त्वया नात्र मिथ्या किञ्चित्त्वयोदितम् ।
त्रैलोक्याधिपतिः शुम्भो निशुम्भश्चापि तादृशः ॥११८॥

satyam uktaṁ tvayā nātra mithyā kiñcit tvayoditam ।
trailokyādhipatiḥ śumbho niśumbhaś cāpi tādṛśaḥ ॥118॥

'You have spoken the truth; there is nothing false in what you have said. Śumbha is the ruler of the three worlds, and so also is Niśumbha.

किं त्वत्र यत्प्रतिज्ञातं मिथ्या तत्क्रियते कथम् ।।
श्रूयतामल्पबुद्धित्वात्प्रतिज्ञा या कृता पुरा ।।११९।।

kiṁ tvatra yat parijñātam mithyā tat kriyate katham ।।
śrūyatām alpabuddhitvāt pratijñā yā kṛtā purā ।।119।।

But how can I go back on My word? Hear of the vow I once made out of foolishness:

यो मां जयति संग्रामे यो मे दर्पं व्यपोहति ।।
यो मे प्रतिबलो लोके स मे भर्ता भविष्यति ।।१२०।।

yo māṁ jayati saṅgrāme yo me darpaṁ vyapohati ।।
yo me pratibaio loke sa me bhartā bhaviṣyati ।।120।।

He alone Who conquers Me in battle, Who removes My pride, Who equals My strength in the world, will become My husband.

तदागच्छतु शुम्भोऽत्र निशुम्भो वा महासुरः ॥
मां जित्वा किं चिरेणात्र पाणिं गृह्णातु मे लघु ॥१२१॥

tadāgacchatu śumbho 'tra niśumbho vā mahāsuraḥ ॥
māṁ jitvā kiṁ cireṇātra pāṇim gṛhṇātu me laghu ॥121॥

Therefore let Śumbha or the great asura Niśumbha come here. Why delay? Having conquered Me, let him take my hand in marriage.'

दूत उवाच ॥१२२॥

dūta uvāca ॥122॥

The messenger said:

अवलिप्तासि मैवं त्वं देवि ब्रूहि ममाग्रतः ॥
त्रैलोक्ये कः पुमांस्तिष्ठेदग्रे शुम्भनिशुम्भयोः ॥१२३॥

avaliptāsi maivaṁ tvaṁ devi brūhi mamāgrataḥ ॥
trailokye kaḥ pumāṁs tiṣṭhed agre
śumbhaniśumbhayoḥ ॥123॥

'You are arrogant, O Devī. Speak not so in my presence. What man in the three worlds surpasses Śumbha and Niśumbha?

अन्येषामपि दैत्यानां सर्वे देवा न वै युधि ॥
तिष्ठन्ति सम्मुखे देवि किं पुनः स्त्री त्वमेकिका ॥१२४॥

anyeṣām api daityānāṁ sarve devā na vai yudhi ||
tiṣṭhanti sammukhe Devi kim punaḥ strī tvam ekikā ||124||

Even against the other daityas, all the gods cannot stand face to face in battle, O Devī. How then can You, Who are one Woman alone?

इन्द्राद्याः सकला देवास्तस्थुर्येषां न संयुगे ॥
शुम्भादीनां कथं तेषां स्त्री प्रयास्यसि सम्मुखम् ॥१२५॥

indrādyāḥ sakalā devās tasthur yeṣām na saṁyuge ||
śumbhādīnāṁ kathaṁ teṣām strī prayāsyasi sammukham ||125||

Indra and all the other gods could not resist Śumbha and the other demons in battle. How will You, a woman, go forth and confront them?

सा त्वं गच्छ मयैवोक्ता पार्श्वंप शुम्भनिशुम्भयोः ॥
केशाकर्षणनिर्धूतगौरवा मा गमिष्यसि ॥१२६॥

sā tvaṁ gaccha mayaivoktā pārśvaṁ śumbhaniśumbhayoḥ ||
keśākarṣaṇanirdhūtagauravā mā gamiṣyasi ||126||

As I have said, go to Śumbha and Niśumbha's side. Suffer not the indignity of being dragged there by your hair.'

देव्युवाच ॥१२७॥

Devy uvāca ॥127॥

The Devī said:

एवमेतद् बली शुम्भो निशुम्भश्चा ।ातिवीर्यवान् ॥
किं करोमि प्रतिज्ञा मे यदनालोचिता पुरा ॥१२८॥

evam etad balī śumbho niśumbhaś cātivīryavān ॥
kiṁ karomi pratijñā me yad anālocitā purā ॥128॥

'So must it be. Śumbha is mighty and Niśumbha is exceedingly heroic, but what can I do? My rash vow was made long ago.

स त्वं गच्छ मयोक्तं ते यदेतत्सर्वमादृतः ॥
तदाचक्ष्वासुरेन्द्राय स च युक्तं करोतु तत् ॥ॐ ॥१२९॥

sa Tvaṁ gaccha mayoktaṁ te yad etat sarvam ādṛtaḥ ॥
tad ācakṣvāsurendrāya sa ca yuktaṁ karotu tat ॥Om॥129॥

Go back and tell the chief of asuras exactly what I have said. And let him do what is fitting.

इति श्रीमार्कण्डेयपुराणे सावर्णिके मन्वन्तरे देवीमाहात्म्ये देव्या दूतसंवादो नाम पञ्चमोऽध्यायः ॥५॥
उवाच ९, त्रिपान्मन्त्राः ६६, श्लोकाः ५४, एवम् १२९, एवमादितः ॥३८८॥

iti śrīmārkaṇḍeyapurāṇe sāvarnike manvantare devīmāhātmye devyā dūtasamvādo nāma pañcamo'dhyāyaḥ ॥5॥
uvāca 9, tripānmantrāḥ 66, ślokāḥ 54, evam 129, evamāditaḥ ॥388॥

Thus ends the fifth chapter, called "The Dialogue between the Goddess and the Messenger" (devyā dūtasamvādaḥ), in the Devi Mahatmya of the Markandeya Purana, during the reign of Savarni Manu.

।। षष्ठोऽध्याय: ।।

धूम्रलोचन वध

।। Sixth Chapter ।।

The Slaying Of Dhumralochana

।। ध्यानम् ।।

ॐ नागाधीश्वरविष्टरां फणिफणोत्तंसोरुरत्नावली-
भास्वद्देहलतां दिवाकरनिभां नेत्रत्रयोद्भासिताम्।
मालाकुम्भकपालनीरजकरां चन्द्रार्धचूडां परां
सर्वज्ञेश्वरभैरवाङ्कनिलयां पद्मावतीं चिन्तये ।।

।। dhyānam ।।

oṁ nāgādhīśvaraviṣṭarāṁ phaṇiphaṇottaṁsoruratnāvalī-
bhāsvaddehalatāṁ divākaranibhāṁ netratrayodbhāsitām ।।
mālākumbhakapālanīrajakarāṁ candrārdhacūḍāṁ parāṁ
sarvajñeśvarabhairavāṅkanilayāṁ padmāvatīṁ cintaye ।।

I meditate upon Padmāvatī, who is seated on the lord of serpents, whose body shines like a radiant creeper adorned

with a garland of superior gems placed on the raised hoods of serpents, whose form glows like the sun, whose three eyes radiate brilliance, who holds a garland, a water pot, a skull, and a lotus in her hands, who wears the crescent moon on her head, who is the supreme one, and who dwells in the lap of Sarvajñēśvara Bhairava (the all-knowing Lord Bhairava)."

"ॐ" ऋषिरुवाच ॥१ ॥

Om ṛṣir uvāca ॥1॥

The seer said:

इत्याकर्ण्य वचो देव्याः स दूतोऽमर्षपूरितः ॥
समाचष्ट समागम्य दैत्यराजाय विस्तरात् ॥२॥

ity ākamya vaco Devyāḥ sa dūto 'marṣapūritaḥ ॥
samācaṣṭa samāgamya daityarājāya vistarāt ॥2॥

On hearing the Devī's words, the messenger was filled with indignation. He returned to the king of the daityas and related everything in great detail.

तस्य दूतस्य तद्वाक्यमाकर्ण्यासुरराट् ततः ॥
सक्रोधः प्राह दैत्यानामधिपं धूम्रलोचनम् ॥३॥

tasya dūtasya tad vākyam ākarṇyāsurarāṭ tataḥ ||
sakrodhaḥ prāha daityānām adhipaṁ dhūmralocanam ||3||

On hearing his messenger's report, the asura king grew enraged and said to Dhūmralocana, the chieftain of the daityas:

हे धूम्रलोचनाशु त्वं स्वसैन्यपरिवारितः ।।
तामानय बलाद् दुष्टां केशाकर्षणविह्वलाम् ।।४।।

he dhūmralocanāśu tvaṁ svasainyaparivāritaḥ ||
tām ānaya balād duṣṭāṁ keśākarṣaṇavihvalām ||4||

Dhūmralocana, hasten with your army and bring that vile woman here by force, dragging her by the hair, kicking and screaming.

तत्परित्राणदः कश्चिद्यदि वोत्तिष्ठतेऽपरः ।।
स हन्तव्योऽमरो वापि यक्षो गन्धर्व एव वा ।।५।।

at paritrāṇadah kaścid yadi vottiṣṭhate 'parah||
sa hantavyo 'maro vāpi yakṣo gandharva eva vā||5||

If anyone rises up to save her, even a god or other celestial being, he is to be slain.

ऋषिरुवाच ॥६॥

ṛṣir uvāca ॥6॥

The seer said:

तेनाज्ञप्तस्ततः शीघ्रं स दैत्यो धूम्रलोचनः ॥
वृतः षष्ट्या सहस्राणामसुराणां द्रुतं ययौ ॥७॥

tenājñaptas tataḥ śīghraṁ sa daityo dhūmralocanaḥ॥
vṛtaḥ ṣaṣṭyā sahasrāṇām asurāṇām drutaṁ yayau॥7॥

Commanded thus by Śumbha, the daitya Dhūmralocana quickly set off, accompanied by sixty thousand asuras.

स दृष्ट्वा तां ततो देवीं तुहिनाचलसंस्थिताम् ॥
जगादोच्चैः प्रयाहीति मूलं शुम्भनिशुम्भयोः ॥८॥

sa dṛṣṭvā tāṁ tato Devīṁ tuhinācalasaṁsthitām॥
jagādoccaiḥ prayāhīti mūlaṁ śumbhaniśumbhayoḥ॥8॥

And when he saw the Devī stationed on the snowy mountain, he thundered, ‘Come to the presence of Śumbha and Niśumbha’.

न चेत्प्रीत्याद्य भवती मद्भर्तारमुपैष्यति ॥
ततो बलान्नयाम्येष केशाकर्षणविह्वलाम् ॥९॥

na cet prītyādya bhavatī madbhartāram upaiṣyati ॥
tato balān nayāmy eṣa keśākarṣaṇavihvalām ॥9॥

And if Her highness will not come in gladness to my master now, then I will take Her by force, dragging Her by the hair, kicking and screaming.

देव्युवाच ॥१०॥

Devy uvāca ॥10॥

The Devī said:

दैत्येश्वरेण प्रहितो बलवान् बलसंवृतः ॥
बलान्नयसि मामेवं ततः किं ते करोम्यहम् ॥११॥

daityeśvareṇa prahito balavān balasaṁvṛtaḥ ॥
balān nayasi mām evaṁ tataḥ kiṁ te karomy aham ॥11॥

'You who are sent by the lord of the daityas are mighty yourself and accompanied by your army. If you take me by force, what can I do to you?'

ऋषिरुवाच ॥१२॥

ṛṣir uvāca ॥12॥

The seer said:

इत्युक्तः सोऽभ्यधावत्तामसुरो धूम्रलोचनः ।
हुंकारेणैव तं भस्म सा चकाराम्बिका ततः ॥१३॥

ity uktaḥ so 'bhyadhāvat tāṁ asuro dhūmralocanaḥ ।
huṅkāreṇaiva taṁ bhasma sā cakārāmbikā tataḥ ॥13॥

Thus addressed, the asura Dhūmralocana rushed at Her.
Thereupon, with a contemptuous outcry,
Ambikā reduced him to ashes.

अथ क्रुद्धं महासैन्यमसुराणां तथाम्बिका ।
ववर्ष सायकैस्तीक्ष्णैस्तथा शक्तिपरश्वधैः ॥१४॥

atha kruddhaṁ mahāsainyam asurāṇāṁ tathāmbikām ।
vavarṣa sāyakais tīkṣṇais tathā śaktiparaśvadhaiḥ ॥14॥

The great army of asuras, now provoked, rained
sharp arrows, spears, and axes upon Ambikā.

ततो धुतसटः कोपात्कृत्वा नादं सुभैरवम् ॥
पपातासुरसेनायां सिंहो देव्याः स्ववाहनः ॥१५॥

tato dhutasaṭaḥ kopāt kṛtvā nādaṁ subhairavam ॥
papātāsurasenāyāṁ siṁho Devyāḥ svavāhanaḥ ॥15॥

Then the lion, the Devī's mount, angrily shook its mane. Emitting a terrifying roar, it fell upon the demon army

❧

कांश्चित् करप्रहारेण दैत्यानास्येन चापरान् ॥
आक्रम्य' चाधरेणान्यान्' स जघान' महासुरान् ॥१६॥

kāṁścit karaprahāreṇa daityān āsyena cāparān ॥
ākrāntyā cādhareṇānyān sa jaghāna mahāsurān ॥16॥

With blows of its paws, it slew some daityas and crushed others in its jaws. And it trampled other great asuras under its hind legs.

❧

केषांचित्पाटयामास नखैः कोष्ठानि केसरी ॥
तथा तलप्रहारेण शिरांसि कृतवान् पृथक् ॥१७॥

keṣāñcit pāṭayāmāsa nakhaiḥ koṣṭhāni kesarī ॥
tathā talaprahāreṇa śirāṁsi kṛtavān pṛthak ॥17॥

With its claws, the lion tore into the entrails of some and beheaded others with the stroke of a paw.

❧

विच्छिन्नबाहुशिरसः कृतास्तेन तथापरे ।।
पपौ च रुधिरं कोष्ठादन्येषां धुतकेसरः ।।१८।।

vicchinnabāhuśirasaḥ kṛtās tena tathāpare ।।
papau ca rudhiraṁ koṣṭhād anyeṣām dhutakesaraḥ ।।18।।

It tore the arms and heads off others still, and tossing its mane, it lapped up the blood from the bellies of others.

क्षणेन तद्बलं सर्वं क्षयं नीतं महात्मना ।।
तेन केसरिणा देव्या वाहनेनातिकोपिना ।।१९।।

kṣaṇena tad balaṁ sarvaṁ kṣayaṁ nītaṁ mahātmanā ।।
tena kesariṇā Devyā vāhanenātikopinā ।।19।।

In an instant that noble, infuriated lion which bore the Devī wreaked destruction on all the army.

श्रुत्वा तमसुरं देव्या निहतं धूम्रलोचनम् ।।
बलं च क्षयितं कृत्स्नं देवीकेसरिणा ततः ।।२०।।

śrutvā tam asuraṁ Devyā nihataṁ dhūmralocanam ।।
balaṁ ca kṣayitaṁ kṛtsnaṁ Devīkesariṇā tataḥ ।।20।।

When he heard that the Devī had slain the asura Dhūmralocana and that Her lion had destroyed his entire army

चुकोप दैत्याधिपतिः शुम्भः प्रस्फुरिताधरः ॥
आज्ञापयामास च तौ चण्डमुण्डौ महासुरौ ॥२१॥

cukopa daityādhipatiḥ śumbhaḥ prasphuritādharaḥ ॥
ājñāpayāmāsa ca tau caṇḍamuṇḍau mahāsurau ॥21॥

Śumbha, the king of daityas, shook with rage. His lower lip quivering, he commanded the two great asuras, Caṇḍa and Muṇḍa:

हे चण्ड हे मुण्ड बलैर्बहुभिः परिवारितौ ॥
तत्र गच्छत गत्वा च सा समानीयतां लघु ॥२२॥

he caṇḍa he muṇḍa balair bahulaiḥ parivāritau ॥
tatra gacchataṁ gatvā ca sā samānīyatāṁ laghu ॥22॥

Caṇḍa! Muṇḍa! Go there with immense forces, and bring Her here at once.

केशेष्वाकृष्य बद्ध्वा वा यदि वः संशयो युधि ॥
तदाशेषायुधैः सर्वैरसुरैर्विनिहन्यताम् ॥२३॥

keśeṣvākṛṣya baddhvā vā yadi vaḥ saṁsayo yudhi ॥
tadāśeṣāyudhaiḥ sarvair asurair vinihanyatām ॥23॥

seizing Her by the hair or tying Her up. But if you hesitate to do this, then let all the asuras with all their weapons strike Her down in battle.

तस्यां हतायां दुष्टायां सिंहे च विनिपातिते ॥
शीघ्रमागम्यतां बद्ध्वा गृहीत्वा तामथाम्बिकाम् ॥ॐ ॥२४॥

tasyāṁ hatāyāṁ duṣṭāyām simhe ca vinipātite ||
śīghram āgamyatāṁ baddhvā gṛhītvā tāṁ athāmbikām ||Om||24||

When that vile Woman has been wounded and Her lion slain, seize Her, bind Her, and bring Her here without delay!

इति श्रीमार्कण्डेयपुराणे सावर्णिके मन्वन्तरे देवीमाहात्म्ये ॥
शुम्भनिशुम्भसेनानीधूम्रलोचनवधो नाम षष्ठोऽध्याय: ॥२५॥

iti śrīmārkaṇḍeyapurāṇe sāvarnike manvantare devīmāhātmye ||
śumbhaniśumbhasenānīdhūmralocanavadho nāma ṣaṣṭho'dhyāyaḥ ||25||

Thus ends the sixth chapter, named 'The Slaying of Dhūmralocana, the Commander of the Armies of Śumbha and Niśumbha', in the Devi Mahatmya, in the Sāvārṇika Manvantara, of the Śrī Mārkaṇḍeya Purāṇa.

॥ सप्तमोऽध्यायः ॥

चण्डमुण्ड वध

॥ Seventh Chapter ॥

Slaying Of Chanda and Munda

॥ ध्यानम् ॥

ॐ ध्यायेयं रत्नपीठे शुककलपठितं शृण्वतीं श्यामलाङ्गीं
न्यस्तैकाङ्घ्रिं सरोजे शशिशकलधरां वल्लकीं वादयन्तीम् ।
कह्लाराबद्धमालां नियमितविलसच्चोलिकां रक्तवस्त्रां
मातङ्गीं शङ्खपात्रां मधुरमधुमदां चित्रकोद्भासिभालाम् ॥

॥ dhyānam ॥

oṁ dhyāyeyaṁ ratnapīṭhe śukakalapathitaṁ
śṛṇvatīṁ śyāmalāṅgīṁ
nyastaikāṅghriṁ saroje śaśiśakaladharāṁ
vallakīṁ vādayantīm ।
kahlārābaddhamālāṁ niyamitavilasaccholikāṁ
raktavastrāṁ

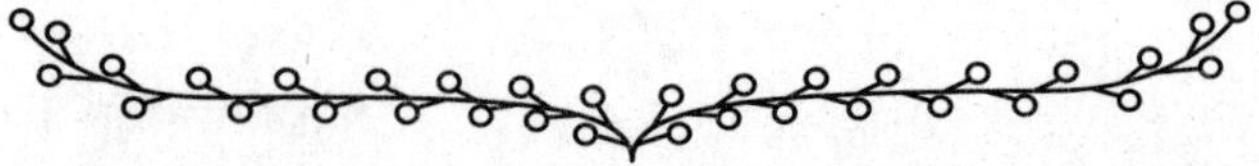

mātaṅgīṁ śaṅkhapātrāṁ madhuramadhumadāṁ
citrakodbhāsibhālām ॥

I meditate upon Goddess Mātaṅgī, who is seated on a jeweled throne, listening to the recitations of parrots, with a dark-hued (śyāma) complexion. She gracefully rests one foot on a lotus, bears the crescent moon on her forehead, and plays the veena. Adorned with a garland of blue lotuses and wearing shining red garments, she has a flowing silken scarf and holds a conch-shaped vessel. Mātaṅgī radiates divine sweetness, intoxicating like nectar, with her forehead glowing brilliantly with wondrous markings.

"ॐ" ऋषिरुवाच ॥१॥

ṛṣir uvāca ॥1॥

The seer said:

आज्ञप्तास्ते ततो दैत्याश्चण्डमुण्डपुरोगमाः ॥
चतुरङ्गबलोपेता ययुरभ्युद्यतायुधाः ॥२॥

ājñaptāste tato daityāś caṇḍamuṇḍapurogamāḥ ॥
caturaṅgabalopetā yayur abhyudyatāyudhāḥ ॥2॥

Headed by Caṇḍa and Muṇḍa, the daityas' fourfold army of elephants, charioteers, cavalry, and infantry went forth at Śumbha's command, brandishing weapons.

ददृशुस्ते ततो देवीमीषद्धासां व्यवस्थिताम् ।।
सिंहस्योपरि शैलेन्द्रशृङ्गे महति काञ्चने ।।३।।

dadṛśus te tato Devīm īṣaddhāsāṁ vyavasthitām ।।
simhasyopari śailendraśṛṅge mahati kāñcane ।।3।।

They saw The Devī Smiling Gently, Seated Upon Her Lion Atop the great, golden peak of the highest mountain.

ते दृष्ट्वा तां समादातुमुद्यमं चक्रुरुद्यताः ।।
आकृष्टचापासिधरास्तथान्ये तत्समीपगाः ।।४।।

te dṛṣtvā tāṁ samādātum udyam añcakrur udyatāḥ ।।
ākṛṣṭacāpāsidharās tathānye tat samīpagāḥ ।।4।।

Seeing Her, they contrived to Carry Her Off. While some approached with swords drawn and bows poised in readiness.

ततः कोपं चकारोच्चैरम्बिका तानरीन् प्रति ।।
कोपेन चास्या वदनं मषी'वर्णमभूत्तदा ।।५।।

tataḥ kopaṁ cakāroccair Ambikā tān arīm prati ।।
kopena cāsyā vadanaṁ maṣīvarṇam abhūt tadā ।।5।।

Ambikā cried out angrily against those foes, and In Wrath Her Face Turned As Black As Ink.

भ्रुकुटीकुटिलात्तस्या ललाटफलकाद्द्रुतम् ।।
काली करालवदना विनिष्क्रान्तासिपाशिनी ।।६।।

bhrukuṭīkuṭilāt tasyā lalāṭaphalakād drutam ।।
Kālī karālavadanā viniṣkrāntāsipāśinī ।।6।।

From Her Scowling Brow, Kālī Sprang Forth, Frightful Of Countenance And Armed With Sword And Noose.

विचित्रखट्वाङ्गधरा नरमालाविभूषणा ।।
द्वीपिचर्मपरीधाना शुष्कमांसातिभैरवा ।।७।।

vicitrakhaṭvāṅgadharā naramālāvibhūṣaṇā ।।7।।
dvīpicarmaparīdhānā śuṣkamāṁsātibhairavā ।।

Bearing A Strange Skull-Topped Staff, Adorned With A Garland Of Skulls, And Clad In A Tiger's Skin. Her Emaciated Flesh Appalling.

अतिविस्तारवदना जिह्वाललनभीषणा ।।
निमग्नारक्तनयना नादापूरितदिङ्मुखा ।।८।।

ativistāravadanā jihvālalanabhīṣaṇā ।।
nimagnāraktanayanā nādāpūritadiṅmukhā ।।8।।

Her Mouth Gaping, Her Lolling Tongue Horrifying, Her Sunken Eyes Glowing red, She Filled the four quarters of the sky With Her Roars.

सा वेगेनाभिपतिता घातयन्ती महासुरान् ॥
सैन्ये तत्र सुरारीणामभक्षयत तद्बलम् ॥९॥

sā vegenābhipatitā ghātayantī mahāsurān ॥
sainye tatra surāriṇām abhakṣayata tad balam ॥9॥

Swiftly Falling Upon the great asuras in that army, She Slew And Devoured Those hosts of the Gods' foes.

पार्ष्णिग्राहाङ्कुशग्राहियोधघण्टासमन्वितान् ॥
समादायैकहस्तेन मुखे चिक्षेप वारणान् ॥१०॥

pārṣṇigrāhāṅkuśagrāhiyodhaghaṇṭāsamanvitān ॥
samādāyaikahastena mukhe cikṣepa vāraṇān ॥10॥

Attacking the rear guard and Seizing the elephants with their drivers, warriors, and bells, She Flung them Into Her Mouth With A Single Hand.

तथैव योधं तुरगै रथं सारथिना सह ॥
निक्षिप्य वक्त्रे दशनैश्चर्वयन्त्य*तिभैरवम् ॥११॥

tathaiva yodhaṁ turagai rathaṁ sārathinā saha ॥
nikṣipya vaktre daśanaiś carvayaty atibhairavam ॥11॥

In like Manner, She Tossed the cavalry with its horses and the charioteers with their chariots Into Her Mouth and Ground them Furiously Between Her Teeth.

एकं जग्राह केशेषु ग्रीवायामथ चापरम् ॥
पादेनाक्रम्य चौवान्यमुरसान्यमपोथयत् ॥१२॥

ekaṁ jagrāha keśeṣu grivāyām atha cāparam ॥
pādenākramya caivānyam urasānyam apothayat ॥12॥

She Seized one asura by the hair and another by the throat. Crushing another Underfoot, She Slammed yet another Against Her breast.

तैर्मुक्तानि च शस्त्राणि महास्त्राणि तथासुरैः ॥
मुखेन जग्राह रुषा दशनैर्मथितान्यपि ॥१३॥

tair muktāni ca śastrāṇi mahātrāṇi tathāsuraiḥ ॥
mukhena jagrāha ruṣā daśanair mathitāny api ॥13॥

The weapons and great missiles the asuras hurled She Caught In Her Mouth and Ground Angrily Between Her Teeth.

बलिनां तद् बलं सर्वमसुराणां दुरात्मनाम् ॥
ममर्दाभक्षयच्चान्यानन्यांश्चाताडयत्तथा ॥१४॥

balināṁ tad balaṁ sarvam asurāṇāṁ durātmanām ॥
mamardābhakṣayac cānyān anyāṁś cātāḍayat tathā ॥14॥

All that army of mighty and evil-natured asuras She Ravaged, Devouring some and Beating others Severely

असिना निहता: केचित्केचित्खट्वाङ्गताडिता: ॥
जग्मुर्विनाशमसुरा दन्ताग्राभिहतास्तथा ॥१५॥

asinā nihatāḥ kecit kecit khaṭvāṅgatāḍitāḥ ॥
jagmur vināśam asurā dantāgrābhihatās tathā ॥15॥

She Struck Down some With Her Sword and Battered others with Her SkullTopped Staff. Other asuras met their destruction Between Her Gnashing Teeth.

क्षणेन तद् बलं सर्वमसुराणां निपातितम् ॥
दृष्ट्वा चण्डोऽभिदुद्राव तां कालीमतिभीषणाम् ॥१६॥

kṣaṇena tad balaṁ sarvam asurāṇāṁ nipātitam ॥
dṛṣṭvā caṇḍo 'bhidudrāva tāṁ Kālīm atibhīṣaṇām ॥16॥

When Caṇḍa saw the entire army of asuras swiftly struck down, he rushed at The Terrifying Kālī.

शरवर्षैर्महाभीमैर्भीमाक्षीं तां महासुरः ॥
छादयामास चक्रैश्च मुण्डः क्षिप्तैः सहस्रशः ॥१७॥

śaravarṣair mahābhīmair bhīmākṣīm tāṁ mahāsuraḥ ॥
chādayāmāsa cakraiś ca muṇḍaḥ kṣiptaiḥ sahasraśaḥ ॥17॥

With a formidable deluge of arrows, that great asura engulfed The Glowering Kālī while Muṇḍa hurled discuses at Her by the thousands.

तानि चक्राण्यनेकानि विशमानानि तन्मुखम् ॥
बभुर्यथार्कबिम्बानि सुबहूनि घनोदरम् ॥१८॥

tāni cakrāṇy anekāni viśamānāni tan mukham ॥
babhur yathā 'rkabimbāni subahūni ghanodaram ॥18॥

Myriad discs entered her mouth like countless solar orbs dissolving into the thickness of a cloud.

ततो जहासातिरुषा भीमं भैरवनादिनी ॥
कालीकरालवक्त्रान्तर्दुर्दर्शदशनोज्ज्वला ॥१९॥

ato jahāsātiruṣā bhīmaṁ bhairavanādinī ॥
Kālī karālavaktrāntar durdarśadaśanojjvalā ॥19॥

With A Terrifying Roar, Kālī Laughed In Fury, Her Fearsome Teeth Gleaming Within Her Ghastly Mouth.

उत्थाय च महासिं हं देवी चण्डमधावत ।।
गृहीत्वा चास्य केशेषु शिरस्तेनासिनाच्छिनत् ।।२०।।

utthāya ca mahāsimhaṁ Devī Daṇḍam adhāvata ।।
gṛhītvā cāsya keśeṣu śiras tenāsinācchinat ।।20।।

Mounting Her Great Lion, The Devī Rushed at Caṇḍa, seized him by the hair, and Severed his head With Her Sword.

अथ मुण्डोऽभ्यधावत्तां दृष्ट्वा चण्डं निपातितम् ।।
तमप्यपातयद्भूमौ सा खड्गाभिहतं रुषा ।।२१।।

atha muṇḍo 'bhyadhāvat tāṁ dṛṣṭvā caṇḍam nipātitam ।।
tam apyapātayad bhūmau sā khaḍgābhihataṁ ruṣā ।।21।।

Seeing Caṇḍa slain, Muṇḍa attacked Her. She Pushed him to the ground and Struck him In Fury With Her Sword.

हतशेषं ततः सैन्यं दृष्ट्वा चण्डं निपातितम् ।।
मुण्डं च सुमहावीर्यं दिशो भेजे भयातुरम् ।।२२।।

hataśeṣam tataḥ sainyaṁ dṛṣṭvā caṇḍaṁ nipātitam ।।
muṇḍaṁ ca sumahāvīryaṁ diśo bheje bhayāturam ।।22।।

Seeing Caṇḍa and also the most valorous Muṇḍa slain, the remaining army panicked and fled in all directions.

शिरश्चण्डस्य काली च गृहीत्वा मुण्डमेव च ।।
प्राह प्रचण्डाट्टहासमिश्रमभ्येत्य चण्डिकाम् ।।२३।।

śiraś caṇḍasya Kālī ca gṛhītvā muṇḍam eva ca ।।
prāha pracaṇḍāṭṭahasamiśram abhyetya Caṇḍikām ।।23।।

And Kālī, Grasping the heads of Caṇḍa and Muṇḍa, Approached Caṇḍikā. Mingling her words with fierce, resounding laughter, she said:

मया तवात्रोपहृतौ चण्डमुण्डौ महापशू ।।
युद्धयज्ञे स्वयं शुम्भं निशुम्भं च हनिष्यसि ।।२४।।

mayā tavātropahṛtau caṇḍamuṇḍau mahāpaśū ।।
yuddhayajñe Svayaṁ śumbhaṁ niśumbhaṁ
ca haniṣyasi ।।24।।

I Here Present To You Caṇḍa and Muṇḍa As Two Great Offerings in the sacrifice of battle. You Yourself Shall Slay Śumbha and Niśumbha.

ऋषिरुवाच ।।२५।।

ṛṣir uvāca ।।25।।

The seer said:

तावानीतौ ततो दृष्ट्वा चण्डमुण्डौ महासुरौ ॥
उवाच कालीं कल्याणी ललितं चण्डिका वचः ॥२६॥

tāv ānītau tato dṛṣṭvā caṇḍamuṇḍau mahāsurau ॥
uvāca Kālīṁ kalyāṇī lalitaṁ Caṇḍikā vacaḥ ॥26॥

When She Saw Those two great asuras, Caṇḍa and Muṇḍa, Brought Before Her, The Auspicious Caṇḍikā Spoke These Playful Words To Kālī:

~

यस्माच्चण्डं च मुण्डं च गृहीत्वा त्वमुपागता ॥
चामुण्डेति ततो लोके ख्याता देवि भविष्यसि ॥ॐ ॥२७॥

yasmāc caṇḍaṁ ca muṇḍaṁ ca gṛhītvā Tvam upāgatā ॥
Cāmuṇḍeti tato loke khyātā Devi bhaviṣyasi ॥27॥

'Because You Have Overpowered Caṇḍa and Muṇḍa And Delivered Them To Me, You, O Devī, Will Henceforth Be Known In The World As Cāmuṇḍā'.

~

इति श्रीमार्कण्डेयपुराणे सावर्णिके मन्वन्तरे देवीमाहात्म्ये
चण्डमुण्डवधो नाम सप्तमोऽध्यायः ॥७॥

iti śrīmārkaṇḍeyapurāṇe sāvarṇike
manvantare devīmāhātmye
caṇḍamuṇḍavadho nāma saptamo'dhyāyaḥ ॥7॥

Thus ends the seventh chapter, titled 'The Slaying of Caṇḍa and Muṇḍa', in the Devī Māhātmya of the Mārkaṇḍeya Purāṇa, during the Sāvarṇi Manvantara.

|| अष्टमोऽध्यायः ||

रक्तबीज वध

|| Eighth Chapter ||

The Slaying Of Raktabija

|| ध्यानम् ||

ॐ अरुणां करुणातरङ्गिताक्षीं
धृतपाशाङ्कुशबाणचापहस्ताम् ।
अणिमादिभिरावृतां मयूखै-
रहमित्येव विभावये भवानीम् ॥

||dhyānam||

oṁ aruṇāṁ karuṇātaraṅgitākṣīṁ
dhṛtapāśāṅkuśabāṇacāpahastām ।
aṇimādibhirāvṛtāṁ mayūkhair-
ahamityeva vibhāvaye bhavānīm ॥

I meditate upon Goddess Bhavānī, who has a radiant reddish complexion and eyes flowing with deep compassion. She holds in her hands a noose, goad, bow,

and arrows, symbolizing control, guidance, and protection. Surrounded by shining rays of light and attended by the eight mystical powers (siddhis) such as Aṇimā, she reveals her divine presence. Realized through the awareness "I am She," Bhavānī is the embodiment of both power and grace, inviting the devotee into a state of unity with the divine.

"ॐ" ऋषिरुवाच ॥१॥

ṛṣir uvāca ॥1॥

The seer said

चण्डे च निहते दैत्ये मुण्डे च विनिपातिते ॥
बहुलेषु च सैन्येषु क्षयितेष्वसुरेश्वरः ॥२॥

caṇḍe ca nihate daitye muṇḍe ca vinipātite ॥
bahuleṣu ca sainyeṣu kṣayiteṣv asureśvaraḥ ॥2॥

After Caṇḍa was killed, Muṇḍa slain, and the vast armies annihilated, the lord of asuras

ततः कोपपराधीनचेताः शुम्भः प्रतापवान् ॥
उद्योगं सर्वसैन्यानां दैत्यानामादिदेश ह ॥३॥

tataḥ kopaparādhīnacetāḥ śumbhaḥ pratāpavān ॥
udyogaṁ sarvasainyānām daityānām ādideśa ha ॥3॥

Burned with rage. His reason overcome, Śumbha ordered the marshaling of all the demon hosts:

अद्य सर्वबलैर्दैत्याः षडशीतिरुदायुधाः ॥
कम्बूनां चतुरशीतिर्निर्यान्तु स्वबलैर्वृताः ॥४॥

adya sarvabalair daityāḥ ṣaḍaśītir udāyudhāḥ ॥
kambūnāṁ caturasītir niryāntu svabalair vṛtāḥ ॥4॥

'Now let the daitya clans with all their troops go forth, the eighty-six Udāyudha and the eighty-four Kambu families, together with their forces'.

कोटिवीर्याणि पञ्चाशदसुराणां कुलानि वै ॥
शतं कुलानि धौम्राणां निर्गच्छन्तु ममाज्ञया ॥५॥

koṭivīryāṇi pañcāśad asurāṇāṁ kulāni vai ॥
śataṁ kulāni dhaumrāṇāṁ nirgacchantu mamājnayā ॥5॥

Let the fifty Koṭivīrya families and the hundred Dhaumra clans depart at my command

कालका दौर्हृद मौर्याः कालकेयास्तथासुराः ॥
युद्धाय सज्जा निर्यान्तु आज्ञया त्वरिता मम ॥६॥

kālakā daurhṛdā mauryāḥ kālakeyās tathāsurāḥ ||
yuddhāya sajjā niryāntu ājñayā tvaritā mama ||6||

So also at my command, let the Kālaka, Daurhṛda, Maurya, and Kālakeya asuras set out in haste, armed for battle.'

इत्याज्ञाप्यासुरपतिः शुम्भो भैरवशासनः ॥
निर्जगाम महासैन्यसहस्रैर्बहुभिर्वृतः ॥७॥

ity ājñāpyāsurapatiḥ śumbho bhairavaśāsanaḥ ||
nirjagāma mahāsainyasahasrair bahubhir vṛtaḥ ||7||

Having issued his orders, Śumbha, the despotic lord of asuras, went forth, attended by many thousands of mighty troops.

आयान्तं चण्डिका दृष्ट्वा तत्सैन्यमतिभीषणम् ॥
ज्यास्वनैः पूरयामास धरणीगगनान्तरम् ॥८॥

āyāntaṁ Caṇḍikā dṛṣṭvā tat sainyam atibhīṣaṇam ||
jyāsvanaiḥ pūrayāmāsa dharaṇīgaganāntaram ||8||

Seeing that most formidable army approach, Caṇḍikā filled the space between earth and sky with the resonance of Her bowstring

ततः सिंहो महानादमतीव कृतवान् नृप ॥
घण्टास्वनेन तन्नादमम्बिका चोपबृंहयत् ॥९॥

tataḥ siṁho mahānādam atīva kṛtavān nṛpa ॥
ghaṇṭāsvanena tānnādānAmbikā copabṛṁhayat ॥9॥

Thereupon her lion emitted a deafening roar, O king, and Ambikā heightened the noise with Her clanging bell.

धनुर्ज्यासिंहघण्टानां नादापूरितदिङ्मुखा ॥
निनादैर्भीषणैः काली जिग्ये विस्तारितानना ॥१०॥

dhanurjyāsiṁhaghaṇṭānāṁ nādāpūritadiṅmukhā ॥
ninādair bhīṣanaiḥ Kālī jigye vistāritānanā ॥10॥

From Her gaping mouth poured dreadful howls, overwhelming the clamour of bowstrings, lion, and bell, and filling all quarters with terror.

तं निनादमुपश्रुत्य दैत्यसैन्यैश्चतुर्दिशम् ॥
देवी सिंहस्तथा काली सरोषैः परिवारिताः ॥११॥

taṁ ninādam upaśrutya daityasainyaiś caturdiśam ॥
Devī siṁhas tathā Kālī saroṣaiḥ parivāritāḥ ॥11॥

Hearing the tumult, the enraged demon armies closed in on the Devī, her lion, and Kālī from all four sides.

एतस्मिन्नन्तरे भूप विनाशाय सुरद्विषाम् ।।
भवायामरसिंहानामतिवीर्यबलान्विताः ।।१२।।

etasminn antare bhūpa vināśāya suradviṣām ।।
bhavāyāmarasiṁhānām ativīryabalānvitāḥ ।।12।।

O king, at that very moment, to insure the well-being of the supreme gods and to annihilate their adversaries, surpassingly brave and powerful

ब्रह्मेशगुहविष्णूनां तथेन्द्रस्य च शक्तयः ।।
शरीरेभ्यो विनिष्क्रम्य तद्रूपैश्चण्डिकां ययुः ।।१३ ।।

brahmeśaguhaviṣṇūnāṁ tathendrasya ca śaktayaḥ ।।
śarīrebhyo viniṣkramya tadrūpaiś Caṇḍikāṁ yayuḥ ।।13।।

śaktis, the gods' embodied powers, sprang forth from the bodies of Brahmā, Śiva, Skanda, Viṣṇu, and Indra, mirroring the form of each. They approached Caṇḍikā.

यस्य देवस्य यद्रूपं यथाभूषणवाहनम् ।।
तद्वदेव हि तच्छक्तिरसुरान् योद्धुमाययौ ।।१४ ।।

yasya devasya yadrūpaṁ yathā bhūṣaṇavāhanam ।।
tad vad eva hi tac chaktir asurān yoddhum āyayau ।।14।।

Whatever that god's form was, whatever his adornments and his mount, in that very form his śakti went forth to combat the asuras.

हंसयुक्तविमानाग्रे साक्षसूत्रकमण्डलुः ॥
आयाता ब्रह्मणः शक्तिर्ब्रह्माणी साभिधीयते ॥१५॥

haṁsayuktavimānāgre sākṣasūtrakamaṇḍaluḥ ॥
āyātā brahmaṇaḥ śaktir Brahmāṇī sābhidhīyate ॥15॥

In a celestial chariot drawn by swans, Brahmā's śakti came forth with prayer beads and waterpot in hand. She is called Brahmāṇī.

माहेश्वरी वृषारूढा त्रिशूलवरधारिणी ॥
महाहिवलया प्राप्ता चन्द्ररेखाविभूषणा ॥१६॥

Māheśvarī vṛṣārūḍhā triśūlavaradhāriṇī ॥
mahāhivalayā prāptā candrarekhāvibhūṣaṇā ॥16॥

Māheśvarī arrived astride a bull, holding the finest trident, wearing great serpents for bracelets, and adorned with the crescent moon.

कौमारी शक्तिहस्ता च मयूरवरवाहना ॥
योद्धुमभ्याययौ दैत्यानम्बिका गुहरूपिणी ॥१७॥

Kaumārī śaktihastā ca mayūravaravāhanā ||
yoddhum abhyāyayau daityān Ambikā guharūpiṇī ||17||

Ambikā, having the war god's form and riding a fine peacock, came forth as Kaumārī with spear in hand to fight against the daityas.

तथैव वैष्णवी शक्तिर्गरुडोपरि संस्थिता ||
शङ्खचक्रगदाशाङ्र्गखड्गहस्ताभ्युपाययौ ||१८||

tathaiva Vaiṣṇavī śaktir garuḍopari saṁsthitā ||
śaṅkhacakragadāśārngakhaḍgahastābhyupāyayau ||18||

Likewise the śakti Vaiṣṇavī, mounted on Garuda, approached holding conch, discus, mace, bow, and sword.

यज्ञवाराहमतुलं रूपं या बिभ्रतो हरेः ||
शक्तिः साप्याययौ तत्र वाराहीं बिभ्रती तनुम् ||१९||

yajñavārāham atulaṁ rūpaṁ yā bibhrato hareḥ ||
śaktiḥ sāpyāyayau tatra Vārāhīṁ bibhratī tanum ||19||

The śakti of Hari, who bears the unique form of the sacrificial boar, came forward as Vārāhī in that boarlike aspect.

नारसिंही नृसिंहस्य बिभ्रती सदृशं वपुः ।।
प्राप्ता तत्र सटाक्षेपक्षिप्तनक्षत्रसंहतिः ।।२०।।

nārasiṁhī nṛsiṁhasya bibhratī sadṛśaṁ vapuḥ ॥
prāptā tatra saṭākṣepakṣiptanakṣatrasaṁhatiḥ ॥20॥

Nārasirhhī, resembling Viṣṇu's embodiment as a man-lion, arrived there, scattering the constellations with the toss of Her mane.

❧

वज्रहस्ता तथैवैन्द्री गजराजोपरि स्थिता ।।
प्राप्ता सहस्रनयना यथा शक्रस्तथैव सा ।।२१।।

vajrahastā tathaivaindrī gajarājopari sthitā ॥
prāptā sahasranayanā yathā śakrastathaiva sā ॥21॥

Thousand-eyed like Indra, and in like manner with thunderbolt in hand, Aindrī arrived riding on the lord of elephants.

❧

ततः परिवृतस्ताभिरीशानो देवशक्तिभिः ।।
हन्यन्तामसुराः शीघ्रं मम प्रीत्याऽऽहचण्डिकाम् ।।२२।।

tataḥ parivṛtas tābhir īśāno devaśaktibhiḥ ॥
hanyantām asurāḥ śīghraṁ mama prītyāha Caṇḍikām ॥22॥

Then Śiva, surrounded by those śaktis of the gods, said to Caṇḍikā, 'Let the asuras quickly be slain for My satisfaction.'

ततो देवीशरीरात्तु विनिष्क्रान्तातिभीषणा ।।
चण्डिकाशक्तिरत्युग्रा शिवाशतनिनादिनी ।।२३।।

tato devīśarīrāt tu viniṣkrāntātibhīṣaṇā ।।
caṇḍikāśaktir atyugrā śivāśataninādinī ।।23।।

Thereupon from the Devī's body there issued forth Caṇḍikā's Own terrifying śakti, savage in her fury and howling like a hundred jackals.

सा चाह धूम्रजटिलमीशानमपराजिता ।।
दूत त्वं गच्छ भगवन् पार्श्वं शुम्भनिशुम्भयोः ।।२४।।

sā cāha dhūmrajaṭilam īśānam aparājitā ।।
dūtas tvaṁ gaccha bhagavan pārśvaṁ
śumbhaniśumbhayoḥ ।।24।।

And She, the unvanquished one, said to Śiva of dark, matted locks, 'Go, My lord, as My messenger to Śumbha and Niśumbha'.

ब्रूहि शुम्भं निशुम्भं च दानवावतिगर्वितौ ॥
ये चान्ये दानवास्तत्र युद्धाय समुपस्थिताः ॥२५॥

brūhi śumbhaṁ niśumbhaṁ ca dānavav atigarvitau ॥
ye cānye dānavās tatra yuddhāya samupasthitāḥ ॥25॥

Say to those two arrogant dānavas, Śumbha and Niśumbha, and to the other dānavas assembled there for battle:

त्रैलोक्यमिन्द्रो लभतां देवाः सन्तु हविर्भुजः ॥
यूयं प्रयात पातालं यदि जीवितुमिच्छथ ॥२६॥

trailoyam indro labhatāṁ devāḥ santu havirbhujaḥ ॥
yūyaṁ prayāta pātālaṁ yadi jīvitum icchatha ॥26॥

Indra must regain the three worlds, the gods must again enjoy the sacrificial oblations, and you must return to the nether world if you wish to live.

बलावलेपादथ चेद्भवन्तो युद्धकाङ्क्षिणः ॥
तदागच्छत तृप्यन्तु मच्छिवाः पिशितेन वः ॥२७॥

balāvalepād atha ced bhavanto yuddhakāṅkṣiṇaḥ ॥
tadāgacchata tṛpyantu macchivāḥ piśitena vaḥ ॥27॥

But if through the conceit of strength you are desirous of battle, then come and let My jackals be satiated with your flesh!

यतो नियुक्तो दौत्येन तया देव्या शिवः स्वयम् ॥
शिवदूतीति लोकेऽस्मिंस्ततः सा ख्यातिमागता ॥२८॥

yato niyukto dautyena tayā Devyā śivaḥ svayam ॥
śivadūtīti loke 'smiṁs tataḥ sā khyātimāgatā ॥28॥

Since the Devī appointed Śiva himself as messenger, she has come to be known in this world as Śivadūtī.

तेऽपि श्रुत्वा वचो देव्याः शर्वाख्यातं महासुराः ॥
अमर्षापूरिता जग्मुर्यत्र' कात्यायनी स्थिता ॥२९॥

te 'pi śrutvā vaco Devyāḥ sarvākhyātaṁ mahāsurāḥ ॥
amarṣāpūritā jagmur yataḥ Kātyāyanī sthitā ॥29॥

Hearing Śiva declare the Devī's words, the great asuras were filled with indignation and went to where Kātyāyanī stood.

ततः प्रथममेवाग्रे शरशक्त्यृष्टिवृष्टिभिः ॥
ववर्षुरुद्धतामर्षास्तां देवीममरारयः ॥३०॥

tataḥ prathamam evāgre śaraśaktyṛṣṭivṛṣṭibhiḥ ॥
vavarṣur uddhatāmarṣās tāṁ Devīṁ amarārayaḥ ॥30॥

At the outbreak of battle, the gods' adversaries, arrogant in their anger, rained torrents of arrows, spears, and lances upon the Devī.

ꕥ

सा च तान् प्रहितान् बाणाञ्छूलशक्तिपरश्वधान् ॥
चिच्छेद लीलयाऽऽध्मातधनुर्मुक्तैर्महेषुभिः ॥३१॥

sā ca tān prahitān bāṇāñ chūlaśaktiparaśvadhān ॥
ciccheda līlayādhmātadhanurmuktair maheṣubhiḥ ॥32॥

And She, with great arrows shot from Her resounding bow, playfully split asunder their hurtling arrows, lances, spears, and axes.

ꕥ

तस्याग्रतस्तथा काली शूलपातविदारितान् ॥
खट्वाङ्गपोथितांश्चारीन् कुर्वती व्यचरत्तदा ॥३२॥

tasyāgratas tathā Kālī śūlapātavidāritān ॥
khaṭvāṅgapothitāṁś cārīn kurvatī vyacarat tadā ॥32॥

32. Kālī roamed about the battlefront, slashing Her enemies to shreds with Her spear and crushing them with Her skull-topped staff

ꕥ

कमण्डलुजलाक्षेपहतवीर्यान् हतौजसः ॥
ब्रह्माणी चाकरोच्छत्रून् येन येन स्म धावति ॥३३॥

kamaṇḍalujalākṣepahatavīryān hataujasaḥ ॥
Brahmāṇī cākaroc chatrān yena yena sma dhāvati ॥33॥

And Brahmāṇī, wherever She went, left Her enemies sapped of strength, disabled by the holy water sprinkled from Her waterpot.

माहेश्वरी त्रिशूलेन तथा चक्रेण वैष्णवी ॥
दैत्याञ्जघान कौमारी तथा शक्तयातिकोपना ॥३४॥

Māheśvarī triśulena tathā cakreṇa Vaiṣṇavi ॥
daityāñ jaghāna Kaumārī tathā śaktyātikopanā ॥34॥

Māheśvarī slew the daityas with Her trident; so, too, did Vaiṣṇavī with Her discus, And Kaumārī with Her spear.

ऐन्द्रीकुलिशपातेन शतशो दैत्यदानवाः ॥
पेतुर्विदारिताः पृथ्व्यां रुधिरौघप्रवर्षिणः ॥३५॥

aindrī kuliśapātena śataśo daityadānavāḥ ॥
petur vidāritāḥ pṛthvyāṁ rudhiraughapravarṣiṇaḥ ॥35॥

Aindrī's thunderbolt rent the daityas and dānavas asunder; hundreds fell, spilling torrents of blood that darkened the earth.

तुण्डप्रहारविध्वस्ता दंष्ट्राग्रक्षतवक्षसः ॥
वाराहमूर्त्या न्यपतंश्चक्रेण च विदारिताः ॥३६॥

tuṇḍaprahāravidhvastā daṁṣṭrāgrakṣatavakṣasaḥ ॥
vārāhamūrtyā nyapataṁś cakreṇa ca vidāritāḥ ॥36॥

They fell, scattered by blows from Vārāhī's boarlike snout, pierced through the chest by Her tusks, and ripped apart by Her discus.

नखैर्विदारितांश्चान्यान् भक्षयन्ती महासुरान् ॥
नारसिंही चचाराजौ नादापूर्णदिगम्बरा ॥३७॥

nakhair vidāritāmś cānyān bhaksayantī mahāsurān ॥
Nārasiṁhī cacārājau nādāpūrṇadigambarā ॥37॥

Nārasiṁhī, tearing other great asuras apart with Her claws and devouring them, roamed about the battlefield, filling the sky with Her roars.

चण्डाट्टहासैरसुराः शिवदूत्यभिदूषिताः ॥
पेतुः पृथिव्यां पतितांस्तांश्चखादाथ सा तदा ॥३८॥

caṇḍāṭṭahāsair asurāḥ śivadūty abhidūṣitāḥ ॥
petuḥ pṛthivyāṁ patitāms taṁś cakhādātha sā tadā ॥38॥

Dazed by Śivadūtī's violent laughter, the asuras fell to the ground, and She devoured those fallen ones.

इति मातृगणं क्रुद्धं मर्दयन्तं महासुरान् ॥
दृष्ट्वाभ्युपायैर्विविधैर्नेशुर्देवारिसैनिकाः ॥३९॥

iti mātṛgaṇaṁ kruddhaṁ mardayantaṁ mahāsurān ॥
dṛṣtvābhyupāyair vividhair neśur Devārisainikāḥ ॥39॥

When the enemy troops saw the enraged band of Mothers crushing the mighty asuras by diverse means, they fled.

पलायनपरान् दृष्ट्वा दैत्यान् मातृगणार्दितान् ॥
योद्धुमभ्याययौ क्रुद्धो रक्तबीजो महासुरः ॥४०॥

palāyanaparān dṛṣṭvā daityān mātṛgaṇārditān ॥
yoddhum abyāyayau kruddho raktabījo mahāsuraḥ ॥40॥

Seeing the remaining daityas flee, tormented thus by the band of Mothers, the great asura Raktabīja went forth in anger to do battle.

रक्तबिन्दुर्यदा भूमौ पतत्यस्य शरीरतः ॥
समुत्पतति मेदिन्यां* तत्प्रमाणस्तदासुरः ॥४१॥

raktabindur yadā bhūmau pataty asya śarīrataḥ ॥
samutpatati medinyāṁ tatpramāṇas tadāsuraḥ ॥41॥

Whenever a drop of blood fell from his body to the ground, an asura of like measure would rise up from the earth.

युयुधे स गदापाणिरिन्द्रशक्तया महासुरः ॥
ततश्चौन्द्री स्ववज्रेण रक्तबीजमताडयत् ॥४२॥

yuyudhe sa gadāpāṇir indraśaktyā mahāsuraḥ ॥
tataś Caindrī svavajreṇa raktabījam aṭādayat ॥42॥

With club in hand the great asura fought with Indra's śakti. Then Aindrī struck Raktabīja with Her thunderbolt.

कुलिशेनाहतस्याशु बहु* सुस्राव शोणितम् ॥
समुत्तस्थुस्ततो योधास्तद्रूपास्तत्पराक्रमाः ॥४३॥

kuliśenāhatasyāśu bahu susrāva śoṇitam ॥
samuttasthus tato yodhās tadrūpās tatparākramāḥ ॥43॥

Blood streamed in torrents from the stricken asura, and from that blood rose up warriors of identical form and might.

यावन्तः पतितास्तस्य शरीराद्रक्तबिन्दवः ॥
तावन्तः पुरुषा जातास्तद्वीर्यबलविक्रमाः ॥४४॥

yāvantaḥ patitās tasya śarīrād raktabindavaḥ ॥
tāvantaḥ puruṣā jātās tadvīryabalavikramāḥ ॥44॥

As many drops of blood fell from his body, so many beings of equal valor, strength, and courage arose.

~

ते चापि युयुधुस्तत्र पुरुषा रक्तसम्भवाः ॥
समं मातृभिरत्युग्रशस्त्रपातातिभीषणम् ॥४५॥

te cāpi yuyudhus tatra puruṣā raktasambhavāḥ ॥
samaṁ mātṛbhir atyugraśastrapātātibhīṣaṇam ॥45॥

And those who sprang up from his blood battled there with the Mothers ever more fiercely, hurling the most formidable of weapons.

~

पुनश्च वज्रपातेन क्षतमस्य शिरो यदा ॥
ववाह रक्तं पुरुषास्ततो जाताः सहस्रशः ॥४६॥

punaś ca vajrapātena kṣatam asya siro yadā ॥
vavāha raktaṁ puruṣās tato jātāḥ sahasraśaḥ ॥46॥

When the Devī's thunderbolt struck Raktabīja's head, blood flowed again, and from it asuras were born by the thousands

~

वैष्णवी समरे चौनं चक्रेणाभिजघान ह।।
गदया ताडयामास ऐन्द्री तमसुरेश्वरम् ।।४७।।

vaiṣṇavī samare cainaṁ cakreṇābhijaghāna ha ।।
gadayā tāḍayāmāsa Aindrī tam asureśvaram ।।47।।

In the combat Vaiṣṇavī attacked the lord of asuras with Her discus, and Aindri beat him with Her mace.

वैष्णवीचक्रभिन्नस्य रुधिरस्रावसम्भवैः ।।
सहस्रशो जगद्व्याप्तं तत्प्रमाणैर्महासुरैः ।।४८।।

vaiṣṇavīcakrabhinnasya rudhirāsravasambhavaiḥ ।।
sahasraśo jagad vyāptaṁ tatpramāṇair mahāsuraiḥ ।।48।।

Blood flowed from the cuts of Vaiṣṇavī's discus, and there from great asuras of equal measure arose by the thousands and filled the world.

शक्त्या जघान कौमारी वाराही च तथासिना ।।
माहेश्वरी त्रिशूलेन रक्तबीजं महासुरम् ।।४९।।

śaktyā jaghāna Kaumārī Vārāhī ca tathāsinā ।।
Māheśvarī triśūlena raktabījaṁ mahāsuram ।।49।।

Kaumārī with her spear, Vārāhī with her sword, and Māheśvarī with her trident struck the great asura Raktabīja.

स चापि गदया दैत्यः सर्वा एवाहनत् पृथक् ॥
मातृः कोपसमाविष्टो रक्तबीजो महासुरः ॥५०॥

sa cāpi gadayā daityaḥ sarvā evāhanat pṛthak ॥
mātṝḥ kopasamāviṣṭo raktabījo mahāsuraḥ ॥50॥

And he, the mighty, rage-filled daitya, struck all the Mothers one by one with his club.

तस्याहतस्य बहुधा शक्तिशूलादिभिर्भुवि ॥
पपात यो वै रक्तौघस्तेनासञ्छतशोऽसुराः ॥५१॥

tasyāhatasya bahudhā śaktiśūlādibhir bhuvi ॥
papāta yo vai raktaughas tenāsañ chataśo 'surāḥ ॥51॥

Out of the blood that streamed upon the earth from the relentless wounds of spear, lance, and other weapons, asuras sprang up by the hundreds.

तैश्चासुरासृक्सम्भूतैरसुरैः सकलं जगत् ॥
व्याप्तमासीत्ततो देवा भयमाजग्मुरुत्तमम् ॥५२॥

taiś cāsurāsṛksambhūtair asuraiḥ sakalaṁ jagat ॥
vyāptam āsīt tato devā bhayam ājagmur uttamam ॥52॥

And those demons born from this one demon's flowing blood pervaded all the world. Utter terror seized the gods.

तान् विषण्णान् सुरान् दृष्ट्वा चण्डिका प्राह सत्वरा ।।
उवाच कालीं चामुण्डे विस्तीर्णं' वदनं कुरु ।।५३।।

tān viṣaṇṇān surān dṛṣṭvā Caṇḍikā prāhasat tvarā ।।
uvāca kālīṁ Cāmuṇḍe vistīrṇaṁ vadanaṁ kuru ।।53।।

Caṇḍikā burst into laughter at their despair and said to Kālī, 'O Cāmuṇḍā, open wide your mouth

मच्छस्त्रपातसम्भूतान् रक्तबिन्दून्महासुरान् ।।
रक्तबिन्दोः प्रतीच्छ त्वं वक्त्रेणानेन वेगिना* ।।५४।।

macchastrapātasambhūtān raktabindūn mahāsurān ।।
raktabindoḥ pratīccha tvaṁ vaktreṇānena vegitā ।।54।।

And quickly drink in the drops of blood from my weapons' blows and the great asuras born therefrom.

भक्षयन्ती चर रणे तदुत्पन्नान्महासुरान् ।।
एवमेष क्षयं दैत्यः क्षीणरक्तो गमिष्यति ।।५५।।

bhakṣayantī cara raṇe tadutpannān mahāsuran ।।
evam eṣa kṣayaṁ daityaḥ kṣīṇarakto gamiṣyati ।।55।।

Roam about on the battlefield and devour the great demons sprung from Raktabīja. So shall this daitya, drained of blood, go to his destruction.

भक्ष्यमाणास्त्वया चोग्रा न चोत्पत्स्यन्ति चापरे ।।
इत्युक्त्वा तां ततो देवी शूलेनाभिजघान तम् ।।५६।।

bhakṣyamāṇās tvayā cogrā na cotpatsyanti cāpare ।।
ity uktvā tāṁ tato Devī śūlenābhijaghāna tam ।।56।।

As you consume those fierce asuras, others shall not arise.' Having spoken thus, the Devī attacked Raktabīja with her lance

मुखेन काली जगृहे रक्तबीजस्य शोणितम् ।।
ततोऽसावाजघानाथ गदया तत्र चण्डिकाम् ।।५७।।

mukhena Kālī jagṛhe raktabījasya śoṇitam ।।
tato 'sāvājaghānātha gadayā tatra Caṇḍikām ।।57।।

While Kālī avidly lapped up his blood. Raktabīja turned upon Caṇḍikā with his club.

न चास्या वेदनां चक्रे गदापातोऽल्पिकामपि ।।
तस्याहतस्य देहात्तु बहु सुस्राव शोणितम् ।।५८।।

na cāsyā vedanāṁ cakre gadāpāto 'lpikām api ।।
tasyāhatasya dehāt tu bahu susrāva śoṇitam ।।58।।

But his cudgel blows caused Her not even the slightest pain. From his beaten body blood flowed copiously

यतस्ततस्तद्वक्त्रेण चामुण्डा सम्प्रतीच्छति ॥
मुखे समुद्गता येऽस्या रक्तपातान्महासुराः ॥५९॥

yatas tatas tad vaktreṇa Cāmuṇḍā sampratīcchati ॥
mukhe samudgatā ye ’syā raktapātān mahāsurāḥ ॥59॥

In every direction, and Cāmuṇḍā engulfed it with Her mouth. And within Her mouth those great asuras who sprang into being from the flow.

तांश्चखादाथ चामुण्डा पपौ तस्य च शोणितम् ॥
देवी शूलेन वज्रेण' बाणैरसिभिर्ऋष्टिभिः ॥६०॥

tāṁś cakhādātha cāmuṇḍā papau tasya ca śoṇitam ॥
Devī śūlena vajreṇa bāṇair asibhir ṛṣṭibhiḥ ॥60॥

Those She now devoured, even while drinking Raktabīja’s blood. The Devī assailed Raktabīja with lance, thunderbolt, arrows, swords.

जघान रक्तबीजं तं चामुण्डापीतशोणितम् ॥
स पपात महीपृष्ठे शस्त्रसङ्घसमाहतः ॥६१॥

jaghāna raktabījaṁ taṁ cāmuṇḍāpītaśoṇitam ॥
sa papata mahīpṛṣṭhe śastrasaṅghasamāhataḥ ॥61॥

Cāmuṇḍā slew the demon Raktabīja and drank all his blood. Struck by a multitude of weapons, he fell upon the surface of the earth.

नीरक्तश्च महीपाल रक्तबीजो महासुरः ।।
ततस्ते हर्षमतुलमवापुस्त्रिदशा नृप ।।६२।।

nīraktaś ca mahīpāla raktabījo mahāsuraḥ ।।
tatas te harṣamatulam avāpus tridaśā nṛpa ।।62।।

O King, the great demon Raktabīja was left bloodless, and then the gods (Tridaśas) experienced immense and incomparable joy.

तेषां मातृगणो जातो ननर्तासृङ्मदोद्धतः ।।ॐ ।।६३।।

teṣāṁ mātṛgaṇo jāto nanartāsṛṅmadoddhataḥ ।।oṁ।। ।।63।।

Their host of Mātrikās (divine mother goddesses), intoxicated by the blood, began to dance wildly in a frenzy of joy.

इति श्रीमार्कण्डेयपुराणे सावर्णिके मन्वन्तरे देवीमाहात्म्ये
रक्तबीजवधो नामाष्टमोऽध्यायः ।।63।।

iti śrīmārkaṇḍeyapurāṇe sāvarṇike
manvantare devīmāhātmye
raktabījavadho nāmāṣṭamo'dhyāyaḥ ॥8॥

Thus ends the eighth chapter, titled "The Slaying of Raktabīja," in the Devī Māhātmya of the Mārkaṇḍeya Purāṇa, set in the Sāvarṇi Manvantara.

।। नवमोऽध्यायः।।

निशुम्भ वध

।। Ninth Chapter ।।

Slaying of Nishumbha

।। ध्यानम् ।।

ॐ बन्धूककाञ्चननिभं रुचिराक्षमालां
पाशाङ्कुशौ च वरदां निजबाहुदण्डैः।
बिभ्राणमिन्दुशकलाभरणं त्रिनेत्र-
मर्धाम्बिकेशमनिशं वपुराश्रयामि ।।

।। dhyānam ।।

oṁ bandhūkakāñcananibhaṁ rucirākṣamālāṁ
pāśāṅkuśau ca varadāṁ nijabāhudaṇḍaiḥ ।
bibhrāṇam induśakalābharaṇaṁ trinetra-
mardhāmbikeśam aniśaṁ vapur āśrayāmi ।।

Meditation Verse (Dhyānam):

I constantly take refuge in the radiant form of Ardhambikā (the half-form of the Goddess), who shines like bandhūka flowers and gold, adorned with a beautiful rosary, and holding a noose, goad, and offering boons and protection with her arms. She wears the crescent moon as an ornament, has three eyes, and embodies the union of Śiva and Śakti.

"ॐ" राजोवाच ॥१॥

Rājovāca ॥1॥

The king said:

विचित्रमिदमाख्यातं भगवन् भवता मम ॥
देव्याश्चरितमाहात्म्यं रक्तबीजवधाश्रितम् ॥२॥

vicitram idam ākhyātaṁ bhagavan bhavatā mama ॥
Devyāś caritamāhātmyaṁ raktabījavadhāśritam ॥2॥

Wonderful is this, revered sir, that you have told me about the Devī's glorious deed in slaying Raktabīja.

भूयश्चेच्छाम्यहं श्रोतुं रक्तबीजे निपातिते ॥
चकार शुम्भो यत्कर्म निशुम्भश्चातिकोपनः ॥३॥

bhūyaś cecchāmy ahaṁ śroturṁ raktabīje nipātite ।।
cakāra śumbho yatkarma niśumbhaś cātikopanaḥ ।।3।।

I wish to hear more about what Śumbha and the wrathful Niśumbha did after Raktabīja was killed.

ऋषिरुवाच ।।४।।

ṛṣir uvāca ।।4।।

The seer said:

चकार कोपमतुलं रक्तबीजे निपातिते ।।
शुम्भासुरो निशुम्भश्च हतेष्वन्येषु चाहवे ।।५।।

cakāra kopām atulaṁ raktabīje nipātite ।।
śumbhāsuro niśumbhaś ca hateṣv anyeṣu cāhave ।।5।।

After Raktabīja was killed and the others slain in battle, Śumbha and Niśumbha fell into unparalleled rage.

हन्यमानं महासैन्यं विलोक्यामर्षमुद्वहन् ।।
अभ्यधावन्निशुम्भोऽथ मुख्ययासुरसेनया ।।६।।

hanyamānaṁ mahāsainyaṁ vilokyāmarṣam udvahan ।।
abhyadhāvan nisumbho 'tha mukhyayāsurasenayā ।।6।।

Seeing that his mighty army was being slaughtered, Niśumba was overcome with fury and rushed forward with the best of his demon forces.

तस्याग्रतस्तथा पृष्ठे पार्श्वयोश्च महासुराः ।।
संदष्टौष्ठपुटाः क्रुद्धा हन्तुं देवीमुपाययुः ।।७।।

tasyāgratas tathā pṛṣṭhe pārśvayoś ca mahāsurāḥ ।।
sandaṣṭauṣṭhapuṭāḥ kruddhā hantuṁ Devīm upāyayuḥ ।।7।।

In front of him, behind him, and on both sides, great asuras, their lips compressed in anger, advanced to slay the Devī.

आजगाम महावीर्यः शुम्भोऽपि स्वबलैर्वृतः ।।
निहन्तुं चण्डिकां कोपात्कृत्वा युद्धं तु मातृभिः ।।८।।

ājagāma mahāvīryaḥ śumbho 'pi svabalair vṛtaḥ ।।
nihantuṁ Caṇḍikāṁ kopāt kṛtvā yuddhaṁ tu mātṛbhiḥ ।।8।।

Having battled the Mothers, Śumbha, mighty in valor and surrounded by his forces, came forward in fury to attack the Devī.

ततो युद्धमतीवासीद्देव्या शुम्भनिशुम्भयोः ।।
शरवर्षमतीवोग्रं मेघयोरिव वर्षतोः ।।९।।

tato yuddham atīvāsīd Devyā śumbhaniśumbhayoḥ ||
śaravarṣam atīvograṁ meghayor iva varṣatoḥ ||9||

Fierce fighting erupted between them, and like two thunderclouds, Śumbha and Niśumbha rained down torrents of arrows on the Devī.

चिच्छेदास्ताञ्छरांस्ताभ्यां चण्डिका स्वशरोत्करैः ।।
ताडयामास चाङ्गेषु शस्त्रौघैरसुरेश्वरौ ।।१०।।

cicchedāstāñ charāṁs tābhyāṁ Caṇḍikā svaśarotkaraiḥ ||
tāḍayāmāsa cāṅgeṣu śastraughair asureśvarau ||10||

Caṇḍikā intercepted them with Her Own volley of arrows and struck the demon chiefs in the limbs with a stream of weapons.

निशुम्भो निशितं खड्गं चर्म चादाय सुप्रभम् ।।
अताडयन्मूर्ध्नि सिंहं देव्या वाहनमुत्तमम् ।।११।।

niśumbho niśitam khaḍgaṁ carma cādāya suprabham ||
atāḍayan mūrdhni simhaṁ Devyā vāhanam uttamam ||11||

Niśumbha, seizing his sharpened spear and shining shield, struck the lion, the Devī's magnificent mount, on the head.

ताडिते वाहने देवी क्षुरप्रेणासिमुत्तमम् ॥
निशुम्भस्याशु चिच्छेद चर्म चाप्यष्टचन्द्रकम् ॥१२॥

tāḍite vāhane Devī kṣurapreṇāsim uttamam ॥
niśumbhasyāśu ciccheda carma cāpyaṣṭacandrakam ॥12॥

Her lion assaulted, the Devī swiftly cut through Niśumbha's superb sword with Her razor-sharp arrow and through his shield, emblazoned with eight moons.

छिन्ने चर्मणि खड्गे च शक्तिं चिक्षेप सोऽसुरः ॥
तामप्यस्य द्विधा चक्रे चक्रेणाभिमुखागताम् ॥१३॥

chinne carmaṇi khaḍge ca śaktiṁ cikṣepa so 'suraḥ ॥
tām apy asya dvidhā cakre cakreṇābhimukhāgatām ॥13॥

His shield and sword broken, the asura hurled his spear, and as it came toward Her, that, too, the Devī cut in half with Her discus.

कोपाध्मातो निशुम्भोऽथ शूलं जग्राह दानवः ॥
आयातं' मुष्टिपातेन देवी तच्चाप्यचूर्णयत् ॥१४॥

kopādhmāto niśumbho 'tha śūlam jagrāha dànavaḥ ॥
āyāntaṁ muṣṭipātena Devī tac cāpy acūrṇayat ॥14॥

Blustering with rage, the dānava Niśumbha seized his lance, and as it came flying, the Devī crushed it with a blow of Her fist.

आविध्याथ गदां सोऽपि चिक्षेप चण्डिकां प्रति ।।
साऽपि देव्या त्रिशूलेन भिन्ना भस्मत्वमागता ।।१५।।

āvidhyātha gadām so 'pi cikṣepa Caṇḍikām prati ।।
sāpi Devyā triśūlena bhinnā bhasmatvam āgatā ।।15।।

Then swinging his club, Niśumbha flung it at Caṇḍikā. The Devī's trident reduced it to ashes.

ततः परशुहस्तं तमायान्तं दैत्यपुङ्गवम् ।।
आहत्य देवी बाणौघैरपातयत भूतले ।।१६।।

tataḥ paraśuhastaṁ tam āyāntaṁ daityapuṅgavam ।।
āhatya Devī bāṇaughair apātayata bhūtale ।।16।।

After wounding the onrushing demon chief with ax in hand, the Devī forced him to the ground with a volley of arrows.

तस्मिन्निपतिते भूमौ निशुम्भे भीमविक्रमे ।।
भ्रातर्यतीव संक्रुद्धः प्रययौ हन्तुमम्बिकाम् ।।१७।।

tasmin nipātite bhūmau niśumbhe bhīmavikrame ||
bhrātary atīva samkruddhaḥ prayayau hantum Ambikām ||17||

When he saw Niśumbha, his brother of fearsome strength, lying fallen on the ground, Śumbha moved forward, greatly enraged, to slay Ambikā.

स रथस्थस्तथात्युच्चैर्गृहीतपरमायुधैः ॥
भुजैरष्टाभिरतुलैर्व्याप्याशेषं बभौ नभः ॥१८॥

sa rathasthas tathāty uccair gṛhītaparamāyudhaiḥ ||
bhujair aṣṭābhir atulair vyāpyāśeṣaṁ babhau nabhaḥ ||18||

Standing in his chariot and holding aloft magnificent weapons, he shone forth and filled the entire sky with his eight incomparable arms

तमायान्तं समालोक्य देवी शङ्खमवादयत् ॥
ज्याशब्दं चापि धनुषश्चकारातीव दुःसहम् ॥१९॥

tam āyāntaṁ samālokya Devī śankham avādayat ||
jyāśabdaṁ cāpi dhanuṣaś cakārātīva duḥsaham ||19||

While She watched him approach, the Devī sounded Her conch, set off an unbearable reverberation with Her bowstring.

पूरयामास ककुभो निजघण्टास्वनेन च ।।
समस्तदैत्यसैन्यानां तेजोवधविधायिना ।।२०।।

pūrayāmāsa kakubho nijaghaṇṭāsvanena ca ।।
samastadaityasainyānām tejovadhavidhāyinā ।।20।।

And filled the firmament with the ringing of Her bell,
which sapped the strength of the assembled demon armies.

ततः सिंहो महानादैस्त्याजितेभमहामदैः ।।
पूरयामास गगनं गां तथैव' दिशो दश ।।२१।।

tataḥ siṁho mahānādais tyājitebhamahāmadaiḥ ।।
pūrayāmāsa gaganaṁ gāṁ tathopadiśo daśa ।।21।।

Then the lion filled every direction with great roars that
caused even the elephants' mighty prowess to falter.

ततः काली समुत्पत्य गगनं क्ष्मामताडयत् ।।
कराभ्यां तन्निनादेन प्राक्स्वनास्ते तिरोहिताः ।।२२।।

tataḥ Kālī samutpatya gaganaṁ kṣmām atāḍayat ।।
karābhyāṁ tan ninādena prāksvanāste tirohitāḥ ।।22।।

Kālī sprang skyward and alighted, pounding the earth
with Her two hands. The noise drowned out all
the previous sounds.

अट्टाट्टहासमशिवं शिवदूती चकार ह ॥
तैः शब्दैरसुरास्त्रेसुः शुम्भः कोपं परं ययौ ॥२३॥

aṭṭāṭṭahāsam aśivam śivadūtī cakāra ha॥
taiḥ śabdair asurās tresuḥ śumbhaḥ kopaṁ paraṁ yayau॥23॥

Śivadūtī laughed loudly and menacingly. When the asuras grew terrified at the sounds, Śumbha flew into a monstrous rage.

दुरात्मंस्तिष्ठ तिष्ठेति व्याजहाराम्बिका यदा ॥
तदा जयेत्यभिहितं देवैराकाशसंस्थितैः ॥२४॥

durātmaṁs tiṣṭha tiṣṭheti vyājahārāmbikā yadā ॥
tadā jayety abhihitaṁ devair ākāśasaṁsthitaiḥ ॥24॥

Ambikā cried out for him, that evil-natured one, to stop, and the gods cheered Her on to victory from their positions in the sky

शुम्भेनागत्य या शक्तिर्मुक्ता ज्वालातिभीषणा ॥
आयान्ती वह्निकूटाभा सा निरस्ता महोल्कया ॥२५॥

śumbhenāgatya yā śaktir muktā jvālātibhīṣaṇā ॥
āyāntl vahnikūṭābhā sā nirastā maholkayā ॥25॥

But Śumbha approached and hurled a fearsome, flaming spear, an incoming mass of fire that the Devī's own firebrand warded off.

सिंहनादेन शुम्भस्य व्याप्तं लोकत्रयान्तरम् ।।
निर्घातनिःस्वनो घोरो जितवानवनीपते ।।२६।।

śumbhenāgatya yā śaktir muktā jvālātibhīṣaṇā ।।
āyāntl vahnikūṭābhā sā nirastā maholkayā ।।26।।

Sumbha's leonine roar pervaded the space between heaven, earth, and the netherworld, but The Devī's Violent Thunderclap Drowned It Out, O king.

शुम्भमुक्ताञ्छरान्देवी शुम्भस्तत्प्रहिताञ्छरान् ।।
चिच्छेद स्वशरैरुग्रैः शतशोऽथ सहस्रशः ।।२७।।

śumbhamuktāñ charān Devī śumbhas tatprahitān charān ।।
ciccheda svaśarair ugraiḥ śataśo 'tha sahasraśaḥ ।।27।।

The Devī split Śumbha's flying arrows with sharp arrows of
Her own, and likewise he split Hers, each discharging arrows by the hundreds and thousands.

ततः सा चण्डिका क्रुद्धा शूलेनाभिजघान तम् ।।
स तदाभिहतो भूमौ मूर्च्छितो निपपात ह ।।२८।।

tataḥ sā Caṇḍikā kruddhā śūlenābhijaghāna tam ।।
sa tadābhihato bhūmau mūrcchito nipapāta ha ।।28।।

Then the enraged Caṇḍikā pierced Śumbha with Her lance. Wounded, he fainted and fell to the ground.

ततो निशुम्भः सम्प्राप्य चेतनामात्तकार्मुकः ।।
आजघान शरैर्देवीं कालीं केसरिणं तथा ।।२९।।

tato niśumbhah samprāpya cetanām āttakārmukaḥ ।।
ājaghāna śarair Devīṁ Kālīṁ kesariṇaṁ tathā ।।29।।

Meanwhile Niśumbha, regaining consciousness, seized his bow and shot arrows at theDevī, Kālī, and the lion.

पुनश्च कृत्वा बाहूनामयुतं दनुजेश्वरः ।।
चक्रायुधेन दितिजश्छादयामास चण्डिकाम् ।।३०।।

punaś ca kṛtvā bāhūnām ayutaṁ danujeśvaraḥ ।।
cakrāyudhena ditijaś chādayāmāsa Caṇḍikām ।।30।।

And then, creating ten thousand arms for himself, the daitya chief, that son of Diti, engulfed Caṇḍikā with ten thousand discuses.

ततो भगवती क्रुद्धा दुर्गा दुर्गार्तिनाशिनी ।।
चिच्छेद तानि चक्राणि स्वशरैः सायकांश्च तान् ।।३१।।

tato Bhagavatī kruddhā Durgā Durgārtināśiṇī ।।
ciccheda tāni cakrāṇi svaśaraiḥ sāyakāṁś ca tān ।।31।।

Thus provoked, the glorious Durgā, who destroys adversity and afflictions, cut through his discuses and missiles with arrows of Her own.

ततो निशुम्भो वेगेन गदामादाय चण्डिकाम् ।।
अभ्यधावत वै हन्तुं दैत्यसेनासमावृतः ।।३२।।

tato niśumbho vegena gadām ādāya Caṇḍikām ।।
abhyadhāvata vai hantuṁ daityasenāsamāvṛtaḥ ।।32।।

Niśumbha, surrounded by his demon army, swiftly seized his club and rushed at Caṇḍikā to kill Her.

तस्यापतत एवाशु गदां चिच्छेद चण्डिका ।।
खड्गेन शितधारेण स च शूलं समाददे ।।३३।।

tasyāpatata evāśu gadāṁ ciccheda Caṇḍikā ।।
khaḍgena śitadhāreṇa sa ca śūlaṁ samādade ।।33।।

Instantly She split the onrushing Niśumbha's club with Her keen-edged sword. He grasped his lance.

शूलहस्तं समायान्तं निशुम्भममरार्दनम् ॥
हृदि विव्याध शूलेन वेगाविद्धेन चण्डिका ॥३४॥

śūlahastaṁ samāyāntaṁ niśumbham amarārdanam ॥
hṛdi vivyādha śūlena vegāviddhena Caṇḍikā ॥34॥

and as he approached with weapon in hand, Caṇḍikā pierced him, the afflictor of the gods, through the heart with a swiftly hurled spear.

भिन्नस्य तस्य शूलेन हृदयान्निःसृतोऽपरः ॥
महाबलो महावीर्यस्तिष्ठेति पुरुषो वदन् ॥३५॥

bhinnasya tasya śūlena hṛdayān niḥsṛto 'paraḥ ॥
mahābalo mahāvīryas tiṣṭheti puruṣo vadan ॥35॥

From his heart's gaping wound came forth another mighty and valorous being, who shouted for the Devī to stop.

तस्य निष्क्रामतो देवी प्रहस्य स्वनवत्ततः ॥
शिरश्चिच्छेद खड्गेन ततोऽसावपतद्भुवि ॥३६॥

tasya niṣkrāmato Devī prahasya svanavat tataḥ ॥
śiraś ciccheda khaḍgena tato 'sāvapatad bhuvi ॥36॥

Bursting into derisive laughter, She severed his head with Her sword, and the figure who had thus emerged fell to the ground.

ततः सिंहश्चखादोग्रं दंष्ट्राक्षुण्णशिरोधरान् ॥
असुरांस्तांस्तथा काली शिवदूती तथापरान् ॥३७॥

tataḥ siṁhaś cakhādogradaṁṣṭrākṣuṇṇaśirodharān ॥
asurāṁs tāṁs tathā Kālī śivadūtī tathāparān ॥37॥

The lion then devoured the asuras whose necks it had crushed with its fearsome fangs, while Kālī and Śivadūtī devoured others.

कौमारीशक्तिनिर्भिन्नाः केचिन्नेशुर्महासुराः ॥
ब्रह्माणीमन्त्रपूतेन तोयेनान्ये निराकृताः ॥३८॥

Kaumārīśaktinirbhinnāḥ kecin neśur mahāsurāḥ ॥
brahmāṇīmantrapūtena toyenānye nirākṛtāḥ ॥38॥

Great asuras perished, pierced through by Kaumārī's spear; others shrank away from the water sanctified by Brahmāṇī's mantras.

माहेश्वरीत्रिशूलेन भिन्नाः पेतुस्तथापरे ॥
वाराहीतुण्डघातेन केचिच्चूर्णीकृता भुवि ॥३९॥

māheśvarītriśūlena bhinnāḥ petus tathāpare ॥
Vārāhītuṇḍaghātena kecic cūrṇīkṛtā bhuvi ॥39॥

Others fell, ripped open by Māheśvarī's trident; some lay on the ground, smashed by the blows of Vārāhī's snout.

खण्डं खण्डं च चक्रेण वैष्णव्या दानवाः कृताः ।।
वज्रेण चौन्द्रीहस्ताग्रविमुक्तेन तथापरे ।।४०।।

khaṇḍaṁ khaṇḍaṁ ca cakreṇa vaiṣṇavyā dānavāḥ kṛtāḥ ।।
vajreṇa caindrīhastāgravimuktena tathāpare ।।40।।

Dānavas were cut to pieces, some by Vaiṣṇavī's discus and others by the thunderbolt discharged from Aindrī's fingertips.

केचिद्विनेशुरसुराः केचिन्नष्टा महाहवात् ।।
भक्षिताश्चापरे कालीशिवदूतीमृगाधिपैः ।।ॐ ।।४१।।

kecid vineśur asurāḥ kecin naṣṭā mahāhavāt ।।
bhakṣitāś cāpare Kālīśivadūtīmṛgādhipaiḥ।।Om ।।41।।

Some asuras perished, some fled from the great battle, and others were devoured by Kālī, Śivadūtī, and the lion.

इति श्रीमार्कण्डेयपुराणे सावर्णिके मन्वन्तरे देवीमाहात्म्ये
निशुम्भवधो नाम नवमोऽध्याय: ।।९।।

iti śrīmārkaṇḍeyapurāṇe sāvarṇike
manvantare devīmāhātmye
niśumbhavādho nāma navamo'dhyāyaḥ ॥9॥

Thus ends the ninth chapter, titled 'The Slaying of Niśumbha,' in the Devī Māhātmya of the Mārkaṇḍeya Purāṇa, set in the Sāvarṇi Manvantara.

।। दशमोऽध्यायः ।।

शुम्भ-संहार

।। Tenth Chapter ।।

The Slaying of Shumbha

।। ध्यानम् ।।

ॐ उत्तप्तहेमरुचिरां रविचन्द्रवह्नि-
नेत्रां धनुश्शरयुताङ्कुशपाशशूलम्।
रम्यैर्भुजैश्च दधतीं शिवशक्तिरूपां
कामेश्वरीं हृदि भजामि धृतेन्दुलेखाम् ।।

।। dhyānam ।।

oṁ uttaptahemarucirāṁ ravicandravahninetrāṁ
dhanuśśarayutāṅkuśapāśaśūlam ।
ramyair bhujaiś ca dadhatīṁ śivaśaktirūpāṁ
kāmeśvarīṁ hṛdi bhajāmi dhṛtendulekhām ।।

Meditation Verse (Dhyānam):

I worship in my heart Kāmeśvarī, who holds the crescent moon on her head, and whose form shines like molten gold. She has the sun, moon, and fire as her three eyes, and she carries a bow, arrows, goad, noose, and a trident in her beautiful arms. She is the very embodiment of Śiva's power (Śakti), radiating beauty and divine strength.

"ॐ" ऋषिरुवाच ॥१॥

ṛṣir uvāca ॥1॥

The seer said:

निशुम्भं निहतं दृष्ट्वा भ्रातरं प्राणसम्मितम् ।
हन्यमानं बलं चौव शुम्भः क्रुद्धोऽब्रवीद्वचः ॥२॥

niśumbhaṁ nihataṁ dṛṣṭvā bhrātaraṁ prāṇasammitam ।
hanyamānaṁ balaṁ caiva śumbhaḥ kiuddho
'bravld vacaḥ ॥2॥

Seeing the lifeless body of Niśumbha, the brother who was as dear to him as life itself, and seeing his forces being slaughtered, the enraged Śumbha spoke these words:

बलावलेपादुष्टे त्वं मा दुर्गे गर्वमावह ।।
अन्यासां बलमाश्रित्य युद्ध्यसे यातिमानिनी ।।३।।

balāvalepaduṣṭe tvam Mā Durge garvam āvaha ।।
anyāsāṁ balam āśritya yuddhyase yātimāninī ।।3।।

'O Durgā, who are corrupt with the arrogance of power, do not show your pride here, for though you are haughty, you fight depending on the strength of others.'

देव्युवाच ।।४।।

Devy uvāca ।।4।।

The Devī said:

एकैवाहं जगत्यत्र द्वितीया का ममापरा ।।
पश्यैता दुष्ट मय्येव विशन्त्यो मद्विभूतयः ।।५।।

Ekaivāham jagaty atra dvitīyā kā mamāparā ।।
paśyaitā duṣṭa mayy eva viśantyo madvibhūtayaḥ ।।5।।

'I Am Alone Here in the world. Who else is there besides Me? Behold, O vile one! These are but Projections of My Own Power, now Entering Back into Me.'

ततः समस्तास्ता देव्यो ब्रह्माणीप्रमुखा लयम् ।।
तस्या देव्यास्तनौ जग्मुरेकैवासीत्तदाम्बिका ।।६।।

tataḥ samastās tā Devyo Brahmāṇīpramukhā layam ।।
tasyā Devyās tanau jagmur ekaivāsīt Tadāmbikā ।।6।।

Thereupon All Those Goddesses, Led By Brahmāṇī, Merged Into The Devī's Body. Then Ambikā Alone Remained.

देव्युवाच ।।७।।

Devy uvāca ।।7।।

The Devī Said:

अहं विभूत्या बहुभिरिह रूपैर्यदास्थिता ।।
तत्संहृतं मयैकैव तिष्ठाम्याजौ स्थिरो भव ।।८।।

Ahaṁ vibhūtyā bahubhir iha rūpair yadāsthitā ।।
tat saṁhṛtaṁ Mayaikaiva tiṣṭhāmy ājau sthiro Bhava ।।8।।

'I have Now Withdrawn the Many Forms I Inhabited Here, Projected by My power. I Stand Alone. Be resolute in combat'.

ऋषिरुवाच ॥९॥

ṛṣir uvāca ॥9॥

The seer said:

ततः प्रववृते युद्धं देव्याः शुम्भस्य चोभयोः ॥
पश्यतां सर्वदेवानामसुराणां च दारुणम् ॥१०॥

tataḥ pravavṛte yuddhaṁ Devyāḥ śumbhasya cobhayoḥ ॥
paśyatāṁ sarvadevānām asurāṇāṁ ca dāruṇam ॥10॥

Then a horrific battle broke out between the two of them, the Devī and Śumbha, while all the Gods and asuras looked on.

शरवर्षैः शितैः शस्त्रैस्तथास्त्रैश्चैव दारुणैः ॥
तयोर्युद्धमभूद्भूयः सर्वलोकभयङ्करम् ॥११॥

śaravarṣaiḥ śitaiḥ śastrais tathāstraiś caiva dāruṇaiḥ ॥
tayor yuddham abhūd bhūyaḥ sarvalokabhayaṅkaram ॥11॥

With showers of arrows, sharp weapons, and terrifying missiles, the two met again in a combat that frightened all the world.

दिव्यान्यस्त्राणि शतशो मुमुचे यान्यथाम्बिका ॥
बभञ्ज तानि दैत्येन्द्रस्तत्प्रतीघातकर्तृभिः ॥१२॥

Divyāny astrāṇi śataśo mumuce yāny Athāmbikā ॥
babhañja tāni daityendras tatpratīghātakartṛbhiḥ ॥12॥

The Wondrous Weapons That Ambikā Now Unleashed by the hundreds, the daitya chief deflected with defensive strikes.

मुक्तानि तेन चास्त्राणि दिव्यानि परमेश्वरी ॥
बभञ्ज लीलयैवोग्रहुङ्कारोच्चारणादिभिः ॥१३॥

muktāni tena cāstrāṇi Divyāni Parameśvarī ॥
babhañja līlayaivograhuṅkāroccāraṇādibhiḥ ॥13॥

And the magic missiles that he hurled, the Supreme Devī Shattered Playfully With Fierce Cries of Contempt.

ततः शरशतैर्देवीमाच्छादयत सोऽसुरः ॥
सापि तत्कुपिता देवी धनुश्चिच्छेद चेषुभिः ॥१४॥

tataḥ śaraśatair Devīm ācchādayata so 'suraḥ ॥
sāpi tatkupitā Devī dhanuś ciccheda ceṣubhiḥ ॥14॥

Then the asura covered Her with hundreds of arrows. Provoked, the Devī Discharged Her arrows and Split his bow.

छिन्ने धनुषि दैत्येन्द्रस्तथा शक्तिमथाददे ॥
चिच्छेद देवी चक्रेण तामप्यस्य करे स्थिताम् ॥१५॥

chinne dhanuṣi daityendras tathā śaktim athādade ॥
ciccheda Devī cakreṇa tām apy asya kare sthitām ॥15॥

His bow broken, the daitya chief took up his spear, but even as it rested in his hand, the Devī Cut Through it With Her Discus

ततः खड्गमुपादाय शतचन्द्रं च भानुमत् ॥
अभ्यधावत्तदा' देवीं दैत्यानामधिपेश्वरः ॥१६॥

tataḥ khaḍgam upādāya śatacandraṁ ca bhānumat ॥
abhyadhāvat tadā Devīṁ daityānām adhipeśvaraḥ ॥16॥

Then, grasping his sword, emblazoned with a hundred moons, the supreme lord of the daityas rushed at the Devī.

तस्यापतत एवाशु खड्गं चिच्छेद चण्डिका ॥
धनुर्मुक्तैः शितैर्बाणैश्चर्म चार्ककरामलम् ॥१७॥

tasyāpatata evāśu khaḍgaṁ ciccheda Caṇḍikā ॥
dhanurmuktaiḥ śitair bāṇaiś carma cārkakarāmalam ॥17॥

As he advanced, Caṇḍikā Broke his sword with sharp Arrows shot from Her bow, and also his shield that shone as the sun's rays.

हताश्वः स तदा दैत्यश्छिन्नधन्वा विसारथिः ।।
जग्राह मुद्‌गरं घोरमम्बिकानिधनोद्यतः ।।१८।।

hatāśvaḥ sa tadā daityaś chinnadhanvā visārathiḥ ।।
jagrāha mudgaraṁ ghoram Ambikānidhanodyataḥ ।।18।।

His steed slain, his bow broken, his chariot wrecked, the daitya grasped his fearsome mace, intent on destroying Ambikā.

चिच्छेदापततस्तस्य मुद्‌गरं निशितैः शरैः ।।
तथापि सोऽभ्यधावत्तां मुष्टिमुद्यम्य वेगवान् ।।१९।।

cicchedāpatatas tasya mudgaraṁ niśitaiḥ śaraiḥ ।।
tathāpi so 'bhyadhāvat tāṁ muṣṭim udyamya vegavān ।।19।।

With sharp Arrows, She Shattered the onrushing Śumbha's mace. Still, he rushed at Her with fist upraised.

स मुष्टिं पातयामास हृदये दैत्यपुङ्गवः ।।
देव्यास्तं चापि सा देवी तलेनोरस्यताडयत् ।।२०।।

sa muṣṭim pātayāmāsa hṛdaye daityapuṅgavah ॥
Devyās taṁ cāpi sā Devī talenorasy atāḍayat ॥20॥

The daitya chief slammed his fist down on the Devī's Heart, and She Struck him on the chest with Her Palm.

तलप्रहाराभिहतो निपपात महीतले ॥
स दैत्यराजः सहसा पुनरेव तथोत्थितः ॥२१॥

talaprahārābhihato nipapāta mahītale ॥
sa daityarājaḥ sahasā punareva tathotthitaḥ ॥21॥

Struck by that blow, the demon king fell to the ground. At once, he rose up again.

उत्पत्य च प्रगृह्योच्चैर्देवीं गगनमास्थितः ॥
तत्रापि सा निराधारा युयुधे तेन चण्डिका ॥२२॥

utpatya ca pragṛhyoccair Devīṁ gaganam āsthitaḥ ॥
tatrāpi sā nirādhārā yuyudhe tena Caṇḍikā ॥22॥

And springing upward, he seized the Devī and ascended high into the sky. There in midair Caṇḍikā Battled with him.

नियुद्धं खे तदा दैत्यश्चण्डिका च परस्परम् ।।
चक्रतुः प्रथमं सिद्धमुनिविस्मयकारकम् ।।२३।।

niyuddhaṁ khe tadā daityaś Caṇḍikā ca parasparam ।।
cakratuḥ prathamaṁ siddhamunivismayakārakam ।।23।।

In the sky, the daitya and Caṇḍikā fought hand to hand as never before, to the astonishment of saints and sages

ततो नियुद्धं सुचिरं कृत्वा तेनाम्बिका सह ।।
उत्पात्य भ्रामयामास चिक्षेप धरणीतले ।।२४।।

tato niyuddhaṁ suciraṁ kṛtvā tenāmbikā saha ।।
utpāṭya bhrāmayāmāsa cikṣepa dharaṇītale ।।24।।

And after prolonged combat, Ambikā Snatched him up, swung him around, and Flung him to the earth.

स क्षिप्तो धरणीं प्राप्य मुष्टिमुद्यम्य वेगितः ।।
अभ्यधावत दुष्टात्मा चण्डिकानिधनेच्छया ।।२५।।

sa kṣipto dharaṇīm prāpya muṣṭim udyamya vegataḥ ।।
abhyadhāvata duṣṭātmā Caṇḍikānidhanecchayā ।।25।।

Striking the ground, the evil one immediately raised his fist and ran forward, desirous of destroying Ambikā.

तमायान्तं ततो देवी सर्वदैत्यजनेश्वरम् ॥
जगत्यां पातयामास भित्त्वा शूलेन वक्षसि ॥२६॥

tam āyāntaṁ tato Devī sarvadaityajaneśvaram ॥
jagaty āṁ pātayāmāsa bhitvā śūlena vakṣasi ॥26॥

The Devī thrust Her Spear through his chest and Threw that onrushing lord of all demonic creatures to the ground.

स गतासुः पपातोर्व्यां देवीशूलाग्रविक्षतः ॥
चालयन् सकलां पृथ्वीं साब्धिद्वीपां सपर्वताम् ॥२७॥

sa gatāsuḥ papātorvyāṁ Devī śūlāgravikṣataḥ ॥
cālayan sakalāṁ pṛthvīṁ sābdhidvīpām saparvatām ॥27॥

Pierced through by The Devī's Weapon, his life-breath gone, he fell to the ground, shaking all the earth together with its oceans, islands, and mountains.

ततः प्रसन्नमखिलं हते तस्मिन् दुरात्मनि ॥
जगत्स्वास्थ्यमतीवाप निर्मलं चाभवन्नभः ॥२८॥

tataḥ prasannam akhilaṁ hate tasmin durātmani ॥
jagat svāsthyam atīvāpa nirmalaṁ cābhavan nabhaḥ ॥28॥

When the evil one was slain, all the universe became calm, regaining its natural order, and the sky cleared.

उत्पातमेघाः सोल्का ये प्रागासंस्ते शमं ययुः ।।
सरितो मार्गवाहिन्यस्तथासंस्तत्र पातिते ।।२९।।

utpātameghāḥ solkā ye prāgāsaṁs te śamaṁ yayuḥ ।।
sarito mārgavāhinyas tathāsaṁs tatra pātite ।।29।।

The flaming clouds of portent that formerly gathered now subsided, and rivers again flowed along their courses when Śumbha fell slain.

ततो देवगणाः सर्वे हर्षनिर्भरमानसाः ।।
बभूवुर्निहते तस्मिन् गन्धर्वा ललितं जगुः ।।३०।।

tato devagaṇāḥ sarve harṣanirbharamānasāḥ ।।
babhūvur nihate tasmin gandharvā lalitaṁ jaguḥ ।।30।।

All the hosts of Gods were overjoyed when he lay slain, and the celestial musicians sang sweetly

अवादयंस्तथैवान्ये ननृतुश्चाप्सरोगणाः ।।
ववुः पुण्यास्तथा वाताः सुप्रभोऽभूद्दिवाकरः ।।३१।।

avādayaṁs tathaivānye nanṛtuś cāpsarogaṇāḥ ।।
vavuḥ puṇyās tathā vātāḥ suprabho 'bhūd divākaraḥ ।।31।।

Others sounded their instruments, and throngs of heavenly nymphs danced. Favorable winds blew, and the sun shone in glory.

जज्वलुश्चाग्नयः शान्ताः शान्ता दिग्जनितस्वनाः ॥ॐ ॥३२॥

jajvaluś cāgnayaḥ śāntāḥ śāntadigjanitasvanāḥ॥Om ॥32॥

The sacred fires glowed peacefully, and the sounds born of the four directions faded away.

इति श्रीमार्कण्डेयपुराणे सावर्णिके मन्वन्तरे देवीमाहात्म्ये शुम्भवधो नाम दशमोऽध्यायः ॥१०॥

iti śrīmārkaṇḍeyapurāṇe sāvarṇike
manvantare devīmāhātmye
śumbhavādho nāma daśamo'dhyāyaḥ ॥10॥

Thus ends the tenth chapter, titled 'The Slaying of Śumbha,' in the Devī Māhātmya of the Mārkaṇḍeya Purāṇa, set in the Sāvarṇi Manvantara.

॥ एकादशोऽध्यायः ॥

देवताओं द्वारा देवी की सतुति तथा देवी द्वारा देवताओं को वरदानः

नारायणी-स्तुति

॥ Eleventh Chapter ॥

Hymn to Narayani

The gods' praise of the Goddess and the boon granted by the Goddess to the gods.

॥ ध्यानम् ॥

ॐ बालरविद्युतिमिन्दुकिरीटां तुङ्गकुचां नयनत्रययुक्ताम् ।
स्मेरमुखीं वरदाङ्कुशपाशाभीतिकरां प्रभजे भुवनेशीम् ॥

॥ dhyānam ॥

oṁ bālaravidyutim indukirīṭāṁ
tuṅgakucāṁ nayanatrayayuktām ।
smeramukhīṁ varadāṅkuśapāśābhītikarāṁ
prabhaje bhuvaneśīm ॥

I worship the Queen of the world (Bhuvaneśī), who wears a moon-shaped crown and shines with the youthful radiance of lightning. She has three eyes and a smiling face. She grants boons and holds a goad and noose that inspire awe and protection.

"ॐ" ऋषिरुवाच ॥१॥

ṛṣir uvāca ॥1॥

The seer said:

देव्या हते तत्र महासुरेन्द्रे सेन्द्राः
सुरा वह्निपुरोगमास्ताम् ॥
कात्यायनीं तुष्टुवुरिष्टलाभाद्
विकाशिवक्त्राब्जविकाशिताशाः ॥२॥

Devyā hate tatra mahāsurendre
sendrāḥ surā vahnipurogamās tāṁ ॥
kātyāyanīṁ tuṣṭuvur iṣṭalābhād
vikāsivaktrābjavikāsitāśāḥ ॥2॥

After the Devī had slain the great asura chief, Indra and the other gods, led by Agni, praised Kātyāyanī for granting their wishes. With hopes fulfilled, their faces beamed.

देवि प्रपन्नार्तिहरे प्रसीद प्रसीद मातर्जगतोऽखिलस्य ॥
प्रसीद विश्वेश्वरि पाहि विश्वं त्वमीश्वरी देवि चराचरस्य ॥३॥

Devi prapannārtihare prasīda prasīda mātar
jagato 'khilasya ||
prasīda viśveśvari pāhi viśvam tvam īśvarī
Devi carācarasya ||3||

'O Devī, Who remove the sufferings of those who take refuge in you, be gracious. Be Gracious, Mother of the entire world. Be Gracious, Ruler of All. Protect the universe, O Devī, Who is the Ruler of the Moving and The Unmoving'.

आधारभूता जगतस्त्वमेका महीस्वरूपेण यतः स्थितासि ॥
अपां स्वरूपस्थितया त्वयैत-दाप्यायते कृत्स्नमलङ्घ्यवीर्ये ॥४॥

ādhārabhūtā jagatas tvam ekā
mahīsvarūpeṇa yataḥ stithāsi ||
apāṁ svarūpasthitayā tvayaitad
āpyāyate kṛtsnam alaṅghyavīrye ||4||

You Alone Are The Sustaining Power Of The World, for You Abide In The Form Of The Earth. By You, Who Exist In The Form Of Water, all this universe prospers, O Devī Of Unsurpassable Strength.

त्वं वैष्णवी शक्तिरनन्तवीर्या
विश्वस्य बीजं परमासि माया ॥
सम्मोहितं देवि समस्तमेतत्
त्वं वै प्रसन्ना भुवि मुक्तिहेतुः ॥५॥

tvaṁ Vaiṣṇavī śaktir anantavīryā
viśvasya bījam paramāsi Māyā ॥
sammohitaṁ Devi samastam etat tvaṁ
vai prasannā bhuvi muktihetuḥ ॥5॥

Of Boundless Might, You Are Viṣṇu's Power, The Source Of All, The Supreme Māyā. Deluded, O Devī, is all this universe. In this world, You Alone, When Pleased, Are The Cause Of Liberation.

विद्याः समस्तास्तव देवि भेदाः
स्त्रियः समस्ताः सकला जगत्सु ॥
त्वयैकया पूरितमम्बयैतत्
का ते स्तुतिः स्तव्यपरा परोक्तिः ॥६॥

vidyāḥ samastās tava Devi bhedāḥ
striyaḥ samastāḥ sakalā jagatsu ॥
tvayaikayā pūritam Ambayaitat kā
te stutiḥ stavyaparāparoktiḥ ॥6॥

All Forms Of Knowledge Are Your Aspects, O Devī, as are All Women In The world. By You Alone, The Mother, Is

This world filled. What praise can be sung to You Who Are Beyond Praise?

सर्वभूता यदा देवी स्वर्गमुक्तिप्रदायिनी ॥
त्वं स्तुता स्तुतये का वा भवन्तु परमोक्तयः ॥७॥

sarvabhūtā yadā Devī bhuktimuktipradāyinī ॥
Tvaṁ stutā stutaye kā vā bhavantu paramoktayaḥ ॥7॥

O Devī, Who Have Become All Things, Who Bestow Enjoyment And Liberation—when You are praised, what Words, however excellent, can extol You?

सर्वस्य बुद्धिरूपेण जनस्य हृदि संस्थिते ॥
स्वर्गापवर्गदे देवि नारायणि नमोऽस्तु ते ॥८॥

sarvasya buddhirūpeṇa janasya hṛdi saṁsthite ॥
svargāpavargade Devi Nārāyaṇī namo 'stu te ॥8॥

Salutation be To you, Devī Nārāyaṇī, Who Abide As Intelligence In The Hearts Of All Beings, Granting Heavenly Reward And Final Liberation.

कलाकाष्ठादिरूपेण परिणामप्रदायिनि ॥
विश्वस्योपरतौ शक्ते नारायणि नमोऽस्तु ते ॥९॥

kalākāṣṭhādirūpeṇa pariṇāmapradāyini ॥
viśvasyoparatau śakte Nārāyaṇi namo 'stu te ॥9॥

Salutation be To You, Nārāyaṇī, Who Bring Change As The Moments Of EverPassing Time, Who Are The Power At The Cessation of the universe.

सर्वमङ्गलमंङ्गल्ये शिवे सर्वार्थसाधिके ॥
शरण्ये त्र्यम्बके गौरि नारायणि नमोऽस्तु ते ॥१०॥

sarvamaṅgalamāṅgalye śive sarvārthasādhike ॥
saraṇye tryambake Gauri Nārāyaṇi namo 'stu te ॥10॥

Salutation be To You, Nārāyaṇī, Who Are The Good Of All Good, The Auspicious One; To You Who Accomplish Every Intent; To You, The Refuge, The All-Knowing, Shining Gauri!

सृष्टिस्थितिविनाशानां शक्तिभूते सनातनि ॥
गुणाश्रये गुणमये नारायणि नमोऽस्तु ते ॥११॥

sṛṣṭisthitivināśānāṁ śaktibhūte sanātani ॥
Guṇāsraye Guṇamaye Nārāyaṇi namo 'stu te ॥11॥

Salutation be To You, Nārāyaṇī, Who Are The Power Of Creation, Sustenance, And Destruction; Who Are Eternal;

Who Are The Source And Embodiment
Of The Threefold Energy.

शरणागतदीनार्तपरित्राणपरायणे ।।
सर्वस्यार्तिहरे देवि नारायणि नमोऽस्तु ते ।।१२।।

śaraṇāgatadīnārtaparitrāṇaparāyaṇe ।।
sarvasyārtihare Devi Nārāyaṇi namo 'stu te ।।12।।

Salutation be To You, Nārāyaṇī, Who Are Intent On Rescuing the distressed and afflicted that take refuge in You; to You, O Devī, Who Remove the suffering of all.

हंसयुक्तविमानस्थे ब्रह्माणीरूपधारिणि ।।
कौशाम्भःक्षरिके देवि नारायणि नमोऽस्तु ते ।।१३।।

haṁsayuktavimānasthe Brahmāṇīrūpadhāriṇi ।।
kauśāmbhaḥkṣarike Devi Nārāyaṇi namo 'stu te ।।13।।

Salutation be To You, Nārāyaṇī, Who Assume The Form Of Brahmāṇi, Riding In A Swanky Chariot, O Devī, And Sprinkling sanctified water.

त्रिशूलचन्द्राहिधरे महावृषभवाहिनि ।।
माहेश्वरीस्वरूपेण नारायणि नमोऽस्तु ते ।।१४।।

triśūlacandrāhidhare Mahāvṛṣabhavāhini ।।
Māheśvarīsvarūpeṇa Nārāyaṇi namo 'stu te ।।14।।

Salutation be To You, Nārāyaṇī, who have the form of Māheśvari, bearing trident, moon, and serpent, and Riding a mighty bull.

मयूरकुक्कुटवृते महाशक्तिधरेऽनघे ।।
कौमारीरूपसंस्थाने नारायणि नमोऽस्तु ते ।।१५।।

mayūrakukkuṭavṛte mahāśaktidhare 'naghe ।।
Kaumārīrūpasaṁsthāne Nārāyaṇi namo 'stu te ।।15।।

Salutation be To You, Nārāyaṇī, Who Have The Form Of Kaumāri, The Faultless One attended by peacock and cock, and Bearing A Great Spear.

शङ्खचक्रगदाशार्ङ्गगृहीतपरमायुधे ।।
प्रसीद वैष्णवीरूपे नारायणि नमोऽस्तु ते ।।१६।।

śaṅkhacakragadāśārṅgagṛhītaparamāyudhe ।।
prasīda Vaiṣṇavīrūpe Nārāyaṇi namo 'stu te ।।16।।

Salutation be To you, Nārāyaṇī, Who Have The Form Of Vaisṇavi, Holding The Supreme Weapons of conch, discus, mace, and bow. Be Gracious!

गृहीतोग्रमहाचक्रे दंष्ट्रोद्धृतवसुंधरे ॥
वराहरूपिणि शिवे नारायणि नमोऽस्तु ते ॥१७॥

gṛhītogramahācakre daṁṣṭroddhṛtavasundhare ||
Varāharūpiṇi śive Nārāyaṇi namo 'stu te ||17||

Salutation be To You, Nārāyaṇī, Auspicious One, Who
Have Viṣṇu's Boarlike Form, Grasping
A Great, Formidable Discus and Uplifting
The Earth With Your tusks.

नृसिंहरूपेणोग्रेण हन्तुं दैत्यान् कृतोद्यमे ॥
त्रैलोक्यत्राणसहिते नारायणि नमोऽस्तु ते ॥१८॥

Nṛsiṁharūpeṇogreṇa hantuṁ daityān kṛtodyame ||
trailokyatrāṇasahite Nārāyaṇi namo 'stu te ||18||

Salutation be To You, Nārāyani, Who In The Ferocious
Form Of The Man-Lion Are Intent On Killing the daityas
and Protecting the three worlds.

किरीटिनि महावज्रे सहस्रनयनोज्ज्वले ॥
वृत्रप्राणहरे चैन्द्रि नारायणि नमोऽस्तु ते ॥१९॥

kirīṭini mahāvajre sahasranayanojjvale ||
vṛtraprāṇahare Caindri Nārāyaṇi namo 'stu te ||19||

Salutation be To You, Nārāyaṇī, Who is Adorned With Diadem, great thunderbolt, and Thousand-Eyed Radiance; to You, O Aindrī, Who Took the demon Vṛtra's life-breath!

शिवदूतीस्वरूपेण हतदैत्यमहाबले ॥
घोररूपे महारावे नारायणि नमोऽस्तु ते ॥२०॥

śivadūtīsvarūpeṇa hatadaityamahābale ॥
Ghorarūpe mahārāve Nārāyaṇi namo 'stu te ॥20॥

Salutation be To You, Nārāyaṇī, Who In The Form Of Śivadūtī, Of Frightful Visage and Piercing Shrieks, Slew the mighty demon army.

दंष्ट्राकरालवदने शिरोमालाविभूषणे ॥
चामुण्डे मुण्डमथने नारायणि नमोऽस्तु ते ॥२१॥

daṁṣṭrākarālavadane śiromālāvibhūṣaṇe ॥
Cāmuṇḍe muṇḍamathane Nārāyaṇi namo 'stu te ॥21॥

Salutation be To You, Nārāyaṇī, Whose Mouth Bares Its Terrifying Teeth and Whose Neck Is Adorned With A Garland Of Skulls; To You, O Cāmuṇḍā, Destroyer of Muṇḍa!

लक्ष्मि लज्जे महाविद्ये श्रद्धे पुष्टिस्वधे ध्रुवे ॥
महारात्रि महाऽविद्ये नारायणि नमोऽस्तु ते ॥२२॥

Lakṣmi lajje mahāvidye śraddhe puṣṭi svadhe dhruve ॥
Mahārātri Mahāmāye Nārāyaṇi namo 'stu te ॥22॥

Salutation be To You, Nārāyaṇī, Who Are Good Fortune, Modesty, Great Knowledge, Faith, Prosperity, Satisfaction to the ancestral spirits, Constancy, The Great Night, and The Great Illusion.

मेधे सरस्वति वरे भूति बाभ्रवि तामसि ॥
नियते त्वं प्रसीदेशे नारायणि नमोऽस्तु ते ॥२३॥

medhe Sarasvati vare bhūti bābhravi tāmasi ॥
niyate Tvaṁ prasīdeśe Nārāyaṇi namo 'stu te ॥23॥

Salutation be To You, Nārāyaṇī, Most Excellent Sarasvatī, Who Are Intelligence and Well-Being, The Divine Consort and The Dark One, Ever Constant. Be gracious, O You Who Are Supreme!

सर्वस्वरूपे सर्वेशे सर्वशक्तिसमन्विते ॥
भयेभ्यस्त्राहि नो देवि दुर्गे देवि नमोऽस्तु ते ॥२४॥

Sarvasvarūpe Sarveśe sarvaśaktisamanvite ॥
bhayebhyas trāhi no Devi Durge Devi namo 'stu te ॥24॥

O Devī, Who Exist In The Form Of All, Who Are The Ruler Of All, Possessing All Power, protect us from fears. O Devī Durgā, salutation be to You!

एतत्ते वदनं सौम्यं लोचनत्रयभूषितम् ॥
पातु नः सर्वभीतिभ्यः कात्यायनि नमोऽस्तु ते ॥२५॥

etat te vadanaṁ saumyaṁ locanatrayabhūṣitam ॥
pātu naḥ sarvabhūtebhyaḥ Kātyāyani namo 'stu te ॥25॥

May This Gentle Face Of Yours, Adorned With Three Eyes, protect us in every way. O Kātyāyanī, salutation be to you!

ज्वालाकरालमत्युग्रमशेषासुरसूदनम् ॥
त्रिशूलं पातु नो भीतेर्भद्रकालि नमोऽस्तु ते ॥२६॥

jvālākarālam atyugram aśeṣāsurasūdanam ॥
triśūlam pātu no bhlter Bhadrakāli namo 'stu te ॥26॥

May Your Terrible, Flaming Trident, Exceedingly Sharp and Destroying all asuras, protect us from dread. O Bhadrakālī, salutation be to You!

हिनस्ति दैत्यतेजांसि स्वनेनापूर्य या जगत् ॥
सा घण्टा पातु नो देवि पापेभ्योऽनः सुतानिव ॥२७॥

hinasti daityatejāṁsi svanenāpūrya yā jagat ॥
sā ghaṇṭā pātu no Devi pāpebhyo naḥ sutāniva ॥27॥

May Your bell that destroys the daityas' life-force and fills the world with its ringing protect us from all evils, O Devī, even as a mother protects her children.

असुरासृग्वसापङ्कचर्चितस्ते करोज्ज्वलः ॥
शुभाय खड्गो भवतु चण्डिके त्वां नता वयम् ॥२८॥

asurāsṛgvasāpaṅkacarcitas te karojjvalaḥ ॥
śubhāya khaḍgo bhavatu Caṇḍike Tvāṁ natā vayam ॥28॥

May Your Sword, smeared with the mire of asuras' blood and fat and blazing as the sun's rays, be for our welfare. O Caṇḍikā, we bow to You!

रोगानशेषानपहंसि तुष्टा
रुष्टा* तु कामान् सकलानभीष्टान् ॥
त्वामाश्रितानां न विपन्नराणां
त्वामाश्रिता ह्याश्रयतां प्रयान्ति ॥२९॥

rogān aśesān apahaṁsi tuṣṭā ruṣṭā
tu kāmān sakalān abhīṣṭān ॥
Tvām āśritānāṁ na vipannarāṇām
tvām āśritā hy āśrayatāṁ prayānti ॥29॥

When pleased, You Destroy All Afflictions, but when Displeased, You Thwart all aspirations. No calamity befalls those who have taken refuge In You, and they who resort To You become a refuge to others.

एतत्कृतं यत्कदनं त्वयाद्य
धर्मद्विषां देवि महासुराणाम् ॥
रूपैरनेकैर्बहुधाऽऽत्ममूर्तिं
कृत्वाम्बिके तत्प्रकरोति कान्या ॥३०॥

etat kṛtaṁ yat kadanam tvayādya
dharmadviṣām Devi mahāsurāṇām ॥
rūpair anekair bahudhātmamūrtiṁ
kṛtvāmbike tat prakaroti kānyā ॥30॥

O Devī, Multiplying Your Own Form Into Many, You Have Wrought Destruction on the mighty asuras who hate righteousness. O Ambikā, Who Else can accomplish that?

विद्यासु शास्त्रेषु विवेकदीपे-ष्वाद्येषु वाक्येषु च का त्वदन्या ॥
ममत्वगर्तेऽतिमहान्धकारे विभ्रामयत्येतदतीव विश्वम् ॥३१॥

vidyāsu śāstreṣu vivekadīpeṣv
ādyeṣu vākyeṣu ca kā tvad anyā ॥
mamatvagarte 'timahāndhakāre
vibhrāmayaty etad atīva viśvam ॥31॥

Who Other Than You Abides In All Forms of learning,
In The Sacred Texts that Are Lights Of Understanding,
In The Primordial Wisdom Of The Vedas? yet Who Else
confounds this universe in the darkest abyss of attachment?

रक्षांसि यत्रोग्रविषाश्च नागा यत्रारयो दस्युबलानि यत्र ।।
दावानलो यत्र तथाब्धिमध्ये तत्र स्थिता त्वं परिपासि विश्वम् ।।३२।।

Rakṣāmsi yatrogravisạ̄s ca nāgā
yatrārayo dasyubalāni yatra ।।
dāvānalo yatra tathābdhimadhye
tatra sthitā tvaṁ paripāsi viśvam ।।32।।

Where malevolent beings and venomous serpents lurk, where enemies and thieves abound, where forest conflagrations rage, there and even in mid-ocean You Stand And Protect the universe.

विश्वेश्वरि त्वं परिपासि विश्वं विश्वात्मिका धारयसीति विश्वम् ।।
विश्वेशवन्द्या भवती भवन्ति विश्वाश्रया ये त्वयि भक्तिनम्राः ।।३३।।

viśveśvari tvaṁ paripāsi viśvaṁ
viśvātmikā dhārayasīti viśvam ।।
viśveśavandyā bhavatī bhavanti
viśvāśrayā ye tvayi bhaktinamrāḥ ।।33।।

O Ruler Of The Universe, You Protect the universe. You Are The Essence Of all things, and You Support All that is. All kings must praise You, O Revered One, and those who bow to You in devotion become the refuge of all.

देवि प्रसीद परिपालय नोऽरिभीते-र्नित्यं यथासुरवधादधुनैव सद्यः ॥
पापानि सर्वजगतां प्रशमं नयाशु उत्पातपाकजनितांश्च महोपसर्गान् ॥३४॥

Devi prasīda paripālaya no 'ribhīter
nityaṁ yathāsuravadhād adhunaiva sadyaḥ ॥
pāpāni sarvajagatāṁ praśamaṁ nayāśu
utpātapākajanitāṁś ca mahopasargān ॥34॥

Be Gracious, O Devī. Even As You Have destroyed the asuras, protect us always from the fear of enemies. May You Subdue the evils of all the worlds and great disasters born of ominous portents.

प्रणतानां प्रसीद त्वं देवि विश्वार्तिहारिणि ॥
त्रैलोक्यवासिनामीड्ये लोकानां वरदा भव ॥३५॥

praṇatānāṁ prasīda Tvaṁ Devi viśvārtihāriṇi ॥
trailokyavāsinām īḍye lokānāṁ varadā bhava ॥35॥

To those who bow down To You, Be Gracious, O Devī, Who Remove the afflictions of all and Who Are Worthy of

praise by the dwellers of the three worlds.
Confer Your Boons Upon The Worlds.

देव्युवाच ॥३६॥

Devy Uvāca ॥36॥

The Devī Said:

वरदाहं सुरगणा वरं यन्मनसेच्छथ ॥
तं वृणुध्वं प्रयच्छामि जगतामुपकारकम् ॥३७॥

Varadāhaṁ Suragaṇā Varaṁ Yan Manasecchatha ॥
Taṁ Vṛṇudhvaṁ Prayacchāmi Jagatām Upakārakam ॥37॥

O hosts of gods, I Am The Giver Of Boons. whatever blessing is your heart's desire, choose that, and I Will Grant it for the welfare of the world.

देवा ऊचुः ॥३८॥

devā ūcuḥ ॥38॥

The gods said:

सर्वाबाधाप्रशमनं त्रैलोक्यस्याखिलेश्वरि ।।
एवमेव त्वया कार्यमस्मद्वैरिविनाशनम् ।।३९।।

sarvābādhāpraśamanaṁ trailokyasyākhilesvari ।।
evam eva tvayā kāryam asmadvairivināśanam ।।39।।

O Ruler of all, may You allay all the miseries of the three worlds and so, too, annihilate our enemies.

देव्युवाच ।।४०।।

Devy Uvāca ।।40।।

The Devī Said:

वैवस्वतेऽन्तरे प्राप्ते अष्टाविंशतिमे युगे ।।
शुम्भो निशुम्भश्चैवान्यावुत्पत्स्येते महासुरौ ।।४१।।

Vaivasvate 'ntare Prāpte Aṣṭāvimśatime Yuge ।।
śumbho niśumbhaś caivānyāv utpatsyete mahāsurau ।।41।।

When the twenty-eighth cycle in the age of the manu Vaivasvata has come, two other great asuras, also named Śumbha and Niśumbha, will arise.

नन्दगोपगृहे जाता यशोदागर्भसम्भवा ।।
ततस्तौ नाशयिष्यामि विन्ध्याचलनिवासिनी ।।४२।।

Nandagopagṛhe jātā Yaśodāgarbhasambhavā ।।
tatas tau nāśayiṣyāmi vindhyācalanivāsinī ।।42।।

Then Shall I Be Born in the home of the Cowherd Nanda, brought forth From Yaśodā's womb; and Dwelling in the Vindhya Mountains, I Shall Destroy the two asuras.

पुनरप्यतिरौद्रेण रूपेण पृथिवीतले ।।
अवतीर्य हनिष्यामि वैप्रचित्तांस्तु दानवान् ।।४३।।

punar apy atiraudreṇa rūpeṇa pṛthivītale ।।
avatīrya haniṣyāmi vaipracittāṁs tu dānavān ।।43।।

Again, having Incarnated on earth in a surpassingly horrific form, I Shall Slay the demons descended from Vipracitti.

भक्षयन्त्याश्च तानुग्रान् वैप्रचित्तान्महासुरान् ।।
रक्ता दन्ता भविष्यन्ति दाडिमीकुसुमोपमाः ।।४४।।

bhakṣayantyās ca tān ugrān vaipracittān mahāsurān ।।
Raktā Dantā bhaviṣyanti dāḍimīkusumopamāḥ ।।44।।

Upon devouring those fierce asuras, my teeth will become red like pomegranate flowers.

ततो मां देवता: स्वर्गे मर्त्यलोके च मानवा: ।।
स्तुवन्तो व्याहरिष्यन्ति सततं रक्तदन्तिकाम् ।।४५।।

tato māṁ Devatāḥ svarge Martyaloke ca mānavāḥ ।।
stuvanto vyāhariṣyanti satataṁ Raktadantikām ।।45।।

Thereafter, In Praise Of Me, the Gods in heaven and the humans in the mortal realm will forever call me Raktadantikā.

भूयश्च शतवार्षिक्यामनावृष्ट्यामनम्भसि ।।
मुनिभि: संस्तुता भूमौ सम्भविष्याम्ययोनिजा ।।४६।।

bhūyas ca śatavārṣikyām anāvṛṣṭyām anambhasi ।।
munibhiḥ saṁstutā bhūmau sambhaviṣyāmy ayonijā ।।46।।

Again, when no rain has fallen for a hundred years and there is no water on earth, Then Praised by sages, I Shall Appear, But Not Born Of A Womb.

तत: शतेन नेत्राणां निरीक्षिष्यामि यन्मुनीन् ।।
कीर्तयिष्यन्ति मनुजा: शताक्षीमिति मां तत: ।।४७।।

tataḥ śatena netrāṇāṁ nirīkṣiṣyāmi yan munīn ।।
kīrtayiṣyanti manujāḥ śatākṣīm iti māṁ tataḥ ।।47।।

Since I Shall Behold the Sages With A Hundred Eyes, humankind Will Glorify Me As Śatāksī.

ततोऽहमखिलं लोकमात्मदेहसमुद्भवैः ।।
भरिष्यामि सुराः शाकैरावृष्टेः प्राणधारकैः ।।४८।।

tato 'ham akhilaṁ lokam ātmadehasamudbhavaiḥ ।।
bhariṣyāmi surāḥ śākair āvṛṣṭeḥ prāṇadhārakaiḥ ।।48।।

Causing the rains to fall, O gods, I shall support the entire world with life sustaining vegetables brought forth from my own substance.

शाकम्भरीति विख्यातिं तदा यास्याम्यहं भुवि ।।
तत्रैव च वधिष्यामि दुर्गमाख्यं महासुरम् ।।४९।।

śākambharīti vikhyātiṁ tadā yāsyāmy ahaṁ bhuvi ।।
tatraiva ca vadhiṣyāmi durgamākhyaṁ mahāsuram ।।49।।

Thus Shall I Be Celebrated On Earth As Śākambharī, and then also shall I Slay a great asura called Durgama

दुर्गा देवीति विख्यातं तन्मे नाम भविष्यति ।।
पुनश्चाहं यदा भीमं रूपं कृत्वा हिमाचले ।।५०।।

durgā devīti vikhyātaṁ tanme nāma bhaviṣyati ॥
punaś cāhaṁ yadā bhīmaṁ rūpaṁ kṛtvā himācale ॥50॥

The Goddess known as Durgā will be known by this name for me. Again, when I take on a fearsome form on the Himalayas.

रक्षांसि भक्षयिष्यामि मुनीनां त्राणकारणात् ॥
तदा मां मुनयः सर्वे स्तोष्यन्त्यानम्रमूर्तयः ॥५१॥

rakṣāṁsi bhakṣayiṣyāmi munīnāṁ trāṇakāraṇāt ॥
tadā māṁ munayaḥ sarve stoṣyanty anaramūrtayaḥ ॥51॥

I will devour the demons to protect the sages. At that time, all the sages and formless beings will praise me.

भीमा देवीति विख्यातं तन्मे नाम भविष्यति ॥
यदारुणाख्यस्त्रैलोक्ये महाबाधां करिष्यति ॥५२॥

bhīmā devīti vikhyātaṁ tanme nāma bhaviṣyati ॥
yadāruṇākhyastrailokye mahābādhāṁ kariṣyati ॥52॥

I will be known as Bhīmā—the terrible one— Who will cause great distress in the three worlds with her fiery form.

तदाहं भ्रामरं रूपं कृत्वाऽसंख्येयषट्पदम् ।।
त्रैलोक्यस्य हितार्थाय वधिष्यामि महासुरम् ।।५३।।

tadāhaṁ bhrāmaraṁ rūpaṁ kṛtvā'sankhyeṣaṭpadam ।।
trailokyasya hitārthāya vadhiṣyāmi mahāsuram ।।53।।

Then I will take the form of a bee (Bhrāmarī), with countless six feet, To kill the great demons for the welfare of the three worlds.

भ्रामरीति च मां लोकास्तदा स्तोष्यन्ति सर्वतः ।।
इत्थं यदा यदा बाधा दानवोत्था भविष्यति ।।५४।।

bhrāmarīti ca māṁ lokās tadā stoṣyanti sarvataḥ ।।
itthaṁ yadā yadā bādhā dānavotthā bhaviṣyati ।।54।।

At that time, the whole world will praise me as Bhrāmarī. Thus, whenever a demon causes trouble.

तदा तदावतीर्याहं करिष्याम्यरिसंक्षयम् ।।ॐ ।।५५।।

tadā tadāvātīryāhaṁ kariṣyāmy arisaṁkṣayam।।oṁ।।55।।

I will descend and destroy the enemies. Om.

इति श्रीमार्कण्डेयपुराणे सावर्णिके मन्वन्तरे देवीमाहात्म्ये
देव्याः स्तुतिर्नामैकादशोऽध्यायः ।।११।।

iti śrīmārkaṇḍeyapurāṇe sāvarṇike
manvantare devīmāhātmye
devyāḥ stutir nāma ekādaśo'dhyāyaḥ ||11||

Thus ends the eleventh chapter, titled "The Praise of the Goddess," in the Devī Māhātmya of the Mārkaṇḍeya Purāṇa during the Sāvarṇi Manvantara.

॥ द्वादशोऽध्यायः ॥

देवी-चरित्रों के पाठ का माहात्म्यः

॥ Twelfth Chapter ॥

Eulogy of the Merits

॥ ध्यानम् ॥

ॐ विद्युद्दामसमप्रभां मृगपतिस्कन्धस्थितां भीषणां
कन्याभिः करवालखेटविलसद्धस्ताभिरासेविताम् ।
हस्तैश्चक्रगदासिखेटविशिखांश्चापं गुणं तर्जनीं
बिभ्राणामनलात्मिकां शशिधरां दुर्गां त्रिनेत्रां भजे ॥

॥ dhyānam ॥

oṁ vidyuddāmasamaprabhāṁ
mṛgapatiskandhasthitāṁ bhīṣaṇāṁ
kanyābhiḥ karavālakhētavilasaddhastābhirāsevitām ।
hastaiś cakragadāsikhetaviśikhāṁ ścāpaṁ guṇaṁ tarjanīṁ
bibhṛṇāmanalātmikāṁ śaśidharāṁ durgāṁ trinetrāṁ bhaje ॥

Meditation Verse (Dhyānam):

I meditate on Goddess Durgā, who shines like a flash of lightning, seated on the mountain of the Lord of beasts (Śiva), terrifying in form.
She is served by maidens with shining hands, adorned with glowing nails. With hands bearing the discus, mace, and spear, a bow, a flag, and a raised index finger, she embodies the essence of fire, wears the crescent moon, has three eyes, and
is fiercely powerful.

"ॐ" देव्युवाच ॥१॥

Devy uvāca ॥1॥

The Devī said:

❧

एभिः स्तवैश्च मां नित्यं स्तोष्यते यः समाहितः ॥
तस्याहं सकलां बाधां नाशयिष्याम्यसंशयम् ॥२॥

ebhiḥ stavaiś ca māṁ nityaṁ stoṣyate yaḥ samāhitah ॥
tasyāhaṁ sakalām bādhāṁ nāsayiṣyāmy asaṁśayam ॥2॥

I shall without doubt destroy every misfortune of those who with collected mind will praise Me always with these hymns.

❧

मधुकैटभनाशं च महिषासुरघातनम् ॥
कीर्तयिष्यन्ति ये तद्वद् वधं शुम्भनिशुम्भयोः ॥३॥

madhukaiṭabhanāśam ca mahiṣāsuraghātanam ॥
kīrtayiṣyanti ye tadvad vadhaṁ śumbhaniśumbhayoḥ ॥3॥

Those who recite the destruction of Madhu and Kaiṭabha, the killing of Mahiṣāsura, and the slaying of Śumbha and Niśumbha

~

अष्टम्यां च चतुर्दश्यां नवम्यां चौकचेतसः ॥
श्रोष्यन्ति चौव ये भक्त्या मम माहात्म्यमुत्तमम् ॥४॥

aṣṭamyāṁ ca caturdaśyāṁ navamyāṁ caikacetasaḥ ॥
śroṣyanti caiva ye bhaktyā mama māhātmyam uttamam ॥4॥

with singleness of mind on the eighth, ninth and fourteenth days of the lunar fortnight, and those who listen with devotion to this supreme poem of My glory

~

न तेषां दुष्कृतं किञ्चिद् दुष्कृतोत्था न चापदः ॥
भविष्यति न दारिद्र्यं न चौवेष्टवियोजनम् ॥५॥

na teṣāṁ duṣkṛtaṁ kiñcid duṣkṛtotthā na cāpadaḥ ॥
bhaviṣyati na dāridryaṁ na caiveṣṭaviyojanam ॥5॥

will have no evil befall them, nor any misfortunes arising from wrongdoing. For them there will be neither poverty nor separation from loved ones.

शत्रुतो न भयं तस्य दस्युतो वा न राजतः ॥
न शस्त्रानलतोयौघात्कदाचित्सम्भविष्यति ॥६॥

śatruto na bhayaṁ tasya dasyuto vā na rājataḥ ॥
na śastrānalatoyaughāt kadācit sambhaviṣyati ॥6॥

Nor danger from enemies, robbers, or kings. Nor at any time will danger arise from weapons, fire, or flood.

तस्मान्ममैतन्माहात्म्यं पठितव्यं समाहितैः ॥
श्रोतव्यं च सदा भक्त्या परं स्वस्त्ययनं हि तत् ॥७॥

tasmān mamaitan māhātmyaṁ paṭhitavyaṁ samāhitaiḥ ॥
śrotavyaṁ ca sadā bhaktyā paraṁ svastyayanaṁ hi tat ॥7॥

Therefore this poem of My glory is to be recited by those of concentrated mind and heard always with devotion, for it is the supreme way to well-being.

उपसर्गानशेषांस्तु महामारीसमुद्भवान् ॥
तथा त्रिविधमुत्पातं माहात्म्यं शमयेन्मम ॥८॥

upasargān aśeṣāṁs tu mahāmārīsamudbhavān ॥
tathā trividham utpātaṁ māhātmyaṁ śamayen mama ॥8॥

May this glorification of Mine put to rest all misfortunes born of pestilence, and also the three kinds of calamity.

यत्रैतत्पठ्यते सम्यङ्नित्यमायतने मम ॥
सदा न तद्विमोक्ष्यामि सांनिध्यं तत्र मे स्थितम् ॥९॥

yatraitat paṭhyate samyaṅ nityam āyatane mama ॥
sadā na tad vimokṣyāmi sānnidhyaṁ tatra me sthitam ॥9॥

Where My praise is always and rightly uttered in My sanctuary, that place I shall not forsake. There abides My eternal presence.

बलिप्रदाने पूजायामग्निकार्ये महोत्सवे ॥
सर्वं ममैतच्चरितमुच्चार्यं श्राव्यमेव च ॥१०॥

balipradāne pūjāyām agnikārye mahotsave ॥
sarvaṁ mamaitac caritam uccāryaṁ śrāvyam eva ca ॥10॥

In the offering of oblations, in worship, in the fire ceremony, and in the great festival, all these deeds of Mine are to be proclaimed and heard.

जानताऽजानता वापि बलिपूजां तथा कृताम् ॥
प्रतीच्छिष्याम्यहं' प्रीत्या वह्निहोमं तथा कृतम् ॥११॥

jānatājānatā vāpi balipūjāṁ tathā kṛtām ॥
pratīcchiṣyāmy ahaṁ prītyā vahnihomaṁ tathākṛtam ॥11॥

When offerings are made in worship, with or without proper knowledge, I shall receive them gladly and also the fire oblation performed in like manner.

शरत्काले महापूजा क्रियते या च वार्षिकी ॥
तस्यां ममैतन्माहात्म्यं श्रुत्वा भक्तिसमन्वितः ॥१२॥

śaratkāle mahāpūjā kriyate yā ca vārṣikī ॥
tasyāṁ mamaitan māhātmyaṁ śrutvā bhaktisamanvitaḥ
॥12॥

At the great annual worship which is performed in the autumn season, those who hear this poem of My glory and are filled with devotion

सर्वाबाधा विनिर्मुक्तो धनधान्यसुतान्वितः ॥
मनुष्यो मत्प्रसादेन भविष्यति न संशयः ॥१३॥

sarvābādhāvinirmukto dhanadhānyasutānvitaḥ ॥
manuṣyo matprasādena bhaviṣyati na saṁśayaḥ ॥13॥

Will be freed by My grace from all afflictions and endowed with wealth, grain, and progeny. Of this there is no doubt.

श्रुत्वा ममैतन्माहात्म्यं तथा चोत्पत्तयः शुभाः ।।
पराक्रमं च युद्धेषु जायते निर्भयः पुमान् ।।१४।।

śrutvā mamaitan māhātmyaṁ tathā cotpattayaḥ śubhāḥ ।।
parākramaṁ ca yuddheṣu jāyate nirbhayaḥ pumān ।।14।।

Hearing of My glory, My auspicious manifestations, and My prowess in battles, they become fearless.

रिपवः संक्षयं यान्ति कल्याणं चोपपद्यते ।।
नन्दते च कुलं पुंसां माहात्म्यं मम शृण्वताम् ।।१५।।

ripavaḥ samkṣayaṁ yānti kalyāṇaṁ copapadyate ।।
nandate ca kularh puṁsāṁ māhātmyaṁ mama śṛṇvatām ।।15।।

For those who hear My glorification, their adversaries go to utter destruction. Well-being comes to them, and their families rejoice.

शान्तिकर्मणि सर्वत्र तथा दुःस्वप्नदर्शने ।।
ग्रहपीडासु चोग्रासु माहात्म्यं शृणुयान्मम ।।१६।।

śāntikarmaṇi sarvatra tathā duḥsvapnadarśane ।।
grahapīḍāsu cogrāsu māhātmyaṁ śṛṇuyān mama ।।16।।

For those troubled by nightmares or the ill-boding of stars, at rituals for averting evil this poem of My glory should always be heard.

उपसर्गाः शमं यान्ति ग्रहपीडाश्च दारुणाः ।।
दुःस्वप्नं च नृभिर्दृष्टं सुस्वप्नमुपजायते ।।१७।।

upasargāḥ śamaṁ yānti grahapīḍāś ca dāruṇāḥ ।।
duḥsvapnaṁ ca nṛbhir dṛṣtaṁ susvapnam upajāyate ।।17।।

It causes misfortunes and evil portents to subside, and it turns nightmares into sweet dreams.

बालग्रहाभिभूतानां बालानां शान्तिकारकम् ।।
संघातभेदे च नृणां मैत्रीकरणमुत्तमम् ।।१८।।

bālagrahābhibhūtānāṁ bālānāṁ śāntikārakam ।।
saṅghātabhede ca nṛṇāṁ maitrīkaraṇam uttamam ।।18।।

It pacifies children overcome by seizures, and wherever discord divides, it best restores friendship.

दुर्वृत्तानामशेषाणां बलहानिकरं परम् ॥
रक्षोभूतपिशाचानां पठनादेव नाशनम् ॥१९॥

durvṛttānām aśeṣāṇāṁ balahānikaraṁ paraṁ ॥
rakṣobhūtapiśācānāṁ paṭhanād eva nāśanam ॥19॥

It is unsurpassed in diminishing the might of all evildoers. Truly its recitation brings about the destruction of fiends, ghosts, and ghouls.

सर्वं ममैतन्माहात्म्यं मम सन्निधिकारकम् ॥
पशुपुष्पार्घ्यधूपैश्च गन्धदीपैस्तथोत्तमैः ॥२०॥

sarvaṁ mamaitan māhātmyam mama sannidhikārakam ॥
paśupuṣpārghyadhūpaiś ca gandhadīpaistathottamaiḥ ॥20॥

All this greatness of mine brings presence and blessings, with offerings of flowers, grains, incense, fragrant lamps, and the best of rituals.

विप्राणां भोजनैर्होमैः प्रोक्षणीयैरहर्निशम् ॥
अन्यैश्च विविधैर्भोगैः प्रदानैर्वत्सरेण या ॥२१॥

viprāṇāṁ bhojanair homaiḥ prokṣaṇīyāraharmiśam ॥
anyaiś ca vividhair bhogaiḥ pradānair vatsareṇa yā ॥21॥

With meals for the Brahmins, sacred fires, and constant sprinklings, Along with various other offerings and gifts throughout the year.

प्रीतिर्मे क्रियते सास्मिन् सकृत्सुचरिते श्रुते ॥
श्रुतं हरति पापानि तथाऽऽरोग्यं प्रयच्छति ॥२२॥

prītirme kriyate sāsmin sakṛtsucarite śrute ॥
śrutaṁ harati pāpāni tathā'rōgyaṁ prayacchati ॥22॥

Here, love is born of sacred rites and holy lore; by hearing it, sins are dissolved and well-being is bestowed.

रक्षां करोति भूतेभ्यो जन्मनां कीर्तनं मम ॥
युद्धेषु चरितं यन्मे दुष्टदैत्यनिबर्हणम् ॥२३॥

rakṣāṁ karoti bhūtebhyo janmanāṁ kīrtanaṁ mama ॥
yuddheṣu caritaṁ yann me duṣṭadaityanibarhaṇam ॥23॥

It protects beings and is praised by births; In battles, it recounts my deeds of slaying evil demons.

तस्मिञ्छ्रुते वैरिकृतं भयं पुंसां न जायते ॥
युष्माभिः स्तुतयो याश्च याश्च ब्रह्मर्षिभिःकृताः ॥२४॥

tasmin śrute vairikṛtaṁ bhayaṁ puṁsāṁ na jāyate ॥
yuṣmābhiḥ stutayo yāś ca yāś ca brahmarṣibhikṛtāḥ ॥24॥

When this is heard, enmity and fear do not arise in men;
Those praised by you and the Brahmarshis
(divine sages) also.

ब्रह्मणा च कृतास्तास्तु प्रयच्छन्ति शुभां मतिम् ॥
अरण्ये प्रान्तरे वापि दावाग्निपरिवारितः ॥२५॥

brahmaṇā ca kṛtāstāstu prayacchanti śubhāṁ matim ॥
araṇye prāntare vāpi dāvāgniparivāritaḥ ॥25॥

Those praised by Brahma himself grant auspicious intellect;
Whether in the forest, wilderness, or surrounded by fire.

दस्युभिर्वा वृतः शून्ये गृहीतो वापि शत्रुभिः ॥
सिंहव्याघ्रानुयातो वा वने वा वनहस्तिभिः ॥२६॥

dasyubhirvā vṛtaḥ śūnye gṛhīto vāpi śatrubhiḥ ॥
siṁhavyākhranuyāto vā vane vā vanahastibhiḥ ॥26॥

Even if surrounded by robbers, or in an empty place, or caught by enemies, Or followed by lions, tigers, or wild elephants in the forest.

राज्ञा क्रुद्धेन चाज्ञप्तो वध्यो बन्धगतोऽपि वा ॥
आघूर्णितो वा वातेन स्थितः पोते महार्णवे ॥२७॥

rājñā kruddhena cājñapto vadhyo bandhagato'pi vā ॥
āghūrṇito vā vātena sthitaḥ pote mahārṇave ॥27॥

Ordered to be killed by an angry king, even if imprisoned,
pierced by arrows or caught in the wind, or cast
into the great ocean.

पतत्सु चापि शस्त्रेषु संग्रामे भृशदारुणे ॥
सर्वाबाधासु घोरासु वेदनाभ्यर्दितोऽपि वा ॥२८॥

patatsu cāpi śastreṣu saṁgrāme bhṛśadāruṇe ॥
sarvābādhāsu ghorāsu vedanābhyardito'pi vā ॥28॥

Or falling in weapons in a fierce battle,
Or struck by painful and terrible afflictions.

स्मरन्ममैतच्चरितं नरो मुच्येत संकटात् ॥
मम प्रभावात्सिंहाद्या दस्यवो वैरिणस्तथा ॥२९॥

smaranmamaitaccharitaṁ naro mucyeta saṅkaṭāt ॥
mama prabhāvātsimhādyā dasyavo vairiṇastathā ॥29॥

Remembering my deeds, a man is freed from danger;
Because of my power, lions and robbers, enemies too,
flee from afar.

दूरादेव पलायन्ते स्मरतश्चरितं मम ॥३०॥

dūrādeva palāyante smarataścaritaṁ mama ॥30॥

Remembering my deeds, they run away far away.

ऋषिरुवाच ॥३१॥

ṛṣir uvāca ॥31॥

The seer said:

इत्युक्त्वा सा भगवती चण्डिका चण्डविक्रमा ॥३२॥

ity uktvā sā Bhagavatī Caṇḍikā Caṇdavikramā ॥32॥

Having spoken thus, the blessed Caṇḍikā.

पश्यतामेव देवानां तत्रैवान्तरधीयत ॥
तेऽपि देवा निरातङ्काः स्वाधिकारान् यथा पुरा ॥३३॥

paśyatām eva devānāṁ tatraivāntaradhīyata ॥
te 'pi devā nirātaṅkāḥ svādhikārān yathā purā ॥33॥

Fierce in valor, vanished from the sight of the gods,
Their enemies struck down, the gods were
delivered from affliction.

यज्ञभागभुजः सर्वे चक्रुर्विनिहतारयः ।।
दैत्याश्च देव्या निहते शुम्भे देवरिपौ युधि ।।३४।।

yajñabhāgabhujaḥ sarve cakrur vinihatārayaḥ ।।
daityāś ca Devyā nihate śumbhe devaripau yudhi ।।34।।

They reclaimed their own dominions as before, and all partook of their shares in the sacrifices. As for the daityas, after the Devī had slain in battle those two enemies of the gods— Śumbha.

जगद्विध्वंसिनि तस्मिन् महोग्रेऽतुलविक्रमे ।।
निशुम्भे च महावीर्ये शेषाः पातालमाययुः ।।३५।।

jagadvidhvaṁsini tasmin mahogre 'tulavikrame ।।
niśumbhe ca mahāvīrye śeṣāḥ pātālam āyayuḥ ।।35।।

The afflictor of the world, terribly fierce and unequaled in prowess, and Niśumbha, great in valor—the rest of them returned to the netherworld.

एवं भगवती देवी सा नित्यापि पुनः पुनः ।।
सम्भूय कुरुते भूप जगतः परिपालनम् ।।३६।।

evaṁ Bhagavatī Devī sā nityāpi punaḥ punaḥ ।।
sambhūya kurute bhūpa jagataḥ paripālanam ।।36।।

Thus, O king, does the blessed Devī, though eternal, manifest again and again for the protection of the world.

तयैतन्मोह्यते विश्वं सैव विश्वं प्रसूयते ॥
सा याचिता च विज्ञानं तुष्टा ऋद्धिं प्रयच्छति ॥३७॥

tayaitan mohyate viśvaṁ saiva viśvaṁ prasūyate ॥
sā yācitā ca vijñānaṁ tuṣṭā ṛddhiṁ prayacchati ॥37॥

She it is who deludes the universe, and She it is who brings forth all things. To the supplicant She grants right knowledge; to the devoted, prosperity.

व्याप्तं तयैतत्सकलं ब्रह्माण्डं मनुजेश्वर ॥
महाकाल्या महाकाले महामारीस्वरूपया ॥३८॥

vyāptaṁ tayaitat sakalaṁ brahmāṇḍaṁ manujeśvara ॥
mahākālyā mahākāle mahāmārīsvarūpayā ॥38॥

O king, by Her all this universe is pervaded, by Mahākālī, who takes form as the great destroyer at the end of time.

सैव काले महामारी सैव सृष्टिर्भवत्यजा ॥
स्थितिं करोति भूतानां सैव काले सनातनी ॥३९॥

saiva kāle mahāmārī saiva sṛṣṭir bhavaty ajā ||
sthitiṁ karoti bhūtānāṁ saiva kāle sanātanī ||39||

At that time, She herself is the great destroyer. Existing from all eternity, She herself becomes the creation. She, the eternal one, sustains all beings.

भवकाले नृणां सैव लक्ष्मीर्वृद्धिप्रदा गृहे ॥
सैवाभावे तथाऽलक्ष्मीर्विनाशायोपजायते ॥४०॥

bhavakāle nṛṇāṁ saiva lakṣmīr vṛddhipradā gṛhe ||
saivābhāve tathālakṣmīr vināśāyopajāyate ||40||

In times of well-being She is indeed good fortune, granting prosperity in the homes of humankind. In times of privation, She exists as misfortune, bringing about ruin.

स्तुता सम्पूजिता पुष्पैर्धूपगन्धादिभिस्तथा ॥
ददाति वित्तं पुत्रांश्च मतिं धर्मे गतिं' शुभाम् ॥ॐ ॥४१॥

stutā sampūjitā puṣpair dhūpagandhādibhis tathā ||
dadāti vittaṁ putrāṁś ca matim dharme gatim śubhām ||41||

And so, praised and worshiped with flowers, incense, perfumes, and the like, She grants wealth, progeny, and a pure mind established in righteousness.

इति श्रीमार्कण्डेयपुराणे सावर्णिके मन्वन्तरे देवीमाहात्म्ये
फलस्तुतिर्नाम द्वादशोऽध्यायः ॥१२॥

iti śrīmārkaṇḍeyapurāṇe sāvarṇike
manvantare devīmāhātmye
phalastutir nāma dvādaśo'dhyāyaḥ ॥12॥

Thus ends the twelfth chapter, titled 'The Praise of the Fruits (Phala Stuti),' in the Devī Māhātmya of the Mārkaṇḍeya Purāṇa, set in the Sāvarṇi Manvantara.

|| त्रयोदशोऽध्याय: ||

सुरथ-वैश्य-वरदा

|| Thirteenth Chapter ||

The Bestowing of Boons to Suratha and Vaisya

|| ध्यानम् ||

ॐ बालार्कमण्डलाभासां चतुर्बाहुं त्रिलोचनाम् ।
पाशाङ्कुशवराभीतीर्धारयन्तीं शिवां भजे ॥

|| dhyānam ||

oṁ bālarkamandalābhāsāṁ caturbāhuṁ trilocanām
pāśāṅkuśavarābhītīrdhārayantīṁ śivāṁ bhaje ||

"ॐ" ऋषिरुवाच ॥१॥

ṛṣir uvāca ||1||

The seer said:

एतत्ते कथितं भूप देवीमाहात्म्यमुत्तमम् ।।
एवंप्रभावा सा देवी ययेदं धार्यते जगत् ।।२।।

etat te kathitaṁ bhūpa devīmāhātmyamuttamam ।।
evaṁprabhāvā sā devī yayedaṁ dhāryate jagat ।।2।।

O King, this supreme glory of the Goddess has been narrated to you. Thus, by her power alone, this world is sustained.

विद्या तथैव क्रियते भगवद्विष्णुमायया ।।
तया त्वमेष वैश्यश्च तथैवान्ये विवेकिनः ।।३।।

vidyā tathaiva kriyate bhagavadviṣṇumāyayā ।।
tayā tvameṣa vaiśyaśca tathaivānye vivekinaḥ ।।3।।

Knowledge itself arises from the divine Māyā of Lord Viṣṇu; therefore you, the merchant, along with other learned ones, fall under delusion.

मोह्यन्ते मोहिताश्चौव मोहमेष्यन्ति चापरे ।।
तामुपैहि महाराज शरणं परमेश्वरीम् ।।४।।

mohyante mohitāścaiva moham eṣyanti cāpare ।।
tāmupaihai mahārāja śaraṇaṁ parameśvarīm ।।4।।

Some are deluded, some are already deluded, and others will become deluded. Therefore, O great king, seek refuge in that Supreme Goddess.

आराधिता सैव नृणां भोगस्वर्गापवर्गदा ॥५॥

ārādhitā saiva nṛṇāṁ bhogasvargāpavargadā ॥5॥

When worshipped, she grants humans enjoyment, heaven, and liberation.

मार्कण्डेय उवाच ॥६॥

mārkaṇḍeya uvāca ॥6॥

Markandeya said:

इति तस्य वचः श्रुत्वा सुरथः स नराधिपः ॥७॥

iti tasya vacaḥ śrutvā surathaḥ sa narādhipaḥ ॥7॥

Hearing these words, King Suratha, the ruler of men, bowed respectfully to the great sage of exalted vows, disheartened due to the loss of his kingdom and attachment.

प्रणिपत्य महाभागं तमृषिं शंसितव्रतम् ।।
निर्विण्णोऽतिममत्वेन राज्यापहरणेन च ।।८।।

praṇipatya mahābhāgaṁ tamṛṣiṁ śaṁsitavrataṁ ।।
nirviṇṇo'timamatvena rājyāpharaṇena ca ।।8।।

Immediately, he began penance, and so did the merchant, O great sage, to behold the Goddess. They went to the riverbank and stayed there.

जगाम सद्यस्तपसे स च वैश्यो महामुने ।।
संदर्शनार्थमम्बाया नदीपुलिनसंस्थितः ।।९।।

jagāma sadyastapase sa ca vaiśyo mahāmune ।।
saṁdarśanārthamambāyā nadīpulinasaṁsthitaḥ ।।9।।

The merchant performed penance, chanting the supreme hymn to the Goddess. They created a sacred image of the Earth Goddess on the riverbank.

स च वैश्यस्तपस्तेपे देवीसूक्तं परं जपन् ।।
तौ तस्मिन पुलिने देव्याः कृत्वा मूर्तिं महीमयीम् ।।१०।।

sa ca vaiśyastapastepe devīsūktaṁ paraṁ japan ।।
tau tasmin puline devyāḥ kṛtvā mūrtiṁ mahīm ayīm ।।10।।

and worshipped her with flowers, incense,
fire offerings, and libations.

अर्हणां चक्रतुस्तस्याः पुष्पधूपाग्नितर्पणैः ॥
निराहारौ यताहारौ तन्मनस्कौ समाहितौ ॥११॥

arhaṇāṁ cakratu stasyāḥ puṣpadhūpāgnitarpaṇaiḥ ॥
nirāhārau yatāhārau tanmanaskau samāhitau ॥11॥

Fasting or eating very little, with focused minds and
self-discipline, they offered their sacrifices,
even their own blood.

ददतुस्तौ बलिं चैव निजगात्रासृगुक्षितम् ॥
एवं समाराधयतोस्त्रिभिर्वर्षैर्यतात्मनोः ॥१२॥

dadatustau baliṁ caiva nijagātrāsṛgu kṣitam ॥
evaṁ samārādhayotstribhirvarṣairyatātmanoḥ ॥12॥

Thus, performing this devotion for
three years with determination,

परितुष्टा जगद्धात्री प्रत्यक्षं प्राह चण्डिका ॥१३॥

parituṣṭā jagaddhātrī pratyakṣaṁ prāha caṇḍikā ॥13॥

the World-Mother became pleased and
appeared directly as Caṇḍikā.

देव्युवाच ।।१४।।

devyuvāca ।।14।।

The Goddess said:

यत्प्रार्थ्यते त्वया भूप त्वया च कुलनन्दन ।।
मत्तस्तत्प्राप्यतां सर्वं परितुष्टा ददामि तत् ।।१५।।

yatprārthyate tvayā bhūpa tvayā ca kulanandana ।।
mattastatprāpyatāṁ sarvaṁ parituṣṭā dadāmi tat ।।15।।

O King and noble son of your family, whatever you ask from me, I shall grant it all, fully pleased.

मार्कण्डेय उवाच ।।१६।।

mārkaṇḍeya uvāca ।।16।।

Markandeya said:

ततो वव्रे नृपो राज्यमविभ्रंश्यन्यजन्मनि ।।
अत्रैव च निजं राज्यं हतशत्रुबलं बलात् ।।१७।।

tato vavre nṛpo rājyamavibhraṁśyanyajanmani ।।
atraiva ca nijaṁ rājyaṁ hataśatrubalaṁ balāt ।।17।।

The king then requested his kingdom back in this very life, and that he might rule his kingdom here, having defeated his enemies by force.

❧

सोऽपि वैश्यस्ततो ज्ञानं वव्रे निर्विण्णमानसः ।।
ममेत्यहमिति प्राज्ञः सङ्गविच्युतिकारकम् ।।१८।।

so'pi vaiśyastato jñānaṁ vavre nirviṇṇamānasaḥ ।।
mametyahamiti prājñaḥ saṅgavicyutikārakam ।।18।।

The merchant, with a calm mind, requested true knowledge—freedom from attachment and ignorance that causes bondage.

❧

देव्युवाच ।।१९।।

devyuvāca ।।19।।

The Goddess said:

❧

स्वल्पैरहोभिर्नृपते स्वं राज्यं प्राप्स्यते भवान् ॥२०॥

svalpairahobhirnṛpate svaṁ rājyaṁ prāpsyate bhavān ॥20॥

O King, with just a few days of effort,
you will regain your kingdom.

हत्वा रिपूनस्खलितं तव तत्र भविष्यति ॥२१॥

hatvā ripūnas khalitaṁ tava tatra bhaviṣyati ॥21॥

Having slain your enemies, your reign will be secure.

मृतश्च भूयः सम्प्राप्य जन्म देवाद्विवस्वतः ॥२२॥

mṛtaśca bhūyaḥ samprāpya janma devādvivvasvataḥ ॥22॥

After death, you will be born again as the son of the Sun God.

सावर्णिको नाम मनुर्भवान् भुवि भविष्यति ॥२३॥

sāvarṇiko nāma manuḥ bhuvī bhaviṣyati ॥23॥

And become the Manu named Sāvarṇi on Earth.

वैश्यवर्य त्वया यश्च वरोऽस्मत्तोऽभिवाञ्छितः ॥२४॥

vaiśyavarya tvayā yaśca varo'smatto'bhivāñchitaḥ ॥24॥

O chief of merchants, I grant you the boon
you desire—knowledge

तं प्रयच्छामि संसिद्ध्यै तव ज्ञानं भविष्यति ॥२५॥

taṁ prayacchāmi saṁsiddhyai tava jñānaṁ bhaviṣyati ॥25॥

That which leads to perfection shall be yours

मार्कण्डेय उवाच ॥२६॥

mārkaṇḍeya uvāca ॥26॥

Markandeya said:

इति दत्त्वा तयोर्देवी यथाभिलषितं वरम् ॥२७॥

iti dattvā tayordevī yathābhiliṣitaṁ varam ॥27॥

Thus having granted their desired boons,

बभूवान्तर्हिता सद्यो भक्त्या ताभ्यामभिष्टुता ।।
एवं देव्या वरं लब्ध्वा सुरथः क्षत्रियर्षभः ।।२८।।

babhūvāntarhitā sadyo bhaktyā tābhyāmabhiṣṭutā ।।
evaṁ devyā varaṁ labdhvā surathaḥ kṣatriyārṣabhaḥ ।।28।।

The Goddess immediately disappeared from their sight, satisfied by their devotion.

सूर्याज्जन्म समासाद्य सावर्णिर्भविता मनुः ।।२९।।

sūryājjanna samāsādya sāvarṇirbhavitā manuḥ ।।29।।

Having obtained the Goddess's blessings, King Suratha.

एवं देव्या वरं लब्ध्वा सुरथः क्षत्रियर्षभः
सूर्याज्जन्म समासाद्य सावर्णिर्भविता मनुः ।।क्लीं ॐ।।

evaṁ devyā varaṁ labdhvā surathaḥ kṣatriyārṣabhaḥ
sūryājjanna samāsādya sāvarṇirbhavitā manuḥ ।।klīṁ oṁ।।

The foremost among the Kṣatriyas, was born from the Sun God and became the Manu named Sāvarṇi.

इति श्रीमार्कण्डेयपुराणे सावर्णिके मन्वन्तरे देवीमाहात्म्ये
सुरथवैश्ययोर्वरप्रदानं नाम त्रयोदशोऽध्यायः ।।१३।।

iti śrīmārkaṇḍeyapurāṇe sāvarṇike
manvantare devīmāhātmye
surathavaiśyayorvarapradānaṁ nāma
trayodaśo'dhyāyaḥ ॥13॥

Thus ends the thirteenth chapter named 'The Granting of Boons to Suratha and the Merchant' in the Devi Mahatmya of the Markandeya Purana during the Savarnika Manvantara.

देवी अपराधक्षमापनस्तोत्रम्

Devi Aparadha Kshamapana Stotram

न मत्रं नो यन्त्रं तदपि च न जाने स्तुतिमहो
न चाह्वानं ध्यानं तदपि च न जाने स्तुतिकथा: ।।
न जाने मुद्रास्ते तदपि च न जाने विलपनं
परं जाने मातस्त्वदनुसरणं क्लेशहरणम् ।।१।।

ṇa ṃatram ṇo ẏantram ṭad-āpi
Ca ṇa Jāne Stutim-āho
ṇa Ca-[ā]ahvānam ḍhyānam ṭad-āpi
Ca ṇa Jāne Stuti-k̲hathāh ।।
ṇa Jāne ṃudrās-ṭe ṭad-āpi Ca ṇa Jāne Vilapanam
Param Jāne ṃātas-ṭvad-ānusarannam k̲hleśa-ḥarannam ।।1।।

O Mother, I know not Your mantra nor Your yantra; alas, I know not even how to sing Your stuti. I do not know how to invoke You in dhyāna, nor can I recite well the tales of Your glory. I know not Your sacred mudrās, nor even how to weep before You in longing. Yet one thing I know with certainty: that simply by remembering You—even imperfectly—my afflictions shall be lifted from my heart.

विधेरज्ञानेन द्रविणविरहेणालसतया
विधेयाशक्यत्वात्तव चरणयोर्या च्युतिरभूत् ॥
तदेतत् क्षन्तव्यं जननि सकलोद्धारिणि शिवे
कुपुत्रो जायेत क्वचिदपि कुमाता न भवति ॥२॥

Vidher-ājnyānena ḍravinna-Virahenna-ālasatayā
Vidheya-āśakyatvāt-ṭava Carannayoryā Cyutir-ābhūt ॥
ṭad-ĕtat k̲hssantavyam Janani Sakalo[a-ū]ddhārinni ṣive
k̲huputro Jāyeta k̲hvacid-āpi k̲humātā ṇa Bhavati ॥2॥

O Mother, through ignorance of the sacred injunctions, through want of wealth, and through my own indolence, I have failed to serve Your lotus feet. I admit my shortcomings in the duties owed to You. Yet all these, I know, are pardonable by You, O Śivā, auspicious Mother—for You are the saviour of all. There may indeed be a kuputra, a fallen son who turns away from his mother, but never can there be a kumātā, a mother who abandons her son.

पृथिव्यां पुत्रास्ते जननि बहवः सन्ति सरलाः
परं तेषां मध्ये विरलतरलोऽहं तव सुतः ॥
मदीयोऽयं त्यागः समुचितमिदं नो तव शिवे
कुपुत्रो जायेत क्वचिदपि कुमाता न भवति ॥३॥

Prthivyām Putrās-ṭe Janani Bahavah Santi Saralāh
Param ṭessām ṃadhye Virala-ṭaralo[a-ā]ham ṭava Sutah ॥

ṃadīyo-[ā]yam ṭyāgah Samucitam-īdam ṇo ṭava ṣive
k̲huputro Jāyeta k̲hvacid-āpi k̲humātā ṇa Bhavati ।।3।।

O Mother, in this world You have countless sons who are simple and content, yet among them I alone am restless and troubled. For this very reason, O Śivā, it is not fitting that You abandon me. For while there may be a kuputra—a fallen son who turns away from his mother—there can never be a kumātā, a mother who turns away from her son.

जगन्मातर्मातस्तव चरणसेवा न रचिता
न वा दत्तं देवि द्रविणमपि भूयस्तव मया ।।
तथापि त्वं स्नेहं मयि निरुपमं यत्प्रकुरुषे
कुपुत्रो जायेत क्वचिदपि कुमाता न भवति ।।४।।

Jaganmātar-ṃātas-ṭava Caranna-Sevā ṇa r̲acitā
ṇa Vā ḍattam ḍevi ḍravinnam-āpi Bhūyas-ṭava ṃayā ।।
ṭathā-[ā]pi ṭvam Sneham ṃayi ṇirupamam ẏat-Prakurusse
k̲huputro Jāyeta k̲hvacid-āpi k̲humātā ṇa Bhavati ।।4।।

O Jaganmātā, Mother of the world, I have never served Your lotus feet, nor have I, O Devī, laid abundant wealth before them in worship. Yet, despite this, Your boundless motherly love for me has remained steadfast and incomparable. For there may be a kuputra—a fallen son who turns away from his mother—but never a kumātā—a mother who turns away from her son.

परित्यक्ता देवा विविधविधसेवाकुलतया
मया पञ्चाशीतेरधिकमपनीते तु वयसि ।।
इदानीं चेन्मातस्तव यदि कृपा नापि भविता
निरालम्बो लम्बोदरजननि कं यामि शरणम् ।।५।।

Parityaktā ḍevā Vividha-Vidha-Sevā-k̲hulatayā
ṃayā Pan.cāśīter-ādhikam-āpanīte ṭu Vayasi ।।
īdānīm Cenmātas-ṭava ẏadi k̲hrpā ṇa-āpi Bhavitā
ṇirālambo ḻambodara-Janani k̲ham ẏāmi ṣarannam ।।5।।

O Mother, having neglected the ritual worship of the devas, more than eighty-five years of my life have slipped away. Now, even at this final moment, if Your grace does not descend, O Mother of bliss and consciousness, where shall this nirālamba—one without any support—find refuge? O Lambodara Jananī, Mother of Ganeśa, to You alone I turn.

श्वपाको जल्पाको भवति मधुपाकोपमगिरा
निरातङ्को रङ्को विहरति चिरं कोटिकनकैः ।।
तवापर्णे कर्णे विशति मनुवर्णे फलमिदं
जनः को जानीते जननि जपनीयं जपविधौ ।।६।।

ṣvapāko Jalpāko Bhavati ṃadhupāko[a-ū]pama-ġirā
ṇirātangko r̲angko Viharati Ciram k̲hotti-k̲hanakaih ।।
ṭava-āparnne k̲harnne Viśati ṃanu-Varnne Phalam-īdam
Janah k̲ho Jānīte Janani Japanīyam Japa-Vidhau ।।6।।

O Mother, by Your grace, even a śvapāka—a dog-eater, from whose mouth no good words arise—becomes a jalpaka, eloquent, his speech flowing sweet as honey. By Your grace, the destitute raṅka, poor and miserable, becomes niratanka, fearless, moving freely as though endowed with countless treasures of gold. O Aparṇā, when the praise of Your glory enters the ear and takes root in the heart, such wonders unfold—who among men can fathom, O Mother, the destiny that the recitation of Your holy name reveals?

चिताभस्मालेपो गरलमशनं दिक्पटधरो
जटाधारी कण्ठे भुजगपतिहारी पशुपतिः ।।
कपाली भूतेशो भजति जगदीशैकपदवीं
भवानि त्वत्पाणिग्रहणपरिपाटीफलमिदम् ।।७।।

Citā-Bhasmā-ḻepo ġaralam-āśanam ḍik-Patta-ḍharo
Jattā-ḍhārī kḫanntthe Bhujaga-Pati-ḥārī Paśupatih ।।
kḫapālī Bhūteśo Bhajati Jagadīśai[a-ĕ]ka-Padavīm
Bhavāni ṭvat-Pānni-ġrahanna-Paripāttī-Phalam-īdam ।।7।।

O Mother, though Lord Śaṅkara is smeared with cita-bhasma from the cremation ground, though His food is poison and His garment the directions themselves; though His matted locks crown His head and a garland of the serpent-king adorns His neck; though He bears in His hand a begging bowl made of skull, He is still revered as Paśupati, Lord of all beings, worshipped as Bhūteśa, and acclaimed as Jagadīśa—the one Lord of the universe. O Bhavānī, all this glory is but the fruit of Your pāṇi-grahaṇa, when He took Your hand in marriage.

न मोक्षस्याकाङ्क्षा भवविभववाञ्छापि च न मे
न विज्ञानापेक्षा शशिमुखि सुखेच्छापि न पुनः ।।
अतस्त्वां संयाचे जननि जननं यातु मम वै
मृडानी रुद्राणी शिव शिव भवानीति जपतः ।।८।।

ṇa ṃokssasya-[ā]akāngkssā Bhava-
Vibhava-Vān.cā-[ā]pi Ca ṇa ṃe
ṇa Vijnyāna-āpekssā ṣaśi-ṃukhi Sukhe[a-ī]cca-āpi ṇa
Punah ।।
ātas-ṭvām Samyāce Janani Jananam ẏātu ṃama Vai
ṃrddānī ṟudrānnī ṣiva ṣiva Bhavāni-īti Japatah ।।8।।

O Mother, I seek neither mokṣa (liberation), nor worldly fortune, nor even the pursuit of knowledge, O Śaśī-mukhī, moon-faced one. I desire not the fleeting comforts of this world again. Instead, I implore You, O Divine Mother—may You turn the course of my life toward the remembrance of Your names. May the sacred garland of Your holy names—Mṛḍānī, Rudrānī, Śivā, Śivā, Bhavānī—ever rest upon my lips. Let my future births be wholly devoted to the ceaseless japa of Your blessed names.

नाराधितासि विधिना विविधोपचारैः
किं रुक्षचिन्तनपरैर्न कृतं वचोभिः ॥
श्यामे त्वमेव यदि किञ्चन मय्यनाथे
धत्से कृपामुचितमम्ब परं तवैव ॥९॥

ṇa-[ā]arādhitāsi Vidhinā Vividho[a-ū]pacāraih
k̲him r̲ukssa-Cintana-Parair-ṇa k̲hrtam Vacobhih ॥
ṣyāme ṭvameva ẏadi k̲hin.cana ṃayy-ānāthe
ḍhatse k̲hrpām-ūcitam-āmba Param ṭavai[a-ĕ]va ॥9॥

O Mother, I have not worshipped You with the rituals laid down by tradition. Instead, my mind has wandered in unworthy thoughts, and my speech has uttered harsh words. Yet, O Śyāmā, if even to a small extent You have bestowed Your grace upon this orphan soul, it is only fitting—for such boundless compassion belongs to You alone, O Supreme Mother.

आपत्सु मग्नः स्मरणं त्वदीयं
करोमि दुर्गे करुणार्णवेशि ॥
नैतच्छठत्वं मम भावयेथाः
क्षुधातृषार्ता जननीं स्मरन्ति ॥१०॥

āapatsu ṃagnah Smarannam ṭvadīyam
k̲haromi ḍurge k̲harunnā-[ā]rnnav[a-ii]eśi ॥

ṇai[a-ĕ]tac-chattha-ṭvam ṃama Bhāvayethāh
khssudhā-ṭrssā-[āa]rtā Jananīm Smaranti ।।10।।

O Mother, sunk deep in misfortune I now remember You—though never before did I call upon Your name. O Mother Durgā, ocean of compassion, do not take me for false or think my invocation mere pretence. For when children are stricken with hunger and thirst, to whom else do they turn but to their mother?

जगदम्ब विचित्रमत्र किं
परिपूर्णा करुणास्ति चेन्मयि ।।
अपराधपरम्परापरं
न हि माता समुपेक्षते सुतम् ।।११।।

Jagadamba Vicitram-ātra khim
Paripūrnnā kharunnā-[ā]sti Cenmayi ।।
āparādha-Paramparā-Param
ṇa ḥi ṃātā Samupekssate Sutam ।।11।।

O Jagadambā, what wonder is there in this? The boundless compassion of the blissful Mother is ever full, for though the son errs again and again, the Mother never abandons him.

मत्समः पातकी नास्ति पापघ्नी त्वत्समा न हि ॥
एवं ज्ञात्वा महादेवि यथायोग्यं तथा कुरु ॥१२॥

ṃatsamah Pātakī ṇāsti Pāpa-ġhnī ṭvatsamā ṇa ḥi ॥
ĕvam Jnyātvā ṃahādevi ẏathā-ẏogyam ṭathā k̲huru ॥12॥

O Mother, none is as fallen as I, and none so uplifting as You, who remove all sins. Knowing this, O Mahādevī, do what is most fitting—save me.

दुर्गा मां की आरती

Aarti of Ma Durga

जय अम्बे गौरी मैया, जय श्यामा गौरी
तुमको निशिदिन ध्यावत हरि ब्रह्मा शिवरी ।। जय अम्बे गौरी ।।

Jai Ambe Gauri, Maiya, Jai Shyama Gauri
Tumako Nishidin Dhyavat, Hari Bramha Shivari
|| Jai Ambe Gauri ||

मांग सिंदूर विराजत, टीको मृगमद को ।।
उज्जवल से दोउ नैना, चन्द्रवदन नीको ।। जय अम्बे गौरी ।।

Mang Sinduur Biraajat, Tiko Mrigmadko ||
Ujjvalse Dou Naina, Chandravadan Niko
|| Jai Ambe Gauri ||

कनक सामान कलेवर, रक्ताम्बर राजे ।।
रक्त-पुष्प गलमाला, माला, कण्ठन पर साजै ।। जय अम्बे गौरी ।।

Kanak Saman Kalevar, Raktambar Raje ||
Raktpushp Gal Mala, Kanthan Par Saje
|| Jai Ambe Gauri ||

केहरि वाहन राजत खड्ग खप्पर धारी ।।
सुर-नर-मुनि-जन सेवत तिनके दुखहारी ।। जय अम्बे गौरी ।।

Kehari Vahan Rajat, Khadg Khappar Dhari ||
Sur Nar Munijan Sevat, Tinke Dukhahari
|| Jai Ambe Gauri ||

कानन कुण्डल शोभित नासाग्रे मोती ।।
कोटिक चन्द्र दिवाकर सम राजत ज्योति
।। जय अम्बे गौरी ।।

Kanan Kundal Shobhit, Nasagre Moti ||
Kotik Chandra Divakar, Sam rajat Jyoti
|| Jai Ambe Gauri ||

शुम्भ निशुम्भ विदारे महिषासुर-घाती ।।
धूम्र विलोचन नैना, निशदिन मतमाती ।। जय अम्बे गौरी ।।

Shumbh- Nishumbh Vidare, Mahishasur Ghati ||
Dhumr Vilochan Naina, Nishadin Madamati
|| Jai Ambe Gauri ||

चण्ड मुण्ड संहारे शोणित बीज हरे ।।
मधु-कैटभ दोउ मारे, सुर भयहीन करे ।। जय अम्बे गौरी ।।

Chand-Mund Sanhare, Shonit Bij Hare ||
Madhu-Kaitabh Dou Mare, Sur Bhayahin Kare
|| Jai Ambe Gauri ||

ब्रम्हाणी रूद्राणी, तुम कमला रानी ।।
आगम-निगम-बखानी, तुम शिव पटरानी ।। जय अम्बे गौरी ।।

Bramhani, Rudrani,Tum Kamala Rani ||
Agam Nigam Bakhani,Tum Shiv Patarani
|| Jai Ambe Gauri ||

चौसठ योगिनी गावत, नृत्य करत भैरू ।।
बाजत ताल मृदंगा और बाजत डमरू ।। जय अम्बे गौरी ।।

Chausath Yogini Gavat, Nritya Karat Bhairu ||
Bajat Tal Mridanga, Aur Baajat Damaru
|| Jai Ambe Gauri ||

तुम ही जग की माता, तुम ही हो भरता ।।
भक्तन की दुःख हरता, सुख सम्पत्ति करता ।। जय अम्बे गौरी ।।

Tum Hi Jag Ki Mata, Tum Hi Ho Bharata ||
Bhaktan Ki Dukh Harta, Sukh Sampati Karta
|| Jai Ambe Gauri ||

भुजा चार अति शोभित, वर-मुद्रा धारी ।।
मनवांछित फल पावत, सेवत नर नारी ।। जय अम्बे गौरी ।।

Bhuja Char Ati Shobhit,Varamudra Dhari ||
Manvanchhit Fal Pavat,Sevat Nar Nari
|| Jai Ambe Gauri ||

कंचन थाल विराजत, अगर कपूर बाती ।।
श्रीमालकेतु में राजत, कोटि रतन ज्योति ।। जय अम्बे गौरी ।।

Kanchan Thal Virajat, Agar Kapur Bati ॥
Shrimalaketu Mein Rajat, Koti Ratan Jyoti
॥ Jai Ambe Gauri ॥

श्री अम्बे जी की आरती, जो कोई नर गावे ॥
कहत शिवानन्द स्वामी, सुख-सम्पत्ति पावे ॥ जय अम्बे गौरी ॥

Shri Ambeji Ki Aarti, Jo Koi Nar Gave ॥
Kahat Shivanand Svami, Sukh-Sampatti Pave
॥ Jai Ambe Gauri ॥